Dornford Yates is the pseudonym of ???? into a middle-class Victorian family, his parents scraped together enough money to send him to Harrow. The son of a solicitor, he qualified for the Bar but gave up legal work in favour of his great passion for writing. As a consequence of education and experience, Yates' books feature the genteel life, a nostalgic glimpse at Edwardian decadence and a number of swindling solicitors. In his heyday and as a testament to the fine writing in his novels, Dornford Yates' work was placed in the bestseller list. Indeed, 'Berry' is one of the great comic creations of twentieth-century fiction, and 'Chandos' titles were successfully adapted for television.

Finding the English climate utterly unbearable, Yates chose to live in the French Pyrénées for eighteen years before moving on to Rhodesia where he died in 1960.

ADÈLE AND CO.
AND BERRY CAME TOO
AS BERRY AND I WERE SAYING
B-BERRY AND I LOOK BACK
BERRY AND CO.
THE BERRY SCENE
BLIND CORNER
BLOOD ROYAL
THE BROTHER OF DAPHNE
COST PRICE
THE COURTS OF IDLENESS
AN EYE FOR A TOOTH
FIRE BELOW
GALE WARNING
THE HOUSE THAT BERRY BUILT
JONAH AND CO.
NE'ER DO WELL
PERISHABLE GOODS
RED IN THE MORNING
SHE PAINTED HER FACE

DORNFORD YATES

SHE FELL
AMONG THIEVES

HOUSE OF
STRATUS

This edition published in 2001 by House of Stratus, an imprint of Stratus Holdings plc, 24c Old Burlington Street, London, W1X 1RL, UK.

www.houseofstratus.com

Typeset, printed and bound by House of Stratus.

A catalogue record for this book is available from the British Library.

ISBN 1-84232-980-4

To
JILL

Contents

1

I Make my Bow to Vanity Fair

If one's life is divided into chapters, a chapter of my life ended one fitful April day, when I drove to the aerodrome at Croydon to meet an aeroplane which failed to arrive.

At the time I believed that that was the last of the chapters of which my life was made up, but though for the next twelve months I was more dead than alive, the following spring another chapter opened and I found myself grey-haired at thirty and desperately hungry for action of any kind.

So I turned to Jonathan Mansel.

Though he seemed a man of leisure, I knew him far too well to suppose him an idle man. More. I had seen him in action; we had shared adventure together more than once; and a man of such brilliant enterprise could no more have folded his hands than could water have run uphill.

On an elegant evening in May I dined with him at his flat in Cleveland Row, and when the cloth had been drawn I stated my case. He heard me out in silence, and after a little discussion which has no place in this tale, he got to his feet and started to pace the room.

'Has it ever occurred to you,' he said, 'that there must be required much service which simply cannot be rendered by the ordinary private detective or plain-clothes man? I don't mean military service; I mean the sort of service which deals with crime… Well, I don't suppose it has. People don't think of these things. But now that I've mentioned it, it must be obvious to you that, because of his birth and education, the range of the ordinary detective is strictly limited. You see, crime is not peculiar to the lower classes: felony is frequently – well, launched by people who live much better than you and I; and though, for instance, those people may be waited upon by a footman who is not what he seems, they do not discuss before servants the crimes which they hope to commit. That's a very crude instance, of course. The game's much finer than that. At times it's extremely dangerous; but it's certainly never dull. There's no pay, of course, and if you get into a mess, you've got to get out on your own; but they'll never give you away and, once they know you, they'll trust you – into the blue. I mean, if I rang them up now and advised the arrest of a one-eyed man who would leave the Canton Club at a quarter to ten, two men would be there with a taxi at half-past nine. Well, that's your reward…'

I do not know what I answered and I do not propose to relate the conversation we had, but I know that when I left him, the sky was pale; yet, though I must have been weary, I felt refreshed, for Mansel was soon to set out on a perilous quest and he had done me the honour to ask me to go with him.

And that shall be the prelude of the tale which I am to tell. To this day I do not know whom we worked for or at whose instance we did the things we did, but to them I shall always be grateful, because they made worth living the life I had found a burden and would have been glad to lay down.

My instructions were clear.

Anise is a village in Dordogne, seventy miles from Bordeaux. You will take in petrol there, at six o'clock in the evening of the seventh of June.

It follows that at that hour I brought my car to rest in front of a petrol-pump – so far as I saw, the only one to deface a shy little hamlet, that must have been very old. My servant, Bell, alighted, to see that justice was done, whilst I sat back in my seat, admiring some magnificent plane-trees and wondering what was to happen now I had kept my tryst.

Then –

'William the Careful,' said Mansel. 'I knew you'd be up to time. But you must admit that Anise is hard to find.'

'Hellish,' said I. 'I've been all over the place. I'll swear the maps are wrong.'

'They are,' said Mansel, cheerfully. 'And I can show you a signpost which actually points the wrong way. Anise is admirably hidden. And yet it's only six miles from the *Route de Bordeaux*. And now get out, and we'll walk across to our inn. I think you'll like your room: it commands the sort of country that Morland knew.'

As I left my seat, I heard him speaking to Bell.

'Well, Bell, how are you? Very glad to see you again. Mr Chandos is coming with me. If you berth the car under those limes and walk into that yard, you might see Carson.'

Carson was Mansel's servant, and he and Bell were old friends.

As we strolled to the inn –

'I'm fishing here,' said Mansel. 'When you've had a wash and a drink, you must come and look at the stream. It's very much like another we used to know. And there's our host, waiting to do you honour – he doesn't get many guests.'

Here I should say that Mansel had a flair for good lodging. Except in the bigger cities, he seldom, if ever, would stay at a well-known hotel, but would find some simple house whose clients were very few: his manner was so attractive and his address was so fine that the host would spare no effort to do as he pleased, and before the first day was out, Mansel and those that were with him were lords of all they surveyed. And so it

3

was at Anise. There was, of course, no bathroom, yet all was ready and waiting for me to bathe: some beer was on ice in my bedroom and a plate of most excellent cheese-straws begged me to break my fast, yet not prejudice the dinner to which I should later sit down.

So I drank and bathed and changed, while Mansel sat by the window and smoked and talked of fishing and the trout he had taken that day. And then we went down to the water he liked so well: but not to fish.

I shall never forget the spot, which seemed to me to belong to the golden days, and I well remember thinking that Virgil might have rounded a Georgic in just such a pretty place.

The sun was low, and the effigies of giant poplars lay in a row upon a meadow whose verge they kept. Beyond them the stream was flowing, a lazy, graceful ribbon of brown and gold, that lipped so closely its banks, which were very trim, that it might have been inlaid in the blowing turf. Beyond, again, was woodland, rising to clothe the shoulder which was turning the water aside, for the stream curled out of the forest and, after lacing the meadow, returned to the ward of the trees. On either hand lay pastures, walled by luxuriant hedgerows that must have stood twelve feet high, so that the pleasance, though spacious, was most secure. Since the evening was very still, the comfortable sounds of husbandry travelled to charm the ear: two fields away a reaper was whetting his scythe, a distant cow-bell lifted its time-honoured note, a peasant was cheering his oxen, and now and again the pomp of the stream was fretted by the splash of a leaping trout.

Mansel sat down by the water and took his pipe from his mouth.

'Now these,' he said, 'are the facts.

'Some two hundred miles from here lives a lady called Señora de —. Once her surname was Blonde, and since she was christened Vanity, you won't be surprised to learn that

4

somebody very soon named her "Vanity Fair". And though she's no longer young, the nickname has stuck.

'Before you were born, that name was a household word. Diplomacy. For years she set the rivers of Europe on fire. She was the dazzling enigma of every embassy. Nobody knew in whose service she really was. No Court dared deny her entry. She held positions at two at the very same time. And then, to the general relief, she saw fit to retire – I mean, into private life.

'Well, first you must understand that the lady's immensely rich. Immensely. What is more, she knows how to live. She was very well born, half Russian and half Roumanian. She has outlived no less than three husbands – a Russian, an American and a Spaniard. Her only living child is a girl, twenty-one years old. She was the American's child. By her father's will this girl must inherit most of her mother's wealth – two-thirds on her marriage and the rest on her mother's death.

'Now Vanity Fair spends money – she keeps the most astonishing state. Lives in the mountains as people used to live in Mayfair. But on her daughter's marriage, much more than half her income will disappear. And her daughter's engaged to be married...to the Count of Rachel, a Frenchman, a man of about twenty-five.'

Mansel lay back on the grass and stared at the sky.

'And now,' he said, 'for the strong stuff.

'Vanity Fair has the reputation of being one of the cleverest, most unscrupulous and most ruthless women alive. The death of her second husband was very sudden, and from time to time several other people who were known to have given her offence have come to untimely ends. There is not a tittle of evidence to connect her with their respective fates: but the series of coincidences is curious. Her son caused her great annoyance shortly before he died...'

'Good God,' said I.

'Quite so,' said Mansel. 'If half what I've heard is true, Vanity Fair is some girl. Be that as it may, there are certain quarters in which her – her influence has been causing growing concern and the advisability of a close-up has been growing more and more desirable. But the insurmountable difficulty has always been to get a foot in. The Château Jezreel is rather a close borough.

'Well, now at last Vanity Fair has given "certain quarters" a chance.

'A few weeks ago she wrote to a detective in London who had served her some years ago, asking him to find her a chauffeur – who could keep his eyes and ears open and render her certain reports. She told him to take his time, as she wanted an exceptional man. The detective accepted her order – and went to the powers that be… As a result, in six days' time I shall report at Jezreel as the chauffeur-detective required by Vanity Fair.

'Well, that's much better than nothing: but it isn't nearly enough. A chauffeur is only a chauffeur, and if I'm to do any good I must have someone upstairs. And that is where you come in.

'Vanity Fair has a weakness for nice young men. You needn't be afraid: immodesty is one of the very few failings she hasn't got. For her own sex she's no use at all: but youth and manhood attract her – she loves to hold a young man with her mental charm. And so I hope to arrange that you shall be her guest at Jezreel. If I can bring that off, we shall have won the first round. With you in the salon, with me below stairs, and with Bell as connecting-file between us, we shall have obtained a real footing in the enemy's camp. Carson will stay outside, representing our lines of communication. Anise will be his headquarters, but of course he'll be on the move.

'And that's very nearly all that I've got to say. My instructions are to listen and watch – *and to act*, if what I have heard or seen will give me good cause. Why she should want a detective, I've no idea: but it's going to be a great help – to the other side. As for the role for which you're cast, I've no doubt you find it offensive: to set out to betray your hostess has an unpleasant ring. But please remember this – *you need have no compunction.* If the half I've been told is true, Vanity Fair is a very monster of iniquity: and if you want something to go on – well, I have very little doubt that when she announces the date of her daughter's marriage, it'll mean that she's fixed the date of her daughter's death.'

There was a little silence.

Then –

'You know, you scare me,' said I. 'I'm not slick enough for this job. I don't mind how rough a game is and I used to know how to hit, but I can't take on a woman like Vanity Fair.'

'I hope you won't try,' said Mansel. 'All I want you to do is to sit at her feet. And unless I'm much mistaken, she'll have you there before you've known her a day. She's a very notable woman, is Vanity Fair. She'll never see sixty again, and the beauty she had has gone the way beauty goes: but I understand that she has an astonishing way – a way which "age cannot wither, nor custom stale". I want you to let yourself go, to be entirely natural and play her game. In that way you'll be playing my game. You're under my orders, of course: but my orders will be her desires. As like as not, she'll use you: I hope to God she does – for then, you see, she'll be playing straight into my hands.'

I shifted uneasily.

'I'm desperately afraid,' I said, 'of letting you down.'

'I'm not,' said Mansel: 'and I'm a pretty good judge. I know that you're not an actor. You're far too simple and downright. And if you were to start pretending, she'd see through you in a flash. And so you're not going to pretend. I hope to contrive that she asks you to stay at Jezreel. You'll accept that invitation and just behave as her guest. And from time to time an English chauffeur, called Wright, will ask your servant questions on what you have seen and heard. Mark that. Not Jonathan Mansel, but an English chauffeur, called Wright. He may happen to look like me, but both our lives may depend on your never having seen him before.' He laughed at the look in my eyes and got to his feet. 'And that's enough for this evening. Follow me very quietly. I don't know whether he's out, but I may be able to show you a trout I've been trying to catch for the last two days. He's a wily old swab, all right. I call him "Vanity Fair".'

Two days later, I was strolling alone in the meadow, absently fishing the water and wondering what was to come, for Mansel was gone to London to take up the role of John Wright and, as such, to leave by train for the South of France. He had taken the road to Paris: there he would leave his car and take to the air, and Carson would drive back to Anise the following day. And at Anise I was to stay, until I received my orders to leave for Jezreel.

I confess that I was uneasy.

I found my commission distasteful, and I felt very sure I was not the man for the job. Had anyone other than Mansel proposed to me such an office, I would have refused it point-blank: but Mansel's judgment was so rare and he was so faithful a friend that when he smiled down my objections, I said no more. Still, I think I should have tried to withstand him, had I not been possessed by an instinct for which I can never account. I felt that behind this curtain which we were to seek to lift, there was set a scene which was waiting for Mansel and me: that the play to be rendered was far more grim and momentous than Mansel dreamed, and that he would have need of someone to stand with their back against his, if he and his fortune were not to go down together before, as the Psalmist has it, the terror by night and the arrow that flieth by day.

The last words that he had spoken came into my mind.

'Remember, my son, no compunction. You must take it from me, that emotion would be out of place. Vanity Fair respects neither God nor man, and the only way to get her is by using the sort of weapons she uses herself. And so, be natural,

William. When in doubt, be natural: and always tell her the truth.'

And there I had a rise which I did not deserve, and a moment later I landed a very fine trout.

For a moment I stared at the fish. Then I put a hand to my head. The thing was absurd, yet true. Mansel was a beautiful angler, and I was the worst in the world. But there on the sward was lying 'Vanity Fair'.

Three weeks and one day had gone by, July had come in in splendour, and I was sitting, smoking, by the side of a country road six miles from Jezreel. The Rolls was berthed in the shade on the opposite side of the way, and Bell was thirty yards off at a bend in the road.

As I heard a car coming, I got to my feet.

With my eyes upon Bell I waited, for he could see the car which was out of my sight. But Bell made no sign.

The car came nearer and nearer... Then at last it whipped round the blind bend – to find the Rolls full in its way.

Its chauffeur applied his brakes and did what he could, but the wings of the two cars met with a hollow crash.

Bell came running, and I stepped into the road.

As the chauffeur got out of his car –

'It wasn't my fault, sir,' he said. He pushed back his cap. 'You're on your wrong side, you know: and you shouldn't leave a car on a bend.'

'You're perfectly right,' said I. 'The fault was mine. I don't know what possessed me to do such a stupid thing.'

The three of us examined the damage. Except that the wings were buckled, there seemed to be no harm done.

When I said as much –

'I touched your wheel, sir,' said Mansel. 'My steering'll have to come down, and I think you'd be well advised to do the same.'

'Oh, hell,' said I. And then, 'I don't see any mark.'

9

'I hit your tire with my hub-cap. Look out. Here's another car coming. We don't want another smash.'

He sounded his horn like fury, and Bell ran round the corner with outstretched arms. A moment later a small van crawled into view. As it made its way by, its occupants were minding our business with bulging eyes.

'Could I have your name, sir,' said Mansel. 'I'm sure I don't want to make trouble, but I've only been here two weeks and I don't want to lose my job. Madame de —'s my lady, of the Château Jezreel. I don't know what she'll say. I oughtn't to be driving really – I haven't a French licence yet.'

'Where is the château?' I said. 'I'd better come up myself and tell her the truth.'

'Very kind if you would, sir. It's only about six miles.'

'I can't do much less,' said I, and got into the Rolls. 'You'd better lead the way.'

'I shall go dead slow, sir,' said Mansel. 'If I've got a wheel out of truth, I don't want to make matters worse.'

As he turned the light car about, I started the Rolls: then Bell took his seat beside me, and, feeling much more than nervous, I drew into Mansel's wake.

Jezreel stood among the mountains, retired from the great highways. The single road that approached it served also the tiny village that clung to the castle's skirts – and served it uncommon well, for the road had been remade at the charge of Vanity Fair. Neither castle nor village was hidden, for the mountains stood back on all sides, but both belonged to the lap of a mighty valley which came to a sudden end. Where it ended, the ground fell steeply for three or four hundred feet, so that such as came up from the north could see no sign of building unless or until they climbed the smart by-road, and except from the north the valley could not be approached. As you breasted the lip of the valley, the castle burst upon you in a most astonishing way, for one moment you could see nothing but the tilted meadows about you and the mountains and forests beyond, and the next you found yourself standing before the gates of Jezreel. Except for those that go on foot in the mountains, the belvedere of the castle belonged to the Col de Fer. Using that infamous pass, you could from one spot, if you pleased, command the most of the valley and all the superb domain. From there you could consider Jezreel: from there you could mark her bulwarks and tell her towers and marvel how men and beasts had dragged the stones for her building to such a place.

Following Mansel's lead, I threaded the pocket village, entered a towering gateway of stone and iron, stole up a very short drive, under a low-pitched archway and into a closed courtyard.

As a servant descended some steps, I took out a card. Very shortly I told him my business. The man took the card and withdrew, and I sat awaiting the pleasure of Vanity Fair.

The afternoon was most hot, but the courtyard was pleasantly cool. From what I could see, the castle was old and curious, belonging to no one age, but raised by more than one hand and more to the will of its masters than to that of an architect. All was most spick and span: the walls were as white as snow, and the shutters might have been painted the day before.

The manservant reappeared and came to my side.

'Madame will receive Monsieur.'

He opened the door of the car and bowed.

At the head of the steps a powdered footman received me and led me through a great hall to one of the finest salons I ever saw. Gigantic Persian carpets covered the floor: tapestries glowed upon the walls: a glorious ceiling presented the death of Actaeon. The furniture these were guarding was of the same magnificence – treasure of gilt and brocade, of inlay and precious stone.

Another footman stood by an open window that gave to the terrace without, and the two of them bowed me into the hands of a butler who received me very gravely and then preceded me over the sunlit flags.

The terrace commanded the valley and faced full south: a flight of steps led down to the blowing meadows, and a fountain was dancing in the sunshine and the grey of the long balustrade was alight with flowers. To one side chairs had been set on a carpet spread upon the stone, and above them a pleasant awning rendered a grateful shade.

The butler's bearing suggested that the terrace was holy ground: the canopy confirmed this suggestion: I only hoped I should make a good sacrifice, for there, like any idol, was sitting Vanity Fair.

So still she sat that she might have been carved out of stone. She was dressed in black, and a little hood of black silk was framing her lovely face. Such hoods were worn in England in Hollar's day, and if they demanded beauty, I can only say that they gave as good as they got. The silk lay close to her temples, which might have belonged to marble – they seemed so smooth and so cold, but lower, on either side, a curl of gold and silver declared her magnificent hair. Her nose and her mouth were very finely chiselled, and her skin might well have been envied by women one half her age: but though her face was lovely, it was not young, and I think that she made no attempt to conceal her years. But all this I noticed later. For the moment I could see nothing except her eyes. Large and grey and steady, these glowed like jewels in her head. Dignity, power and charm sat in that level gaze which, though it was not unkindly, yet gave the impression of looking into my heart. And then as I met that gaze, it slid into a stare...

To save my life, I could not have looked away, but I know that I quailed in spirit, for now I seemed to be facing something that was not decent, but should have been draped – a bare personality, that had all the libertine's daring and the brilliance of naked steel. And so I was, for though I did not know it, something that was not human was looking me down…something that learned in heaven to live in hell…a highly dangerous 'make-up'. There were times when a fallen angel looked out of the steady, grey eyes of Vanity Fair.

I bowed, and Vanity Fair inclined her head.

'I understand,' she said, 'that you have a confession to make.'

'That's quite right,' said I. 'I'm sorry,' and with that I told her my tale.

'Why are you here?' she said.

'Partly to apologise,' I said, 'and partly to tell you your chauffeur was not to blame.'

'How came you to be so careless?'

'There you have me,' said I. 'I suppose for the moment I forgot the rule of the road. I can't explain my action. I just went and asked for trouble, and trouble came.'

Vanity Fair smiled.

'And your chauffeur, too?' she said. 'Blind leading the blind?'

'He isn't a chauffeur,' I said. 'He's a body-servant: if need be, he can handle the car and he keeps her clean.'

'Sit down,' said Vanity Fair. I took my seat. 'And now please tell me the damage.'

'Our wings were buckled,' said I. 'So much can be seen. But your chauffeur hit my wheel, and that means that both our front axles ought to come down. I'm very sorry,' I added. 'It's at least a two-day job.'

Vanity Fair shrugged her shoulders.

'I've more than one car,' she said, 'but what about you?'

'I shall go back to Perin,' I said. 'They'll be able to do it there.'

'Where were you bound for?'

'I was making for Lally by way of the Col de Fer. But I can't do a pass like that till I've had my steering down.'

'Are you meeting friends at Lally?'

'Oh, no,' said I. 'I've nothing much to do, so I'm wandering round.'

'I don't think you'll care for Lally – unless you have come to see the nakedness of the land. Lally parades the truth that she's seen better days. I always find that depressing. Where were you going from there?'

'I don't know. I had thought about Spain.'

Vanity Fair inspected a shapely hand.

'You were very careless,' she said. 'My chauffeur – my nice, new chauffeur might have been spoiled.'

'I'm afraid that's true,' said I.

'I think you should be punished for that. Jezreel is extremely dull: I think you might well be confined here for two or three days – until your car has been mended. What do you think?'

'I – '

'Your fellow-prisoners will be my daughter and her fiancé, a most unattractive pair, my secretary and my chaplain, neither of whom has a brain, and myself, who was presented at Court before you were born.'

I got to my feet and bowed.

'Madam,' I said, 'you put a premium upon crime.'

Vanity Fair laughed.

'Wait till you've served your sentence. I tell you, Jezreel is dull.' She touched a bell by her side. 'I've six men in all in the garage: if your wing is sent to Perin, I should think they might manage between them to take your axle down.'

The butler appeared.

'Mr Chandos will stay at Jezreel – in "the corner suite". Inform his servant and send Wright here.'

Two minutes later Jonathan Mansel appeared.

'Mr Chandos has told me what happened this afternoon. He says you were not to blame. The wings, of course, must go to the town to be done: can the rest of the work be done here?'

Mansel hesitated. Then –

'We can take down the axles, madam, and if there's no damage done, we can put them back. But if they're out of alignment, they'll have to go to a forge.'

'Then take them down and see. And look after Mr Chandos' servant.' She turned to me. 'I don't suppose he speaks French.'

'Not a word that I know of,' said I.

'Then he and Wright will get on. Would you like to put your car in the garage, or will you leave it to Wright?'

'I think perhaps I'll do it.'

'Then do. And then ask for your room. Tea will be served here at five o'clock.'

'Thank you very much,' I said feebly.

She smiled and nodded, and I left by the way I had come, with Mansel behind.

As I took my seat in the Rolls, I saw that my baggage was gone.

'You'll be staying here, sir?' said Mansel.

'It seems so,' said I. 'How long will they take with that wing?'

'Four or five days, sir, at least. You'll only get it rough-painted.'

'That doesn't matter,' said I, and started the car.

Mansel took his stand on the step.

'Back through the archway, sir, and then turn sharp to the left.'

Ten minutes later I entered 'the corner suite', to find a luxury which I had never known. All the appointments were royal. I have been led through state bed-chambers in King's houses, but I never saw one that was finer than that in which I was to lie. Poppaea, I think, would have approved my bathroom. The bath was sunk in the floor. It was also full of warm water, and Bell was laying some clothes on the lovely bed.

Thanks to Mansel's most careful preparation, it had proved extremely easy to enter the enemy's camp.

To the Count of Rachel I took an instant dislike.

Had I been in some hotel, I should have supposed him a waiter, but he had not the presence of the servants attached to Jezreel. What hair he had was sandy: his lips were loose: the rims of his eyes were red. So much for his appearance. His manner also betrayed him, as I shall show. The man was offensive, because unsure of himself. So was his flesh. Gaston, Count of Rachel, was highly perfumed.

At a quarter to eight that evening, I entered the gorgeous salon adjoining the dining-room, to find him holding an envelope up to the light. This was a bad beginning, for the letter was plainly not his, but had been laid in the salon with the rest of the evening post. (It was not till later that I learned that the whole of the mail went first to Vanity Fair, who inspected everyone's letters before they were laid in the salon for their owners to claim.)

The fellow started and pitched the letter down. Then, as though to defy the opinion which he knew very well I must hold, he thrust his hands into his pockets, looked me up and down, and actually let out a snort.

I could have burst with laughter. Instead –

'Good evening,' I said gravely. 'My name is Chandos. I expect you're Monsieur de Rachel. When I arrived, I think you were out in your car.'

The man was gravelled. His hands came out of his pockets and the blood came into his face.

'I – I did not know,' he stammered. 'Why are you here?'

His luck was clean out. Before I could make any answer –

'How d'you do, Mr Chandos,' said a voice. 'My mother was telling us about you and how you nearly killed Wright. I see you've made friends with Gaston. My name is Virginia Brooch.'

We shook hands easily, while Gaston strolled on to the terrace, perhaps to seek the composure I hope he found.

The girl had very fair hair, and her close-set eyes were blue. Her features were clean and she was not unattractive, but her manner was inclined to be hearty, not to say rough. For her age she was too well-covered – soon to be fat.

Whilst we were talking together, the secretary and chaplain appeared. These I had met at tea. My hostess had dubbed them fools, and I must confess that the looks and the demeanour of the priest argued a vacant mind. The secretary might have been wise, but his manner was so subdued as to offer no clue. His name was Acorn and that of the priest was Below.

As Gaston returned from the terrace, Vanity Fair came floating into the room. And with her came light. As though some switch had been turned, her blazing personality lit up the atmosphere. Her laughter, her dulcet voice, the flash of her ready wit took hold of the listless scene and fairly shook it into a lively masque. Father Below was grinning. Acorn grew almost gay; Gaston recovered his balance and Virginia began to shout. For myself, I frankly confess I was carried away. I enjoyed the masque very much – and entirely failed to perceive that it was not a masque at all, but a puppet-show. Vanity Fair was as finished a puppet-mistress, as ever was born.

Dinner was served – in a room such as I had heard of, but never seen. The floor was of marble, in the midst of which a lovely refectory table stood on a precious rug. The walls were hung with Gobelin tapestry and a little fountain was dancing in the fireplace of chiselled stone. Four glorious chandeliers were shedding candlelight, and the chairs were no chairs, but stalls – that had come out of some cathedral and had been built and carved to the glory of God. Music was being discoursed by a hidden orchestra, footmen were standing like statues against the walls, but, as was proper, the eye was most held by the board, the polish of which was so high that the sparkle of glass and silver was matched by the flash of the oak.

Here I may say that the chandeliers were all of solid silver and had hung in a palace in Moscow until they came to Jezreel: that more than six hundred candles went to the lighting of that room: that the servants were shod with rubber, so that they made no sound: that the band which was making the music was sitting up in a loft which the tapestry hid.

As the fish appeared –

'Tell me,' said Vanity Fair, 'what does anyone think of my chauffeur – the new man, Wright?'

17

Her words seemed to fill up my cup. Talk of doing business with pleasure…

'I can't say I like him,' said Gaston, taking a trout.

'You wouldn't,' said Vanity Fair. 'He doesn't use scent.'

There was a dreadful silence which I very nearly disgraced. Then –

'I should say he was a gentleman,' said Virginia. 'He's very polite. What do you think, Mr Chandos?'

'There's no doubt about it,' said I. 'But times are hard, you know, and a chauffeur's job is better than walking the streets.'

'I do not agree,' said Gaston. 'I would rather walk the streets than accept a servant's post.'

'We were talking of gentlemen,' said Vanity Fair.

Had I been the Count, I should have left the table and then the house: but Gaston only looked very black and drained his glass.

I began to feel rather dazed…two bombs in one minute are apt to shake a man up…not bricks – bombs…

My hostess turned to Acorn.

'And what do you think?'

'My opinion is valueless, madam.'

'True,' said Vanity Fair, and turned to the priest.

The chaplain blew out his cheeks.

'The man is expert,' he said. 'He mended my braces admirably.'

Before we could laugh –

'That's really why I engaged him,' flashed Vanity Fair. 'And I very much want him to look at your spinal cord. I know that's out of alignment. Bent at birth, I should say. Have some more trout, Mr Chandos. I'm going to take another and miss the meat.'

The meal proceeded.

Hare after hare was started by Vanity Fair, and though I was spared, the efforts of the others to course it were derided with merciless wit. She simply dug the pit-falls and then kicked her victims in, omitting no circumstances of insult, yet all the time displaying the utmost good will. It was an extraordinary business. Here was a queen usurping the functions of court-jester, and doing his job far better because her wit was so rare. In a way it was rather shameful, because, except for Gaston, her victims could hardly hit back, but with it all, she was gracious, and, though bad form is offensive, she never once offended my eyes or ears.

Presently she returned to Mansel.

'I pay Wright five pounds a week. Does anyone think he's worth it?'

'Jean doesn't like him,' said Gaston.

'That's in his favour. Jean is a lazy fool, who would be a knave. His efforts to rob me are really beneath contempt. Anything else?'

'He minds his own business,' said Virginia.

'Which shows that you don't,' said her mother. 'How do you know?'

'From Suzanne,' said the girl. 'He never opens his mouth in the servants' hall.'

'He can't talk French,' said Gaston.

'What of that?' said Vanity Fair. 'More than one of the staff can speak English. I don't suppose he's ashamed of his mother tongue.'

'I'm not,' cried Gaston, furiously.

'Then why be so painfully English?' said Vanity Fair. 'Anywhere outside Paris they'd know you were French.' She turned to me. 'Would you be content to speak French as he speaks English?'

'I should be very thankful,' said I.

This was true. His grammar was very sound.

'I said "content", Mr Chandos,' said Vanity Fair.

'Yes,' I said stoutly, 'I would.'

'Liar,' says she. 'And don't try to save his face. He knows how to do it a great deal better than you. Where did you see Wright last?'

The shock could not have been greater, if she had picked up a hammer and hit me between the eyes.

I seemed to hear Mansel speaking.

Both our lives may depend on your never having seen him before.

It was too late now. She had a sow by the ear. Unless I could make it the wrong one…

My brain was out of action, but instinct caught up the reins.

I heard myself make answer.

'At a village in Wales. I've been trying to remember ever since I saw his face: and now you've jogged my memory.' I put a hand to my eyes. 'I stopped there one evening for petrol and he was standing close to the petrol-pump. I remember he helped the mechanic to get the top off my tank.'

'Was your servant with you?'

I shook my head.

'I was alone,' I said. 'It must be two years ago.'

'What was the name of the village?'

'I've no idea,' said I. 'I was going north from Brecknock.'

'Was he a chauffeur then?'

I opened my eyes.

'Certainly,' said I. 'He was wearing a chauffeur's clothes. I don't remember any car.'

'Did Wright know you?'

'No,' said I. 'I asked him. I told him I was certain I'd seen him before. But he didn't seem to know me. I'll try him again tomorrow.'

'Don't do that. Let him be.'

'As you please,' said I. 'But how on earth did you guess that I'd seen him before?'

Vanity Fair vouchsafed me a dazzling smile.

'There are more things in Jezreel, Mr Chandos, than are dreamt of in your philosophy.'

If I laughed, it was not in my heart. Indeed, I was at my wit's end, for I knew as well as did she that the instant dinner was over, *Vanity Fair was going to send for Mansel to check the truth of my words*. Unless, before he was summoned, Mansel could be apprised of what I had said, Vanity Fair was going to catch him clean out.

As a man in a dream, I helped myself to some dish.

Mansel would have saved the game somehow, but I was beaten and hopeless and could only dwell upon the ruin which I had wrought.

And then a merciful Fate played into my hands.

As a servant made to offer me gravy, Virginia bounced in her stall and touched his arm. The boat slipped off the salver and into my lap.

The confusion that followed was hideous.

The unfortunate servant was trembling: Virginia screamed her dismay: the butler came running with napkins: and Vanity Fair sat glowering in a silence far more scathing than any words.

'It was nobody's fault,' said I: 'but if you'll excuse me, I think I must go and change.'

With my thighs still smoking, I hurried out of the room…

Bell, as luck would have it, was in my suite.

As I tore off my clothes –

'Run some water,' I said, 'and lay out clean things.'

Then I seized a pencil and paper and scrawled a note, reciting exactly the tale I had told to Vanity Fair.

Bell was ready and waiting before I had done.

As I folded the paper –

'Find Captain Mansel at once. Ask him for a gallon of petrol in which you can souse my clothes. And give him this note: it's vital: and he's to read it at once.'

Though I made what haste I could, Bell was back with the spirit before I had done.

'All right?' said I.

'Quite all right, sir.'

I could have thrown up my hat.

Some pudding was being served, as I entered the dining-room...

I found the atmosphere sultry. Virginia was halfway to tears, and Vanity Fair was plainly seething with wrath. But I was exalted. I could, I think, have moved mountains, and after a little Vanity Fair was laughing and Virginia had asked me to use her Christian name.

And then the meal was over, and the ladies rose to their feet.

'Don't sit too long,' said my hostess. 'My daughter has no use for women: neither have I.' She turned to the door. As she passed the butler, 'It may be too late,' she said, 'but I want to see Wright.'

Of such, and worse, was the kingdom of Vanity Fair. She despised and mistrusted her fellows: to declare such scorn and suspicion was her delight: in her eyes of steel, tails were made to be twisted and necks, if need be, to be wrung: she was a ruffler born, whose swordsmanship was so brilliant that no one dared call her out: she revelled in intrigue: power was the breath of her life: she was fearless, unconscionable, charming and deadly shrewd: she would go all lengths – for a whim: to herself, as to everyone else, her will was law. The woman was mediaeval – born out of time: and she kept to herself at Jezreel because the days were modern and she could not do as she pleased without her gates. This limitation must have vexed her – Catharine de Medici cooped in a market-town: still even small fry can be hustled and teased and watched: for want of a duchy to harass and towns to sack, Vanity Fair was playing a game of chess – against herself, of course: her household made her the men, and the board was Jezreel. And now, for the very first time, somebody else had taken a hand in the game...

I wondered how long it would be before she found out that she was being opposed. It occurred to me with a shock that she must never find out. If she did…

As I switched out my light, some clock chimed half-past eleven. As though inspired by its music, an owl cried twice.

I lay back on my pillows, thinking.

She must not find out…

She almost *had* found out about three hours ago…

I wondered what Mansel was thinking. I wished he could have been there at dinner, to see for himself how damnably clever she was…the infinite pains she had taken to put me at ease, to appoint me her gossip to dip in the dish of her gibes…and then, without any warning, the point at my throat…

I lay there, wakeful and pensive, savouring the fine, sweet air with which the great chamber was quick. Now and again a wandering breath would flicker about my temples or flirt with the crimson valance above my head; but these were outlaw zephyrs, for all the winds were still. Somewhere without, a sluice was roaring gently, like Bottom's sucking-dove.

As I turned at length to my slumber, I heard the clock chime again.

A quarter to twelve.

And then I was sitting upright, and every nerve in my body had leapt to life – for again, when the chime was over, some owl had cried twice. And that was not natural.

On my knees at an open window, I studied the night.

The scene was memorable. A fine moon sailed in the sky, to fill the valley with magic and lend the mountains a standing not to be found by day: my eyes were no longer masters of what they saw: Mystery, orbed and sceptred, was holding her shining court, and all things, high and low, were wearing her levée dress: the stage was black with witchcraft: enchantment was in the air.

And something else.

After, perhaps, five minutes, I saw a definite movement...down in the meadows...some seventy yards from the foot of the terrace steps. With my eyes on the spot, I waited, but not for long. Again I saw the movement, nearer the house. Someone was stealthily approaching, passing from shadow to shadow, so as to move unseen.

At the last I saw him plainly, a giant of a man, with the stride of one that spends his life in the mountains and on his feet. Then the wall of the terrace hid him, and I saw his figure no more.

Had I been a guest at Jezreel, and nothing more, I should, I suppose, have gone to seek some servant and tell him what I had seen: it would, of course, have been my duty – to Vanity Fair. But I was more than a guest, and if thieves were to break in and steal, it was no business of mine. What was more, I was very sure that the man I had seen was no thief, but that he had announced his presence – by using the cry of an owl...that he was, in short, one of the pieces upon the board of Jezreel.

For more than an hour I watched, but he never came back: and though I would have waited, the strong air fought against me, and after a while I knew that I could not trust my eyes.

And so I went to my bed – to sleep the sun into the sky.

A wail of horror woke me at seven o'clock – a French servant's declaration of terrible news. As I rushed to a window, I heard him running on the terrace, mouthing his consternation, and calling upon his God.

The poor man was hardly to blame. His duty was to open the shutters, not to remove the dead.

Asprawl on the flags of the terrace was lying the body of a girl, flat on its face. Her pitiful arms were outstretched and a leg was drawn up. She was wearing no clothing at all, and her hair was fair.

2

I am Treated as I Deserve

I ripped a sheet from the bed and ran downstairs: but Mansel was there before me, and two or three servants with him, trembling and peering and holding each other back.

As Mansel laid down the head, I came up with my sheet, and the two of us covered the body without a word.

Then –

'I can't speak French, sir,' said Mansel; 'will you tell them to find a stretcher or something like that? I mean, we can't leave her here.'

Someone thought of the leaf of a table, and this was brought. As Mansel and Bell were laying the body upon it, Acorn came, blowzed and bustling, to take my place.

'Take her to the chapel,' he said. 'And lock the door, if you please, and bring me the key.' As the bearers moved off, he addressed himself to me.

'Mr Chandos, what do you know of this shocking affair?'

I told him shortly enough.

'What a dreadful business,' he said. 'To fall from a window like that! She's only been here a week. Julie, her name was. Julie. A country girl. She was taken as kitchen-maid. Most respectable people, her parents.' He sucked in his breath. 'Madame de — will be most frightfully upset.'

'Naturally enough,' said I. 'You think she fell from a window?'

'That's the report that was brought me.' He stepped to the balustrade and peered at the house. Then he pointed up at a casement set in the steep-pitched roof. 'I rather imagine,' he said, 'that that was her room. If she rose in the night and leaned out… They're highly dangerous, these windows: the sills are so low.'

'She was wearing no nightgown,' I said. 'The body was nude.'

'That would be right,' he said. 'The people here wear no nightclothes of any kind.'

Thoughtfully I withdrew to my suite…

I had food for thought.

I did not believe that Julie had fallen from her window – without any help. Indeed, I felt very sure that the man I had seen in the shadows had caused her death. And I had a dreadful feeling that, if the truth were known, Julie in some way or other had crossed the sinister path of Vanity Fair.

The door of the bed-chamber opened and Bell came into the room.

'A nice show, this,' I said.

'Shocking, sir,' said Bell. 'They say she was only sixteen.'

I told him of the man in the meadows.

'Tell Captain Mansel,' I said. 'Not a breath to anyone else. And ask him this. I suppose I shall be called at the inquest. Am I to mention this man?'

'Very good, sir.'

As I was finishing dressing, Bell reappeared.

'You're to keep what you saw to yourself, sir, at any cost.'

'Right,' said I. 'And the inquest?'

'The Captain says there won't be an inquest,' said Bell.

Brushes in hand, I regarded him.

'No inquest?' I said.

'No, sir.'

For an instant his eyes met mine: then he shrugged his shoulders and picked up my coat.

I stepped to the window and stared at the mountains lifting their sunlit heads.

There won't be an inquest.

I found the saying pregnant. If sudden, violent death was not to be probed, it looked very much as though Mansel had taken his life in his hand.

(In fact, there was no inquest. So far as I know, the police were not even informed. Julie had died – and was buried the following day. Her father and mother were present, in deep distress. Their gratitude to her mistress was very touching: and when Vanity Fair, who received them, showed them a picture of the tombstone which she proposed to erect, the poor peasants were quite overwhelmed. The text to be cut upon the marble she chose herself. 'Suffer little children to come unto me.')

At my hostess' instance, that morning her daughter showed me the house. While the building itself was more curious than sightly, its contents were notable, and I cannot believe that anywhere else in the world were so many lovely pieces in everyday use. I cannot begin to describe them and what they must have been worth I cannot pretend to say, but I know that it seemed presumptuous to live and move in the midst of such precious things. We trod upon Persian carpets that famous museums would have been proud to hang up: we lifted arras that should have been under glass: we sat upon chairs which a king and his queen had honoured – there were the royal arms, which some tireless needle had blazoned four hundred years before. Statuary, paintings and tapestries argued the connoisseur of unlimited means: yet all was for use, not for show, and a clock that had come out of Strasburg in sixteen hundred and one, from whose case a different apostle appeared at each hour of the day, was working perfectly. Several sedan-chairs were employed, of all things, as lampshades; on the floor of the one whose door Virginia opened was a powerful electric lamp, the light of which was projected on to the roof of the chair, and if, she explained, this radiance was not enough, the roof of the chair was opened to let the light on to the ceiling and make the hall or the chamber as bright as day. Of these chairs I counted eleven, all of them very fine: from what her daughter said, I gathered they were a weakness of Vanity Fair's. 'Mother loves them,' she laughed. 'She simply can't resist a good-looking chair.' I only once saw a cabinet-maker at work, but everything's condition was perfect and all the rooms were open and beautifully kept.

By the time we had done, I had a fair idea of the plan of the house and had learned how the household was lodged and which were the private quarters of Vanity Fair. Like that which I had been given, her suite was a 'corner' suite and lay at the opposite end of the south façade, commanding the valley on one hand, and on the other the mountains that soared to the west. In the midst of her suite, however, a tower rose up from the terrace, to pierce the floor above hers and then stand up by itself till its height diminished that of the steep-pitched roof: by using this tower I judged – and I later found I was right – access could be had to her suite from without and below and above, though the principal doors, which gave to the hall and the staircase, were shut and barred.

There was no garden to see, for the countryside was the garden that graced Jezreel: and this I found so attractive that after lunch that day I proposed to go for a walk.

'A long one,' I said. 'If you will excuse me, I won't appear at tea.'

'I told you Jezreel was dull,' said Vanity Fair. 'Where d'you propose to go?'

'Right up the valley,' I said. 'I want to see the back of beyond.'

'You won't appear at dinner if you try to do that. When you get to the head of the valley, you'd better turn right. There you'll find a path which will either break your heart or bring you into the road which leads to the Col de Fer. From what I've seen of you, I'll back your heart, so a car shall be there to meet you from six o'clock on.'

'But that's ideal,' said I. 'Are you sure it's quite convenient?'

'It wouldn't be there if it wasn't,' said Vanity Fair. 'What time shall you start?'

'I thought in about half-an-hour.'

'Make it three-quarters,' she said. 'And come to my salon, will you, before you set out?'

With that, she was gone, leaving me ill at ease. Her command was disconcerting. Why should she want to see me…alone…in her private room?

Thirty-five minutes later, her personal maid, called Esther, a woman with a face like a mask, ushered me into an exquisite little salon which was full of the scent of pot-pourri and fairly ablaze with the sunshine which was not at all shut out.

Vanity Fair was installed in a deep *chaise longue*.

'Sit down, Mr Chandos,' she said. 'I think you'd look very well in that bracket chair.'

I took my seat – facing the light.

'This business this morning,' she said. 'Now who was first on the scene?'

'That I can't tell you,' I said. 'It was somebody's cry that woke me, but by the time I had got to the window, whoever it was was gone. When I got down, Wright was there with three other men.'

'I'm told that she fell from a window. Did what you saw bear that out?'

'It certainly did,' said I, feeling more at my ease.

'But you heard no cry in the night. Do you sleep very sound?'

'Pretty well, I think,' said I, wishing that I knew what was coming, and crossing my legs. 'I certainly heard no cry.'

'What time did you go to sleep?'

So that was it. Vanity Fair wished to know if I had seen the man in the meadows at a quarter to twelve.

Like a fool, I decided to lie.

'I really can't say,' I said. 'Soon after I bade you good night.'

'That was at eleven o'clock.'

'Soon after that,' said I. 'I'd nothing to do.'

'She might have fallen before that. For all you know, she was there when you went to bed.'

'Oh no. I mean – well, I think I should have seen her,' I said, and could have ripped out my tongue.

'Seen her? How could you have seen her?'

'I leaned out of the window,' I said, 'the very last thing. The moon was lighting the terrace: but she wasn't there.'

'Fancy your remembering that.'

I shrugged my shoulders – desperately.

'I just do,' said I. 'And I'll tell you another thing. I can tell you the very time, for the castle clock chimed the quarter whilst I was looking out.'

Another lie – but a good one. If I had retired at a quarter past eleven, I could hardly have seen the man at a quarter to twelve.

'That's more like it,' says she. 'No doubt at all about that?'

'None whatever,' said I, and felt very pleased with myself.

'Good,' says Vanity Fair. She flung me a charming smile. 'I put your mind to the grind-stone, and see how sharp it's become. You heard the clock chime the quarter, and she wasn't there.'

'Quite right,' said I, and grinned back.

'Did you set your watch?'

'I can't say that,' said I.

'Well, do so,' says Vanity Fair. 'Right away – before you go out. Punctuality's one of my failings, and I always go by that clock. And now go and have a good walk. To be honest, I envy you. What does the prophet say? "How beautiful upon the mountains are the feet of him that bringeth good tidings." And if I was half my age, I'd keep you company.'

Thus elegantly dismissed, I took my leave.

Outside her suite, I drew a deep breath of relief. Vanity Fair had annoyed me and frightened me out of my life: for all that, I had won the round, for my monstrous cross-examination had borne her no fruit. I, Richard Chandos, had beaten Vanity Fair.

That lie, of mine, about the clock striking the quarter… I could have hugged myself.

I proposed to leave by the terrace, but first I made for the courtyard, to set my watch. As I came to the steps, Virginia was taking her seat at the wheel of a fast-looking car.

When I had explained my quest –

'Good for you, Richard,' says she. 'And we're very proud of that clock. Did mother tell you the legend?'

'No,' said I, adjusting the hands of my watch.

'Then listen to me,' says Virginia. 'It's very short. Years and years ago the son of this house was to die – at a quarter past six. I don't know what he'd done, but he'd disobeyed his father and so was condemned to death. But the servants were bound they'd save him. So during the night they blocked up the gap in the wheel that controls the chimes: the gap that engaged the hammer when the quarter was due. So that, though the time came and went, the clock never struck the quarter and the life of the boy was saved.'

'What a – what a curious tale,' I stammered. 'And the – the damage was never repaired?'

'Repaired?' screamed Virginia. 'How can you? Would you tear up a dainty legend like that? The piece of oak they fashioned is still in its place, and from that day to this that clock's never chimed the quarter – the quarter past.'

Though the valley was handsome enough, I fear my thoughts were busy with Vanity Fair. It was plain I was in the toils. I was suspected of proposing to play her false: I had, therefore, been carefully tested and, while I thought I had passed, I had broken down. Mansel's words came into my mind. *Always tell her the truth.* I could have done myself violence…

I felt suddenly angry. Vanity Fair was outrageous. How dared she subject a guest to such an ordeal? To be summoned and cross-examined, as though I were one of her servants, suspected of stealing goods… I had, of course, no standing. In fact, I was not a guest. In fact, I was being treated precisely as I deserved. And yet I resented that treatment. It made things so very awkward. I had told her a lie, and she knew it – and was sending a car to meet me, to whisk me back to her table and a dinner fit for a king. The truth was this. I knew I was being played with, and the knowledge was making me cross.

I pulled myself together and sought to review the facts. These were few, but ill-favoured.

An intensely suspicious woman, Vanity Fair suspected that I was a spy, that I was in league with Mansel, that I was aware that a man had come out of the meadows the night before. These suspicions she meant to confirm, and no convention whatever would stand in her way. When she had to deal with strangers, she much preferred to have them within her gates.

The evidence she held at the moment was that I had told her a lie. She had tried to make me clinch it – by saying that when the clock chimed, I had set my watch. By the grace of God, I had avoided that pitfall. All the same, honest guests do not lie: they may make mistakes, of course: but they do not lie. I decided with the utmost reluctance that I must correct my statement – repeat what Virginia had told me and say that the chime I had heard must have been the half-hour.

So much for the moves she had made: now for my own.

It was perfectly clear that she knew of the man in the meadows, because it was perfectly clear that she wanted to know if I knew. She also knew more than I did of Julie's death. Why did she want to know who was first on the scene?

On the whole I supposed that honours were more or less even: but another sitting or two in 'the Star Chamber' would certainly settle my hash. I should have to tell Mansel as much. I was no sort of match for Vanity Fair.

My mind made up, I began to observe such surroundings as must have pleased any man. As is not always the way, the closer you drew to the country, the finer it looked. With a sparkling eye, I marked the sweep of the valley and the depth of the hammercloth forests that covered the mountain sides: the turf I trod was like velvet and the song of unruly water refreshed the ear. The torrent ran to my left – to be tamed lower down to the service of Vanity Fair. It was this laughing water that flowed in the pipes of Jezreel and flooded the castle with light, as well, of course, as providing the gentle, regular music which I had heard from my bedroom the night before. The further I went, the taller the mountains seemed and the more the forests that clad them hung on their sides: the natural grandeur about me grew more superb and impressive with every step, yet the friendly peace of the country was always there, for the meadows were deep and smiling and gentle-eyed cows were grazing and swinging their cumbersome heads to rout the flies.

The object of my walk was threefold. I found the valley lovely and I wished to prove the promise which its recesses held out: I wished to acquaint myself with the outskirts of Jezreel: and I wished to discover the way by which the man I had seen had reached the floor of a valley with walls so sheer. (I knew, of course, of one path: but I felt that Vanity Fair would hardly have told me the way which her man had used.)

Now I had a binocular with me, and when I had covered two miles, I had a sudden whim to survey Jezreel. It was rather late in the day, for, to see any detail at all, I should have looked back when I had gone but three furlongs, or less than that. All the same, my glasses were strong and, since the chance might not come back, I took my seat on a knoll and put them up to my eyes.

Inch by inch I raked the façade and the terrace, upon which I could make out two footmen arranging chairs. I inspected the roof and the tower and I saw that the fatal casement was now fast shut. I could see my bedroom windows, at one of which Bell was standing with something of mine in his hand. I could see the private apartments of Vanity Fair, and something at one of their windows of curious shape: a thick-set cross it looked like...

Vanity Fair lowered her glasses and waved.

Feeling uncommonly foolish, I did the same.

I also swore – for some ridiculous reason, under my breath. And then, with what grace I could summon, I put my glasses away and resumed my walk.

To be so disconcerted was childish, as I very soon saw, but it had not occurred to me that my progress along the valley was to be watched. To take with me and use my glasses was a perfectly natural act: and if it was the way of a knave, it was equally well the way of an honest man. And since, in any event, the damage, if any, was done, from that time on I determined to do as I pleased.

I, therefore, made the most of that afternoon, judging height and distance, marking what cover there was, surveying the sides of the mountains for signs of paths and seeking and finding three places at which one could cross the water by night as by day.

So I came to the head of the valley about a quarter past five.

The head of the valley was closed, except for a deep ravine by which the water came down. The torrent raged in this channel which it had worn and no man on earth could ever have gone that way; but I think, if he could, he would only have come to a cliff, for though, because the gorge curled, I could not see up, above the bellow of the rapids I was almost sure I could hear the roar of a fall. I very soon saw the path which I was to take, but hereabouts there was no other way out and, after a few minutes' rest in the cool which the rapids dispensed, I left the turf to climb to the mountain road.

Now the path was mostly open: it follows that the higher I climbed, the better I viewed the mountains on the opposite side of the valley which I had left. These were most heavily wooded: but, observing them carefully, I presently saw that what I had thought one mountain was really two, and that though, from below, the foliage hid their juncture, there must at that point be a way that a man could take. (I do not mean to say that he could not have climbed straight up the mountain-side, for, steep as it

34

was he could have gone up or come down by passing from tree to tree: but this would have been a most hard and perilous progress and could never have been attempted except by day.) When next I stopped to look, it was clear I was right, for I saw the faint ridge in the pretty green quilt of the tree-tops which tells of a pass.

Now Vanity Fair had not said that the valley was blind, but she had pretty well forced me to take the path on my right. I had little doubt of two things. One was that she did not wish me to find the pass I had marked: and the other that it was by that pass that the man I had seen in the meadows had come to Jezreel.

I was nearing the road now and I stopped once more to gaze across the valley and see what I could.

Now the path had been leading me back, away from the head of the valley towards Jezreel, and when I looked round this last time, I saw directly before me a delicate fall of water which was lacing the hanging forest a crow's mile off. The cascade itself was so slender and the forest about it so deep that unless I had turned at that moment, I should never have known it was there. That was how I had missed it when I had gone by in the valley, because for two or three paces I was looking the other way.

At once I whipped out my glasses and set my back to a rock.

If there *was* a path up to the pass, at some point or other that path had to cross that fall...

And so it did, halfway up. I could see the rough-hewn bridge that carried it over the foam. There was not so much as a handrail: and the bridge was very narrow, just wide enough for one man.

At last I lowered my glasses, to smile at my luck. Three paces more or less, and I should have gone empty away. As it was...

I put my glasses away and turned to the road.

This was closer than I knew. In fact, the boulder had masked it – the rock against which I had leaned, to steady my gaze. As I rounded that comfortable bulwark –

'That's right,' said Vanity Fair. 'Did you set your watch?'

She was sitting alone in the back of an open car. On its step was spread a napkin, on which was standing a glass. As I stepped on to the road, the chauffeur, called Jean, ripped open a bottle of beer.

'I knew you'd be thirsty,' she said. 'And thirst is a healthy emotion which should be indulged. Not a thirst for knowledge, you know. I've known that to be unhealthy.'

I saw my chance and leaped in.

'I never asked her,' I said. 'She volunteered the information.'

An image regarded me straitly.

'Who volunteered what?'

'Virginia,' I said. 'She saw me setting my watch and told me the legend and that the clock doesn't chime the quarter past. If she wasn't pulling my leg, that means that I must be mistaken and that it was the half-hour and not the quarter that I heard chimed last night.'

The eyes of Vanity Fair were like dancing steel.

'Oh, Richard Chandos,' she said, 'when I asked you this afternoon, why ever didn't you say that you'd set your watch by the chime?'

I picked up my glass.

'It wouldn't have been true,' I said.

'I wasn't thinking of that,' said Vanity Fair.

I confess that I drank her health…

On the way down we stopped, to look at Jezreel.

'You can't see it so well from the valley,' said Vanity Fair.

Nearly an hour had gone by when I stopped in the midst of my toilet to stare upon Bell.

'But I saw you,' I said. 'You were standing just there, with something of mine in your hand.'

'It wasn't me, sir,' said Bell. 'I've been down in the garage, at work on the Rolls. I've never come into this room all the afternoon.'

For a moment I stood, still staring. Then I returned to the business of fastening the studs of my shirt. It was no good my being annoyed: again I had been treated exactly as I deserved.

'Well, just run through the drawers,' I said, 'as a matter of form. I don't suppose anything's gone. Whoever it was had orders to search, not steal.'

With that, I continued to dress.

As I got into my jacket, I heard Bell exclaim. Then he turned from an open wardrobe and came to my side. The pistol with which I travelled was in his hand. Its magazine was empty, and the round that had lain in the chamber had been withdrawn.

'So they did come to steal,' said I. 'Have we any spare ammunition?'

'That we have, sir,' said Bell. 'I've got a box in the Rolls.'

'Well, fill it up,' said I, 'and put it where I can reach it, just under the bed.'

'Very good, sir,' said Bell. 'But I think you should lock your doors.'

'I will,' said I. 'And tell Captain Mansel this. I think that I ought to see him. If I can't – well, I can't. But tell him that I'm being played with. He'll understand.'

'That's what you're here for,' said Mansel.

Bell and I jumped like two children and then swung round.

Mansel was sitting on a table, dressed in an old suit of flannels, swinging a leg.

'We're perfectly safe,' he said. 'It's my evening off. I'm believed to be cycling to Perin. That's why I'm late. But when you come up to bed, you shall have your talk.'

'Well, I'm damned glad to see you,' I said. 'But how did you come? By the salon?'

Mansel shook his head.

'Don't lock your doors,' he said. 'It isn't worthwhile.' He walked to a massive pier-glass, heavily framed in gilt and fastened against the wall. 'You know the old riddle,' he said: ' "When is a door not a door?" Well, here's a new answer, William: "When it's a looking-glass".' He laid hold of the frame and pulled. At once the mirror swung inwards, and there was a thin, stone corridor, running both right and left. 'The backstairs, William. You never saw such a system. Takes you all over the house.' He closed the door carefully. 'And now you'll have to be going. Don't let your lady friend bounce you, and listen for all you're worth. I rather think you may get some copy tonight.'

'I've more than enough to go on with,' said I. 'We simply must have a talk. But I mayn't be up for ages. You know what she is.'

'You'll find me here,' said Mansel. 'I'm out on the loose, you know: and I can come in when I please. And, to tell you the truth, I don't care how late you are, for I happen to be very tired and I'm going to sleep – in your room. Don't you worry, William. Bell will look after me.'

Two minutes later I was drinking an excellent cocktail and arguing with Virginia about the various styles in which women dress their hair.

The priest was late for dinner – a breach of duty so grave that, without being told to do so, a servant ran off to his room. He appeared, however, whilst the soup was still on the board, to take his seat in manifest agitation, which I supposed to be due to his failure to be in time.

Vanity Fair knew better.

'I understand you've received a registered letter. Is that the stone which has troubled the stagnant pool?'

With that air of importance which only the unimportant ever take on –

'My presence is required,' said the priest. He breathed very hard. 'If you will allow me, I will leave for England tomorrow.' He sipped his soup. 'As a trustee, you know. There's talk of an aerodrome.'

His mistress sat very still.

' "Leave for England?" ' she said. 'You're out of your mind.'

The chaplain was wagging his head.

' "Leave for England",' he said. 'I confess I shall feel the move. Besides, I've no bags. I used to have one – a brown one: but things get lost. Of course, one shouldn't take root. But business is business, madam, as someone has said.'

He returned to his soup, frowning. The rest of us awaited the earthquake with bated breath.

'Quite so,' said Vanity Fair. 'And business will keep you here, at the Château Jezreel.'

To everyone's horror, the divine saw fit to disgorge a ripple of mirth.

'Madam,' he declared, 'I know you. You think that I shall be lost. But you mustn't seek to dissuade me. As the solicitors say – '

'I never seek to dissuade,' flamed Vanity Fair. 'Be good enough to tell your advisers that the services of my chaplain cannot be spared.'

But the man had no ears to hear. The deference shown in his letter had made him drunk.

'Don't tempt me, madam,' he boomed. 'As trustee, my duty is plain. I have no more desire to leave you than you have to let me go. But it will not be for long. And when my business is concluded – '

'Business be damned. Understand this, Below. If you leave Jezreel tomorrow, you leave for good.'

The chaplain started and choked: for a moment he stared about him: then his benignant satisfaction changed to incredulous dismay. As a baby's whose cake has been taken, his lips went down, and when, at that moment, a servant offered him wine, he waved away the dainty as though such consolation was only fit for the dogs.

'But, madam,' he wailed, 'year after year you have urged me to go on leave: and now that I – '

'That will do,' said Vanity Fair. 'Give your letter to Acorn. He'll write you a suitable answer and send it off.' She turned to me. 'Did Virginia show you the lanterns that came from Prague?'

'She showed me a lot,' I said, 'but – '

'You must see them tomorrow, if you can spare the time. Has Gaston shown you his wardrobe – that came from Bordeaux?'

'I have bought nothing in Bordeaux,' screamed Gaston.

'You may have bought them in Paris, but they are "as worn in" Bordeaux. Have a word with Mr Chandos' servant. He'll bear me out.' She turned to her daughter. 'Where did you go today?'

'We had tea at Moineau,' said Virginia.

'The dog returns to his vomit,' said Vanity Fair. 'Which of you two is it that has this disgusting taste? Or do you both wallow together? Don't think that I'm going to forbid you, but I'd very much rather you drank.'

Virginia prayed me in aid.

'Don't you like dancing, Mr Chandos?'

'Yes,' I lied stoutly. 'I do.'

'Quite so,' said Vanity Fair. 'You also like the Zoological Gardens. But that doesn't mean that you cherish the ways of baboons.' She raised her eyes to heaven. 'The casino at Moineau, when crowded, must be a gorgeous sight.'

'But, mother,' protested Virginia, 'you know you won't let us dance here.'

'You shall dance after dinner, my dear – with Mr Chandos. Gaston's interpretation of the art is rather too simian for me. I know that we're lower than the angels, but why illustrate that truth?'

'I'm very bad,' I said nervously.

'You would be,' said Vanity Fair. 'But not to the pipes of Pan. You danced up the valley today. I saw the spring in your step and the lift of your head.' She returned to Virginia. 'I'm not suggesting that the leopard should change his spots: but so long as you're under my roof, you must behave as my daughter and not as his wife. The servants have to be considered. Once you're married, you'll probably live elsewhere. Gaston might find me exacting, as a resident mother-in-law.'

With a very crooked smile, Gaston expelled a noise which I took to be one of dissent.

'I cannot interpret that sound,' said Vanity Fair. 'Did it mean that you enjoy my society?'

'Of course,' said Gaston.

'I'm glad to hear it. I tell you frankly I take great pleasure in yours. You importune me for trouble – to my delight. When anyone asks me for trouble, I'll feed him until he bursts.' She turned upon me. 'Digest that, Richard Chandos. It may provoke your stomach, but it'll do you good.'

The meal proceeded.

Glancing at Father Below, I observed with relief that the comfort of apples seemed to have had its way. He was eating with evident relish and, whilst he now and then sighed, he stayed himself with champagne. Here was no subject for pity. I could see him at some station-hotel... His mistress knew best. As for her, her reduction of the obstinate fortress had whisked her ill-humour away.

My mind flew suddenly to Julie. I found it indecent that we should be feasting while she lay stark in the chapel within our gates. By rights we should have been fasting. But the tragedy had made no difference to life at Jezreel.

The place seemed suddenly sinister. The breath of the Middle Ages tainted the air... Death was dressed in splendour, and Evil was royally lodged.

Gaston and Acorn were arguing.

'I know you are wrong,' said Gaston.

'Have a care,' said Vanity Fair. 'My secretary is paid to be right.'

'I do not care,' said Gaston. 'I say he is wrong.'

'It's some time ago,' said Acorn, 'but I was at New Orleans when the news came in.'

'What news?' said Vanity Fair.

'That the *Clair de Lune* had been holed on her maiden voyage.'

'No, no,' cried Gaston. 'It was the *Pompadour*.'

The man was right. I knew it. Old friends of mine, the Cheviots, had barely escaped with their lives when the *Pompadour* was holed on her maiden voyage.

Before I could put in an oar –

'Well, what on earth does it matter?' said Vanity Fair.

'But he says I am wrong,' cried Gaston.

'I've no doubt you are. What of that?'

'I am not wrong,' screamed Gaston. 'I – '

'That,' said Vanity Fair, 'is extremely easy to say.'

'But I was on board,' raved Gaston, and struck the oak with his hand.

There was an uncomfortable silence.

Then –

'Indeed,' said Vanity Fair. 'How very disagreeable for the other passengers.' She turned to Virginia. 'Do they throw people out at Moineau? Or can you behave as you please?'

Her daughter set her head on one side.

'I shouldn't risk it, mother: you're very well here.'

To my surprise and relief, Vanity Fair sat back and laughed till she cried.

I confess my respect leaped up. She knew how to lose.

After dinner I danced with Virginia, against my will. This on the terrace, to music most beautifully played and the light of the moon. Vanity Fair applauded the exhibition and made us perform until I was ready to drop. When Gaston sought to withdraw, she called him back and made him sit by her side.

And Julie lay dead.

Mansel let me talk for a quarter of an hour. Then he lay back in his chair and crossed his legs.

'With Vanity Fair,' he said, 'you never know. That is her ace of trumps. She's put her arms about you today. But I wouldn't swear that you're not to be murdered tonight. That you're to be visited I'm certain. That's really why I'm here. I think you're to be half-killed. I can hardly believe that she would dare bump you off.'

'Well, I don't care,' said I. 'You and I know how much I value my life. But, you know, this woman's wearing. She's as good as a raree-show: but she ought to be under glass.'

'That's perfectly true,' said Mansel. 'What I've gone through since you came, I cannot describe. To be weighed by Vanity Fair is to be found wanting – and accordingly weighed again.'

'And your duties,' said I. 'What are you here to detect?'

Mansel sighed.

'Vanity Fair sometimes behaves as a child. I am here to watch de Rachel and pick up what gossip I can in the servants' hall. There's very little gossip – the servants are too much afraid of losing their jobs. She pays them four times as much as they'd get elsewhere; but if one of them puts a foot wrong, he's fired that night. I except friend Jean – as lazy a rogue as you'd meet in a summer's day. But Vanity Fair has his measure: she's using him. As for the sweet-smelling Gaston, anyone can see what he is – a French Count ten times removed from the cousin whose title he bears. I suppose he's a right to bear it. I'm told that, except for him, the family's faded out.'

'Well, there,' said I, 'there's a chance that Titus Cheviot can help,' and, with that, I told him about the *Pompadour*.

'Good,' said Mansel. 'Drop a line to Titus and tell him to write to Anise. That was five or six years ago. De Rachel left France then and he's not got a bean: and he sticks what he does for the money Virginia will bring.'

'By God, he earns it,' said I.

'Serve him right,' said Mansel. 'But why does Virginia want him? Answer me that. She's not too bad, Virginia. But she doesn't seem to be acting under duress.'

'I'm sure she dislikes him,' said I. 'Why, my face is straighter than hers while her mother is twisting his tail.'

'I'd love to hear it,' said Mansel. 'Never mind. What else did you pick up in that wonderful dining-room?'

I told him how Vanity Fair had whipped Father Below.

'That,' said Mansel, 'is what I wanted to hear. She requires Below for the marriage. For some reason best known to herself, the date's not fixed. But he's got to be here on tap, ready to tie the knot at a nod from her. A *locum tenens* might boggle at rushing the business through. But Below will do as he's told – as you saw tonight. That letter he got was written at my request.' He threw back his head and covered his eyes with his hands. 'You know I'm more confused than when I began. I've confirmed an idea or two, but they're in my lady's favour. For one thing, I'm pretty sure that this marriage is going to go through.'

'And Julie?' said I.

'Ah,' said Mansel. 'And Julie. That's a bad show. And there's another riddle. What on earth can Julie have done?'

'She was killed, of course.'

'I think that Julie was smothered, and then thrown out. There were certain signs in her face. I imagine your wallah did it – the wallah you saw in the fields. I don't think he's gone: I think he's up in the tower. And he, no doubt, is the fellow who's coming to see you tonight.' I glanced at the looking-glass. 'You needn't worry. As long as he sees your light burning, he won't come down.'

'But what's the idea?' said I. 'To put me out of action?'

'To frighten you off,' said Mansel. 'Not out of Jezreel, for she likes your company. But off the holy ground of her private affairs.

'Supposing you wake in the night, to find your throat in the grip of a monster you cannot see. You're being choked to death, and you can't as much as cry out. You put up a fight, of course, but what can you do? At last you lose consciousness, and when you come to, you're alone... The next morning you tell your tale. Vanity Fair expresses the utmost concern, declares she can't understand it. "It looks, Mr Chandos, as though you'd offended some god – spied on his private rites, or something like that..." And while she speaks, she's mocking you with those eyes. Pure speculation, of course. But I think I'm right.

'Anyway, you've done very well, and you'll soon be free. Tomorrow night the Rolls will be ready for the road: and the day after that you're going. She'll try to keep you all right, but you mustn't stay, for only your going away will convince her that you are no spy. Once you're gone, she'll miss you – Jezreel is dull – and she'll do her very utmost to get you back. And back you will come, my lad, in the fullness of time. You'll tell her you're going to Biarritz, and thence to Spain.'

'Where in fact am I going?'

'I'm not quite sure,' said Mansel, and got to his feet. 'I'll send you your orders in writing tomorrow night. And now you must go to bed. Time's getting on, and I've got to be up at six.'

My lights had been put out for nearly an hour and, though I was wide awake and straining my ears, I lay with my eyes close shut, as though I were fast asleep.

Beside the curtains that graced the head of my bed Mansel, I knew, was standing as still as death.

I never heard the man enter: I never heard him approach.

The first thing I heard was the smack of Mansel's fist, as he hit someone under the jaw.

In a flash I was out of bed, to find Mansel down on his knees, with his hand on his victim's heart.

'I had to hit hard,' he breathed, 'but he seems all right. He won't come round for some time.'

45

(Here I should say that Mansel was a beautiful boxer, and, as such, had been famous before he had left his school.)

'Where's your torch?' I whispered. 'I don't believe it's my man.'

'I know it isn't,' said Mansel. 'It's a colleague of mine, *called Jean.*'

With that, he drew his torch and lighted the fellow's face.

There was no doubt about it. There were the bull-dog features of the chauffeur who, six hours before, had poured my beer.

Mansel sat back on his heels and fingered his chin.

'I might have known,' he murmured. 'William, my boy, we've done a good night's work. This is going to be very awkward for Vanity Fair.'

Twenty minutes later Mansel was gone and I was again in my bed, and Jean, who was still unconscious, was lying on the tiles of my bathroom, his ankles lashed with his belt and his wrists with mine. The weapon which he had been wearing was back in his sleeve.

It was a curious weapon, carefully sheathed and plainly many years old. There is, I believe, one like it in a private collection in Rome. It was not a lethal weapon. The mark it would have made on the skin would scarce have been seen. It was, however, hollow.

How much liquid this 'syringe' contained I do not know, but the drop which Mansel extracted and placed in a phial was found to be more than sufficient to cause immediate death.

3

The Path in the Mountains

'It's a matter for you, Mr Chandos.'

'The Star Chamber' was cool and dim, for its shutters were shut. Vanity Fair's manner went with the room. Cool, reserved, entirely at my disposal, she might have been my banker – some very giant of finance that, because I was his client, was awaiting my puny instructions to sell or retain some shares.

I crossed my legs and laughed.

'I don't care,' I said. 'So far as I am concerned, my score was settled last night. I'll bet he's got a headache just now that he'd sell for what it'd fetch.'

'Headache?' said Vanity Fair. She drew in her breath. 'He'd have something more than a headache if I had my way.'

Of this I was sure. Vanity Fair had no use for servants that failed.

'What does Acorn think?' said I.

'I don't think he knows what he thinks. As usual, he offers me bread, and gives me a stone. I said the man should be jailed, and he quite agreed. "Then have him jailed," said I. "That's all very well," said Acorn, "but what's he done?" Since I couldn't answer the question, I sent for you. After all, you'll have to charge him.'

'Well, he hasn't done anything,' said I. 'He didn't have time.'

'What d'you think he was going to do?'

'I've no idea,' said I.

Vanity Fair frowned.

'In a way, you know, it's a pity you struck so soon. He was bent on mischief, of course, or he would have knocked at the door. Why did you strike so soon? Wouldn't it have been more normal to challenge him first?'

'His movement was furtive,' said I, 'and that was enough for me.'

Vanity Fair nodded.

'Quite right,' she said. 'Never wait. Well, what's to be done? Acorn is waiting on you. Say the word and he's going to ring up the police.'

I shook my head.

'Don't do it for me,' said I.

'We can do it for nobody else. Unless you're prepared to charge him, it's no good our calling the police.'

I admit the cards were good, but she played them uncommonly well.

'Let the fellow go,' said I, and got to my feet.

'Wait a minute.'

She moved to a table to pick up a telephone.

After a moment's pause –

'Mr Chandos declines to charge him. Pay him his wages and let him be ready to leave at a quarter to twelve. On foot, of course. I'll see the man in the guard-room at twelve o'clock.'

The guard-room lay in the tower that belonged to her suite.

As she replaced her receiver –

'Please rest assured that Jean will never forget this unpleasant affair. I shall see to that. I trust that you'll come to forget it, and please begin by putting it out of your mind. Ask Virginia to show you those lanterns. You can't think of anything else when you're looking at them.'

Before seeking Virginia, I went to look at the Rolls.

As I made my way to the garage, I considered again the nature of Vanity Fair. Yesterday she had done me honour: last night she had sought my life – in the vilest of ways. And yet I was sure that she liked me... Some would have found her mad. But she was not mad. She was as level-headed as Mansel himself. She was not even inconsistent. Her will of iron was her god, and she was its prophetess. To her will all things were subject: the faintest attempt to thwart it had to be crushed. These things were not out of reason. What was out of reason was that I still liked her.

I entered a mighty coach-house and walked to the Rolls.

'She'll be ready tonight, sir,' said Mansel. 'I expect your servant told you there's nothing wrong.'

'All that labour for nothing,' said I.

'It had to be done, sir,' said Mansel. 'There's your wing. I'm afraid it won't look very smart.'

'They've been very quick,' said I.

'They have indeed, sir,' said Mansel. 'But they want to keep our custom, and that's why they did it at once.'

I turned to see Virginia.

'And what,' said she, 'are you doing this afternoon?'

'What you suggest?' said I.

'Have you seen St Albert de Moulin?'

I shook my head.

'Well, you must see that. It's a city – not quite as big as Jezreel. Let Gaston drive us over. It's only forty miles off.'

'With pleasure,' said I. 'And this morning you'll show me the lanterns that came from Prague.'

'I'll show you them now. One moment. Can we have the coupé, Wright, at a quarter to three?'

'Certainly, miss,' said Mansel. 'Will you take a man in the dickey?'

'No, thanks. We'll take her alone.'

'Very good, miss.'

As we left the coach-house –

'I do like that man,' said Virginia. 'I hope mother keeps him on.'

The lanterns hung in a suite on the second floor. To reach this, we had to go by the rooms in which Gaston was lodged. As we were passing these, I heard a girl's agonised cry.

'Let me go, sir, I beg and pray you. Oh, let me go.'

There was only one thing to be done.

'You go on,' I said. 'I'll join you.'

Virginia inclined her head and held on her way.

I opened de Rachel's door…

The fellow had a girl by the wrists – a housemaid, a nice-looking girl. She was straining away from her captor, whose face was wreathed in a grin.

When he saw me, he let her go, and she made her escape.

I shut the door behind her and turned to see the gallant more white in the face than red.

He was swallowing violently.

'What then?' he said thickly, and breathed very hard through the nose.

'This,' said I. 'Virginia heard what was happening, and now I'm going to ask her what she wants done. If she wants you kicked, I'll kick you until you pray for death. If she wants your head knocked off, I'm not too bad with my fists and I'll do what I can. If she asks me not to thrash you, I'll let you go. But I shouldn't do this again, because next time I shan't leave the decision to her.'

With that, I turned and left him, with a hand to his throat.

Virginia was not to be seen, but right at the end of the hall a door which had been shut was standing ajar…

As I pushed it open, I saw her at one of the windows regarding the sunlit fields.

At once I passed to her side.

'I'm sorry,' I said. 'I've taken no action, of course. Is there anything you would like done?'

She shook her head. Then, without looking round, she put out a hand.

I took it naturally.

'I'm sorry, Virginia.'

Her fingers closed upon mine.

'When will your car be ready?'

'This evening,' said I.

'Then go tomorrow morning. Let nothing stop you, Richard. Just go – and forget Jezreel.'

I felt very kindly towards her. She did not know that I knew the risk she was running in giving me such advice.

Appearances, however, had to be preserved.

'I'm not afraid,' I said. 'Besides, he won't try to get back – in your mother's house.'

Virginia shivered.

Then –

'I want you to go for my sake. If you stay, you'll make me unhappy. I mayn't be in love with Gaston; but, at least, at the moment, I care for nobody else.'

What the false suggestion cost her I cannot tell. But this I do know – few girls would have gone so far to save a comparative stranger from possible harm. Virginia had pledged her jewels, in order to force my hand.

She had, of course, succeeded. I had to go now. Not that it mattered, because I had meant to be gone. What did matter was that now I could not come back.

As I put her hand up to my lips, I wondered what Mansel would say...

Virginia caught her breath – she knew how to act. Then she whipped away her fingers.

'And now for the lanterns,' she said.

These were most exquisite things. Each of their seven faces presented a lovely window, glazed with Bohemian glass. The windows were made to open, and each of them had four panes:

and each of the panes was presenting some fable of Aesop's, the detail of which was so fine as to trouble the naked eye.

They had been made, said Virginia, as a wedding gift to some monarch whose name I forget: and now they served to illumine a seldom-used salon belonging to Vanity Fair. Lest the light they shed was too poor, standing between the windows was a sedan chair. This I had marked and admired the day before. The brocade of its cushions…

In spite of myself I started.

The roof of the chair was open, *but the blinds of the chair were drawn.*

As we turned to leave the salon, I know that Virginia was speaking, but I do not know what she said.

To be honest, my brain was recoiling, as a man recoils from a snake.

'Ask Virginia to show you those lanterns.'

The truth was clear, if startling.

Though Virginia herself did not know it, she and I had just kept an appointment with Vanity Fair.

I confess that from that time on I counted the hours. I had had enough of Jezreel. For me, the house was haunted, and that by something more dreadful than any ghost. The place was cursed with the spirit of Vanity Fair.

We are so well accustomed to the safety of modern times that treachery is no longer a household word, and I almost despair of presenting the horrid condition of mind to which I had now been reduced. It was not, I think, bodily fear: it was not the dread of exposure: it was the guilty feeling of one who, by his own act, has witnessed some hideous office not meant to be seen, who knows he is being sought by the officers whom he observed. This on suspicion alone, for Vanity Fair had no proof. As a spy, I deserved no less. But she was using treachery as though it were not an essence, but something which is sold by the quart.

I reported the business to Mansel within the hour. My hasty note concluded, *I firmly believe that all these sedan-chairs are nothing but posts of observation, to be used as required.*

After what had occurred that morning I had, of course, assumed that Virginia's expedition would not take place. De Rachel had insulted Virginia by insulting a decent maid who was paid to sweep, but not garnish, the rooms which his presence fouled: and I had insulted de Rachel by denying his right to bestow his fragrant favours as he saw fit. At luncheon, however, to my surprise and disgust, the arrangement was gaily confirmed by Vanity Fair, and at three o'clock precisely our most uncongenial muster struggled into the coupé and took to the roads.

I shall never forget that drive.

I can only suppose that de Rachel's skin was of the nature of buckram, for his air was as high and as jaunty as though he had in his pocket the patent of chivalry. That he fancied himself as a driver was very clear, and I think the display which he gave was meant as well to awe Virginia as to diminish me and to demonstrate to us both that his skill and dash and daring were idiosyncrasies. Be that as it may, he so much abused the car that I could hardly sit still, while the risks which he took were so shocking that again and again I was frightened out of my life. Mercifully the roads were open, and the traffic which we encountered was very slight, but as we approached St Albert, he preferred to run over a dog to slackening speed. A more wanton piece of cruelty I never saw, and I was not surprised when Virginia, who knew her swain and, while we were some way off, had begged the dog's life, immediately burst into tears. This very natural distress appeared to afford de Rachel matter for mirth and he made the incident into a parable by which was exposed the folly of such as made bold to oppose his strength of will.

Although I was ripe for murder, for Virginia's sake I said nothing – until we were out of the car.

Then I took de Rachel aside.

'Either I drive back,' I said, 'or you travel alone. Don't argue the point, but tell me which you prefer.'

The man looked me up and down.

'And if I refuse,' he said.

'Then I shall decide,' said I, and, with that, I rejoined Virginia, who showed me the little town.

When we returned to the coupé, de Rachel was asprawl in the dickey, pretending to be asleep...

I am glad to record that some ten miles from Jezreel we ran into a thunderstorm. Of malice prepense, I instantly put down my foot. ...When we arrived at the castle, Gaston de Rachel's condition suggested that he was newly risen from the bed of some stream.

As he descended stiffly –

'It serves you right,' said Virginia, 'for killing that dog.'

I had expected that Bell would hand me my orders when I went upstairs to dress, but he told me instead that I should find a note in the Rolls: 'beneath the cushion, sir: but you're not to touch it until you're twenty miles off.'

'All right,' said I. 'Tell Captain Mansel I'll leave about half-past ten.'

'Very good, sir,' said Bell. He hesitated. 'And if you please, I'm to spend the night here in your room.'

'Oho,' said I. 'So he thinks...'

'He didn't say, sir,' said Bell. 'But no one won't be surprised, sir – not after last night.'

'That's true,' said I. 'All right. We'll watch by turns: and if anyone comes, we'll plug him before he can think.'

'Every time, sir,' said Bell, warmly.

But I knew in my heart there was no danger, because Mansel had given no order. My faithful servant was taking his name in vain.

Half-an-hour later, perhaps, my hostess sat back in her stall. 'You're determined to leave us,' she said. 'Hasn't Gaston contrived to induce you to alter your mind?'

'I'm afraid not,' said I, unsteadily.

Vanity Fair shrugged her shoulders.

'He'll miss you terribly,' she said. 'Won't you, Gaston?'

De Rachel was understood to say that he would.

'You don't seem very sure about it.'

'I shall be desolated,' mouthed Gaston.

'I had a feeling you would,' said Vanity Fair. 'Still you ought to have learned quite a lot in forty-eight hours. Did you make the most of your drive?'

'I enjoyed it very much,' said Gaston, with bulging eyes.

Vanity Fair turned to me.

'And you?'

'It was delightful,' said I, shakily. 'The scenery – '

'Yes. I wasn't thinking of the scenery,' said Vanity Fair. 'Never mind. Candle's arriving on Friday – I've just had a wire. The portrait-painter, you know. I want him to paint Virginia.'

'They'll do each other credit,' said I. 'He's awfully good.'

'So I'm told. If he does her well, I'm going to have him do Gaston and Father Below. The two together, you know – a conversational piece.'

'I do not want to be painted,' said Gaston violently.

'That I can well believe. But I think you'll appeal to Candle. There's something about your smile that won't go into words. There's a note of interrogation about it which is curiously repulsive. And Father Below is pure Flemish.'

'I say I do not want to be painted.'

'I know. I heard you just now. If you say it again, I'll point the obvious and have you done in a kilt.'

We all broke down at that, and decency went to the winds. Virginia was simply convulsed. For the fiftieth time I wondered what manner of match this was.

Vanity Fair was speaking.

'Where shall you go, Mr Chandos?'

'To Biarritz, I think. There may be some letters there. And so into Spain.'

Vanity Fair nodded.

'Send me a line,' she said. 'And a postcard of Burgos Cathedral. I was married there, but I haven't seen it for years.'

'Of course,' said I.

Father Below looked up.

'May I ask your servant,' he said, 'to buy me some boots?'

'Ask me,' said I.

'You're very kind,' said the priest. 'Years ago I purchased some boots in Spain. I never knew such comfort. They had elastic sides.'

'I won't forget,' I said, laughing.

The priest blinked across the table.

'I'm sorry you're going,' he said irrelevantly.

'So are we all,' cried Virginia.

'Why?' said Vanity Fair.

'Madam,' said Father Below, 'he's an honest face.'

I felt very much ashamed.

'His face is his fortune,' said Vanity Fair.

'And ours,' said Acorn, suddenly.

'Speech!' shrieked Virginia. 'Richard, you've got right off.'

'Stay and be painted,' said her mother. 'Conversational piece with Virginia. And what did you think of the lanterns that came from Prague?'

Her smile was dazzling: her gaze seemed to pierce my brain.

'I shall never forget them,' said I.

'I think you're rather like them.'

'Like the lanterns?' said I.

'Yes,' said Vanity Fair. Her eyes were like dancing flames. 'They're so very easy to see through, and yet, when one looks, one can hardly believe one's eyes.'

There was a moment's silence.

Then Gaston sniggered.

Quick as a flash, the whip was laid to his back.

'Have I said anything vulgar?' said Vanity Fair.

By noon the next day Lally was peeping below me and Jezreel was twenty miles off. The Col de Fer lay between us... For all that, I berthed the Rolls at a point from which I could see the road back for more than a mile. Such precaution seemed fantastic: but then you never knew – with Vanity Fair.

I left the car and lighted a cigarette. As I threw the match into a runnel, Bell handed me Mansel's note.

The position is most obscure, but I think that the death of Julie offers a definite line.

Julie was undoubtedly murdered.

Jezreel was Julie's first place.

I believe that she was engaged – to be put to death.

If I am right, she must have given offence by something she did at her home, the little village of Carlos, forty miles off, by road.

Her offence must have been the grave one of knowing too much.

I want you to try to find out what Julie knew.

Get a map and see the relation which Carlos bears to Jezreel. Reconnoitre the vicinity of Carlos and follow all paths till you strike the one you saw leading out of the Jezreel valley.

Note.

It is vital that we should be in communication. Let Bell get in touch with Carson, who is in touch with me.

Note.

Your visit has been invaluable. For one thing only, Candle's an acquaintance of mine. Had I not learned that he was coming, I might have walked into his arms.

Without a word, I handed the sheet to Bell.

Then I strolled down the road and started to lay my plans.

My orders were clear. I meant to carry them out with the utmost dispatch. I felt like some prisoner enlarged – that has left his fellow behind in the gloom of the jail. It made me much more than uneasy to think of Mansel alone within the verge of Jezreel.

That night I lay at Bayonne, and at two o'clock the next day Bell set me down at a point three miles from Carlos, where the road was shadowed by beeches and borne by an old stone bridge.

When he had gone about –

'Tomorrow night,' said I, 'between twelve and one. If I'm not here, I'll be here the night after that. If we simply have to write, that crevice there will serve as a letter-box. And now you get off to Anise. And mind you take it easy tomorrow and let the Rolls care for herself.'

'Very good, sir,' said Bell, slowly. And then, 'You will watch out, sir? I – I know you don't care any more, but there's others that value your life.'

'I promise,' I said.

'Good luck, sir,' said Bell, and held his hand to his hat.

Then he let the Rolls steal forward…

A moment later she rounded a bend in the road and passed out of my sight.

The weather seemed set fair, and I was travelling light. My clothes were more easy than handsome, and a little haversack was all the luggage I had. And in that there was food for two days.

Once again I looked at my map. Then I set off up the road, towards the village I sought.

I was in the heart of the mountains, very close to the borders of Spain. The road which the Rolls had been using was little more than a shelf. The country was very lonely, yet showed on every side the traces of man's acceptance of Nature's gifts. A patch of scythe-mown meadow sloped to a belt of forest no axe had touched: sheep, like toys, clung to a strip of pasture neighboured by angry crags: a tumbling rill had been switched to water a field that hung like an apron over this shapely spur, and there was a piled-stone wall, with a barn thrusting up beside it, to house the hay. There were several such barns hereabouts, all standing alone and remote and often perched upon heights to which no waggon could ever have made its way: it was clear that what hay they kept was carried by hand.

For a mile I followed the road: then I turned to strike up a mountain whose top, if the map was faithful, commanded the village of Carlos and, beyond, the marches of Spain.

Once I had viewed the village, I meant to make at once for the head of the valley of Jezreel.

In this way I hoped to short-circuit the system which Mansel had set, for, when I had found the valley, I could take the path that I knew and prove at once the relation it bore to Carlos and where it led.

More than an hour went by before I was able to gain the position I sought. Indeed, for the last hundred yards I had to cover ground which, had I not come so far, I would not have essayed; for I have no head for heights, yet had to go up an array of rock and verdure which was handsome enough to look at, but more like a wall than a slope.

Then I scrambled over a ridge and lay down, spent and panting, to look upon Carlos below me, grey and white in the sunshine, some two miles off.

I wiped the sweat from my face and took out my map...

A compass-bearing showed me that the valley I meant to make for lay almost due north, and after resting five minutes I got to my feet and set out for a sugar-loaf peak, which lay more to the east than I liked, yet made a better landmark than anything else I could see.

That my progress was watched by peasants, I make no doubt, but I never saw man or woman that afternoon. Flocks I saw and cattle, but only so far away that I could not hear their bells. Fountains and crags and forests were all my company, and once and again a meadow that seemed to have strayed from its fellows into a haughty pageant to which it did not belong.

The going was most severe, but I dared not spare myself, because the night was coming when, unless I was sure of my bearings, I could not march. For more than half the time the sugar-loaf peak was wholly out of my sight and, though I have what is called an eye to country, more than once I blundered and had to retrace my steps. By dint, however, of going as hard as I could, I made the foot of my landmark just as the sun went down.

I was now in a tract which was wilder than any that I had trodden that afternoon, and as I sat down by some water to break my fast, I saw that, direction apart, I could not hope to traverse country so rugged when once it was dark. I, therefore, ate no more than a crust of bread and then set about the business of crossing the vigorous torrent which barred my way.

At the price of ten precious minutes I found a spot at which I could leap the stream, but I very soon saw that I might have spared my pains, for that the water was going the way I believed to be mine. For a quarter-of-an-hour I followed its brawling course: then, to my vexation, it curled sharp round to the right and once again barred my way.

Stifling an oath – for the shadows were coming in – I began to cast about for another way over the foam: but here the ground was against me and, what was worse, the water itself was swollen because, since I had crossed it, it had accepted the tribute of two or three lesser streams. Indeed, the head of water was now considerable, and though I was ready to ford it, rather than make my way back, if I had tried I must have lost my footing and might have been badly hurt.

I, therefore, turned to retrace my weary steps, when it suddenly entered my head that this might well be the torrent that entered the very valley to which I was trying to come.

A moment's reflection convinced me that this was so. I could not, I knew, be far from the valley's head, and though I had never before been over this ground, I had seen enough of mountains to know that that two such important streams should be flowing so close together was most improbable.

The water, therefore, would be the most faithful of guides and, what was more, the path which I hoped to discover lay the same side of the torrent as that upon which I now stood.

I hastened down stream excitedly...

I had hoped to spend some of the night in one of the barns, but hereabouts there were none, for the country was much too rude to allow of meadows: now, however, I would not have altered my course for the finest of beds, for if, before night fell, I could strike my path, I could follow this in the darkness without any fear of falling or losing my way.

The light was failing fast when I rounded a precipitous shoulder to hear the roar of a fall.

With a leaping heart I pushed on and, after a gruelling furlong, I stood looking into the gorge at whose mouth I had sat and rested three days before. There was no doubt about it. If I had cared to go down to the foot of the fall and then climb up the mountain that mothered the gorge, I could have seen in the distance the lights of Jezreel.

As I had thought, the water fell over a cliff some forty feet high, to enter at once the ravine which its own immemorial impatience had fretted out of the rock. For the gorge had been but a gully when the hills took up the order they still maintained.

After a swift inspection I set my face to the east, that is to say to my right. At once I observed a dip in the fading skyline, which had the look of a saddle, a mile away. I doubted if I could reach it before the stars came out. But if I could, and if Mansel's theory was good, then the path which I was seeking would be lying right under my nose.

I set out feverishly...

I have often found that when one is bent upon something with all one's might, one is apt to shut one's eyes to the laws of Nature in a way that would discredit an infant of tender years. No mountain goat could have won the ridge I was seeking before night fell. The distance apart, until I came upon it, I could in no sort distinguish the country I had to cross, and before I had gone fifty paces the ground fell sharply away and I had to go down and so lose sight of the saddle I hoped to reach. When I was down, I found that my way was opposed by a spur which I could not scale, and I had to turn south, to round it as best I could. By the time I was round, it was almost too dark to see, and in any event a shoulder of hanging forest was now obscuring the background upon which I was depending for my direction. For all that, I struggled on, but the forest forced me still further out of my course, and when at last I was round, my skyline had gone. Night had come in.

I was now as much disheartened as, a quarter-of-an-hour before, I had been elated. I could not see: I had but the roughest idea of which way to go: another divergence and I should be utterly lost: the spot at which I was standing offered no sort of shelter against the keen, night air: the disorder of the country about me was not so much wild as savage: and the path which I could be treading the whole night long lay, I was sure, but the toss of a biscuit away.

I determined to go on – somehow...

For an hour and twenty minutes I wrestled, as Jacob wrestled, to overcome the darkness and the snares which an unkind Nature spread in my way. That I do not halt today, as Jacob halted, is not my fault, for a score of times I must have missed breaking a leg by the breadth of a hair. I stumbled, I slipped, I fell: I bruised myself upon rocks, I tore my skin upon briers and I sank to the knee in mold which a thousand autumns had been at pains to amass. And then at last I knew that I was beaten – that I had been beaten for more than an hour and a half, and that I should have done far better to pass the night where I was when darkness came down. For now I was lost.

The stars were out now and were shedding a little light, but their radiance was worse than useless and only served to deceive. I, therefore, drew my torch, to look for some cleft or hollow in which I could take some rest.

(Here I should say that when night came in, I had started to use my torch, but when I had fallen twice, I put it away, partly lest I should break it and partly because, if I was to save myself, I needed two hands.)

Where I stood, the turf was marshy, for a rill had sprawled out of its bed, but the ground rose sharply before me, and there wild box was growing and a parcel of rocks was thrusting out of the bushes, to offer at least a lodging which was not wet.

I, therefore, put up my torch and set out to take this shelter for what it was worth, but the slope was more steep than the light of the torch had told and the box bushes fought against me as though they would keep me out. At last, however, my hands encountered a ledge, and, using what strength I had left, I hauled myself on to this lodgment, to sit there, blown and battered, under the lee of the boulders for which I had made.

When I had got my breath, I stood up and took out my torch, to see if I could do better than use the ledge as a bed. And then I saw what, had I had not been so weary, I might have guessed.

The ledge was no ledge, but a path – the path which I had been seeking for seven hours.

I shall never forget that moment or the thrill of relief and excitement which lifted my heart. My weariness fell away and I felt as much refreshed as when I set out. And though I knew I must eat and must take some rest, I decided to walk for a while until I should come to some harbour which would offer me comfort less cold than the parcel of rocks.

The path rose steadily. It was always very narrow and only at very few places could two men have walked abreast: but, its surface was very good and except at one or two points, I do not think a blind man could have gone astray. After my tribulation, I trod upon air.

So for, perhaps, a mile. Then I came to a little hollow where a sudden grove of beeches had laid a carpet of leaves and the wind had swept and gathered them into a bed.

I turned aside from the path and sat down luxuriously.

I intended, when I had eaten, to take some rest, but if my flesh was weary, my spirit was fresh, and, though I shut my eyes, the slumber which I was inviting refused to come. My brain, as a naughty child, would not put away its toys, but played with my late adventure and the gambler's luck I had had. To be honest, I did not much care, for I wanted to be afoot when the dawn came up, and though the chill of that hour was likely enough to rouse me, the chance that I might sleep on presented itself to my mind. And that, no doubt, was why I could not fall asleep. Be that as it may, I presently gave up trying and raised myself up. Then I lighted a pipe and sat musing, relaxed in body and mind, and finding my humble lodging a great deal more to my taste than all the sumptuous appointment of 'the corner suite' at Jezreel.

I knew that I must be at least four thousand feet up, for the spot was wrapped in that lovely mantle of silence which only high places wear. Till now, since I had left Bell, I had hardly been out of earshot of falling water, but now I could hear no springs, and, except when the leaves above me sighed at some fickle air, there was no sound.

I had rested for more than an hour, chewing the cud of fancy and lazily reflecting that the closer you creep to Nature, the more liberal she is of her charms, when, all of a sudden, the lovely shield was smirched.

Somewhere below in the darkness somebody laughed.

I think the hair rose upon my head.

The laughter was wild, and the virtue of the silence it outraged lent it a hideous likeness to the mirth of some unclean spirit in search of rest. For a moment I wondered if the tales of such things were true and if I was to be beset by some power of darkness whose writ was running in the region in which I lay.

Then I heard a man mouthing French – a flurry of violent words.

In that instant I knew three things.

I knew that the man was coming the way I had come, for when I had entered my hollow I had just surmounted a zigzag of two or three bends. I knew that the man was alone, for the style and the tone of his threats were those of soliloquy. And I knew that the speaker was Jean, late chauffeur and private assassin to Vanity Fair.

Because of the leaves below me I dared not move, but unless he was using a torch, I was sure that I could not be seen. Still, to sit there, breathless and waiting for the man to come up and go past was very trying, for I was sitting full in the open and only four feet from the path.

With a pounding heart, I sat peering for the tell-tale glow of a torch…

If the man had a light, I should have to take my pistol and shoot him dead – directly and indirectly in self-defence. But I did not want to do murder, although he did. To judge from the incoherence which he had been letting fly, my lingering death was among his heart's desires. But I did not want him to die. I wanted him to lead me…to lead me up to my goal. Though I knew not what I was seeking, I had no shadow of doubt that if I could follow Jean, I should find it and find it out. He was, of course, hot from Jezreel. And he was bound for the bourn from which 'my wallah' had come, where was springing that fountain of knowledge, a draught of which had cost poor Julie her life.

I could hear his footsteps now, but I saw no light. Then he rounded the last of the zigzag, and I knew I was safe. He raved no more, for he had no breath to spare: the way was steep, and he was fat and unused to such exercise.

He hove into view – I could see him against the stars…

And then he was by…and I was padding behind him…wondering what I had done to deserve such astonishing luck.

I will not describe our progress, but I very soon found that until the moon rose or the dawn came up, I need have no fear of giving my presence away, for I was shod with rubber, but Jean was shod with leather and made enough noise for four.

To my surprise and relief – for now I blessed the darkness as truly as I had cursed it three hours before – the fellow hardly rested and never sat down, but held on his way at a steady two miles an hour; and we must have gone nearly six miles when a radiance began to lighten the dark of the eastern sky.

I had now to be most careful.

The dawn was coming – I knew it. The moon as well, perhaps. But the dawn was coming to peel off the cloak of darkness which was all the cover I had.

And so it did.

I began to be able to see the fellow before me, and once he glanced over his shoulder, to observe the state of the sky and bring my heart into my mouth.

After that, I began to fall back.

Little by little I had to increase my distance: then I had to wait at the bends and peep and crouch and use the traditional aids of a man who is stalking his prey.

For more than an hour now we had been going downhill, and since we had on the whole been moving south, I knew we must be close to the frontier, if indeed we were not in Spain. Where Carlos lay, I had but the faintest idea.

The daylight was growing broad when I rounded a rockbound spur to see my man before me crossing a little plain. The path was gone, the soil was poor and stony, and the plain was ringed with mountains the sides of which were most sheer. Except for the way we had come, there seemed to be no entry, and since the plain was round and the walls which kept it were steep, the place had the look of a circus perhaps three furlongs in width.

It was a most curious and something sinister sight, for though it belonged to Nature, there was no sign of life. There were no birds or beasts, no foliage or running water to ruffle by sound or movement the trance which lay like a mantle upon this unearthly spot: but what was more strange and more compelling, I could have sworn that once it was not deserted... The empty bed of a torrent seemed to confirm this view.

If the bed of the torrent was empty, the ground was bare. There was no cover at all. And I saw at once that cost what it might, I must advance no further till Jean was out of my sight.

He was now some sixty yards off.

Trembling with impatience, I took out my glasses and set my back to a rock...

He was heading straight for the opposite side of the circus, where a slender cascade fell down in a single leap: but even this died before it could reach the plain, for half-way down it lost its elegant form and came to a lovely end in a mist that hung like smoke at the foot of the cliff.

In vain I raked the crag for some sign of a path...

I lowered my glasses, to see if I dared advance, but the sun was about to rise and had the man turned when once I was out on the plain, he could no more have failed to see me than if, two hours before, I had crossed with a lamp in my hand.

Cursing this change of fortune, I took again to my glasses, to see what I could.

The man walked on, without swerving, straight for the elegant fall. At its foot he paused for a moment, and raised his eyes. Then he hunched his shoulders and disappeared in the smoke.

For ten minutes or more I watched the face of the cliff. Then I put up my glasses and crossed the plain.

Not until I was close to the fall, was I able to read the riddle which Jean's disappearance had set.

There was a cleft or fissure, the foot of which was masked by the mist of the fall. Thousands of years ago the mountain had been riven by some supernatural shock. As those of a flint that is struck with a hammer, its halves had started apart – no more than that. The cleft thus formed was irregular, doubling upon itself, so that no light was appearing between its sides: from end to end it was less than five feet wide: and since Nature had been at some pains to cover the damage up, very few men, I think, would have seen that the mountain was split, and none, I am sure, would have dreamed that there was a natural passage, not quite two hundred yards long.

The exit was clothed with bushes of great luxuriance, and when I had picked my way clear, I saw before me what I can only describe as a rolling park. It seemed to be as fast land-locked as the circus which I had left, but there the resemblance ended, for here was as lovely a pleasance as ever made glad the heart of man. I have seldom seen finer timber or richer turf, and in all my life I never saw two such beauties so well disposed. The flower-starred fields gave to the trees a standing beyond compare: the grateful trees turned meadows into glades fit for a king's pleasures: and the two together made vistas like those which Watteau has limned. That there was water abundant was very clear, and a long way off I could see a lively ribbon sunk in the vivid leafage with which the mountains were hung.

And something more I could see – a splash of white against the trunk of a chestnut, a furlong away.

In a flash I had found my glasses...

A girl was standing, peering at something out of my field. I could see that her hair was fair, but her back was turned to me and she stood behind the chestnut, as though she wished to see, yet not to be seen. One hand was against the trunk and the other was holding a dog, a huge Great Dane. Between the leaves of the chestnut I could see the flash of a rill that fell into a pool.

I had no doubt she was looking after the chauffeur and at once I turned my glasses to follow her gaze.

But the fellow was out of my sight.

And out of hers, too, I fancy, for when I returned to the girl, she was standing stripped to the skin on the edge of the pool.

If I lowered my glasses of instinct, I had my reward.

I have seen many lovely pictures, but the rarest of all was the picture I saw at that moment in the heart of a thousand hills.

The sun was up and over the mountain-tops and was laying long, clean-cut shadows upon the dew: the majestic trees stood breathless: the meadows were quick with the magic that night had left: and in the midst of this beauty, a slim, straight, girlish figure remembered Artemis.

The pleasance became her temple: the groves and lawns and fountains became her courts: and she became the darling for whom the dawn had discovered a golden world.

For a moment she stood like an arrow. Then –

The snap of a twig behind me brought me about in a flash.

Twelve feet away was crouching a giant of a man. He was very dark and though he was not ill-favoured, I shall see the look on his face till my dying day. It shook me more, I think, than the look of the knife he was holding close to his ribs.

4

We Find Out What Julie Knew

I owe my life to the fact that the grass was wet.

As the fellow launched himself at me, I made to leap to one side, but I slipped and fell. Unable to stop himself – for he had expected my body to check his rush – he measured his length across mine, and his knife drove into the turf a foot from my groin. But, as he fell, I had the time and the instinct to turn on my back, and before he could strike again, I let him have my binocular full in his face.

The glasses were very heavy and weighed between three and four pounds. I had often cursed the day when I bought them, because of their weight. But now, as a knuckle-duster, they were beyond all price.

Because I was lying, no strength was behind the blow, but the weight of them knocked him sideways, and I was up before he.

I think the man must have been dazed or else was no sort of fighter and only good at exploiting the upper hand, for I well remember that, as he rose, he had a hand to his head and that, just before I struck him again, he took it away to stare at the blood upon his fingers as though he was loth to believe the tale it told.

His blood was the last thing he saw.

As a man puts the weight, I planted those heavy glasses full on the side of his head, not letting them go, but with all my weight behind them – and I am a heavy man.

I believe that he died there and then, but I cannot be sure. From that time on he certainly never moved. But, though I was shaken, I felt no compunction at all, for the fellow had sought to kill me behind my back. As for Julie... He was, of course, 'my wallah', the man I had seen in the meadows the night before Julie died.

As I stood, nursing my hand, which was very much bruised, I began to wonder what Vanity Fair would say...

Suddenly I thought of the girl, but she was not to be seen. Only the hound lay couched by the white of her frock. This suggested that she had seen nothing: but since I had run risk enough, I dragged the body into a dip of the ground and then sat down close by behind a swell of the turf.

It was then that I realised how badly shaken I was, and when I had found my brandy, I had to take two hands to hold the flask to my mouth.

This was, no doubt, reaction, for I had just walked with Death. It had been a very near thing. There had, in fact, been no fight. The man had allowed me to kill him, as the ox allows the butcher to take his life. But, but for the grace of God, our roles would have been reversed. Had the grass not hidden the twig upon which he had stepped, he would have played the butcher, and I the ox: and my body would have lain in the hollow, and he would have been sitting down and draining my flask. It had been a very near thing.

I wiped my face and my hands and tried to think what to do.

I had, it seemed, scrambled home – by the skin of my teeth. I had made a discovery which I had survived to recount. I had found out 'what Julie knew'.

This park was a private domain of Vanity Fair's. And Julie had found it – had found the secret way in.

That I was right in this, I had next to no doubt. If Carlos was not very far...

I decided to look for Carlos without delay. Once I had found the village, my job was done. Before I began, however, I had to dispose of my dead. Burial was out of the question. Yet if they sought for the man and employed the dog...

I decided to look for a pool.

This made me remember the girl, but when I peered at the chestnut, the dog and her dress were gone. Straining my eyes – for, apart from their horrid condition, my glasses were out of shape – I thought I could see in the distance a flutter of white.

I could hardly employ the pool which the girl had used, but I could find no other, search as I would. I dared not go far, of course: I had no desire to be seen. And in the end I could do no more than drag the corpse into the bushes, perhaps twenty paces beyond the mouth of the cleft.

I had some hazy idea of bringing back Bell that night to help me to other rites, but the honest truth is that I was too tired to think. My one idea was to locate the village and then repair to the bridge and sleep until Bell arrived. I must be there by midnight, whatever befell. But first I had to find Carlos. Till then I dared not rest, for such was my state that if once I had closed my eyes, I should, as like as not, have slept the sun out of the sky.

As I shambled across the circus, I tried to determine the angle at which I should bear to the west... And that shows the state I was in. Nearly two hours went by before it entered my head to look at my map.

Upon this the circus was marked – a natural colosseum entitled the *Cirque des Morts*. And Carlos lay two miles west. Of the park I had found, the map showed no sign at all.

It was nearly eleven o'clock when I stumbled into the road and plodded down to the bridge by which I had spoken with Bell.

On its coping I scrawled a note.

Don't go. I'm asleep in the leaves by the side of the rill.

I folded it up and stuffed it into the crevice. Then I left the road, to slide and scramble into a drift of leaves.

A touch on my arm woke me, and I started up, blinking and helpless before the glare of a torch.

'Are you all right, sir?' said Bell.

'Yes,' I said, yawning. 'I think so. I'm still damned tired. Did you get to Anise all right?'

'There's blood on your sleeve, sir.'

'Is there?' said I, sitting up. 'Well, it isn't mine.'

'Tell me the worst,' said Mansel. 'Whom have you hurt?'

That brought me up to my feet.

'By Jove,' I cried, 'I'm thankful to hear your voice. You're not going back, are you?'

'Well, I was,' said Mansel slowly: 'but now I'm less sure. Come to the Rolls, William. Bell's got some beer.'

As we scrambled on to the road, Carson rose out of the shadows and touched his hat.

'Hullo, Carson,' I said. And then, 'Hullo, it's your car.'

'Yours is at Anise,' said Mansel. 'We didn't need two, and I didn't want your number-plates showing round here. And now you get in and sit down.'

Though he must have been very eager to hear my news, since I was very hungry, he made me eat: and whilst I ate, I listened to what he said.

'My hand has been forced, William. For twenty-four hours I tried to find a way out, but it couldn't be done. Vanity Fair never mentioned Candle to me, but he's due to arrive tomorrow at ten o'clock. Well, I couldn't put him off, so I had to go. Candle knows me quite well. If I could have seen him alone, I might have stopped his mouth: but that would have been no good, for Vanity Fair would have had it open all right. And so I had to be gone.

'Well, that was easy enough. I've always a bolt-hole ready, by day and night. I said I was in touch with Carson. Well, off he goes to Bordeaux and gets on the telephone: and last night I get a wire to say that my little girl is dangerously ill. You know I've no little girl: but Vanity Fair has seen her photograph... So this morning I left – much to her suspicion and entirely to her disgust. I certainly meant to go back, when Candle had gone: but now that depends on your news. Who did you have your scrap with?'

' "My wallah," ' said I. 'The fellow I saw in the fields.'

'Dead?' said Mansel.

I nodded.

'I killed him in self-defence.'

'That I can well believe. Does anyone know?'

'Nobody saw,' said I. 'But I couldn't bury the body. I hid it as well as I could.'

'And the shot,' said Mansel. 'Was anyone thereabouts?'

'I didn't shoot him,' said I. 'I did him in with my glasses. Cracked his skull.'

'Did you, though?' said Mansel. He laughed. 'History repeats itself. Your prototype did his damage with the jawbone of an ass. And when and where did this happen?'

'At five o'clock this morning, five miles from here.'

'Then I can go back,' said Mansel. 'I've got a good alibi. All the same... And now you get on with your meal, and I'll tell you the news of Jezreel.

'Vanity Fair is peevish. She misses you very much, as I knew she would. She rang up Bayonne this morning, but they said that you'd left for Spain. Virginia is also peevish, and Gaston is getting the wet. He disparaged you yesterday: and she choked him off in terms that I wouldn't have thought she knew. No love lost there. She's marrying the man by order – no doubt about that. But why? That's where I'm damned well stuck. They both hate de Rachel – loathe him, as he deserves. Yet they have agreed together, the one to become his wife and the other to make him a virtual millionaire. De Rachel has no hold upon them: that I'll swear. Yet each is going to make him a present. Virginia is going to be joined, to use her own words, "to a dirty shop-soiled mutt that ought to be pushing soap in a fourth-rate store": and Vanity Fair is going to part with a fortune which he will proceed to debauch with the hideous finesse of his kind.'

He lay back and closed his eyes.

'Of course there's a snag somewhere: but I'm damned if I see where it is.

'Oh, and poor old Below is peevish. At least he laments your loss. He talked to me about you, after you'd gone. He knew your father at Oxford.'

'He never said so,' said I.

'I know. It was rather pathetic. "It would have seemed boastful," he said: "and in the absence of proof…" '

'Poor old fellow,' said I. 'She's got him where he belongs.'

'Perhaps she has. D'you pity the bears at the Zoo? They're a damned sight better off there than taking their chance in the mountains. Look at the buns they get.'

'I've broken my fast,' said I, laughing. 'And now you shall hear my tale. I'll eat again presently.'

With that, I told him the truth from beginning to end.

When I had done –

'Well, there you are,' said Mansel. 'And now you must see what I meant when I talked at Cleveland Row. *Only* an amateur could ever have done so well. No money on earth could ever buy service like that. Never mind. What a glorious show. But I'd like to have a look at that girl. Not a peasant, you say. Well bred. It looks to me as if *she* was "what Julie knew".'

'I never thought of that,' said I.

'You would have,' said Mansel, 'if you hadn't been so tired. And why is she there? And what has she to do with Vanity Fair?'

'And Jean?' said I.

Mansel frowned.

75

'Exactly,' he said. 'And Jean. Assassins don't go with dryads…
Can you eat as we go? I'll drive. And I'm devilish glad I brought
Carson, because we'll have need of Bell.' He asked for my map.
'How close can you get to this pleasance, using the road?'

'To within three miles,' said I.

'That's not too bad,' said Mansel. 'When we take to our feet,
d'you think you can find the way?'

'I'll do it somehow.'

'That's the stuff,' said Mansel. 'Now if you were being paid,
you'd want a private bathroom and a couple of days in bed.'

The sky was not yet pale when Mansel and Bell and I passed
under the fine cascade and into the cleft.

The corpse was as I had left it.

Mansel said it was that of a Spaniard, the moment he saw its
face: then he went on his knees and proceeded to search the
body with infinite care. The pockets yielded nothing, but the
sash of coarse, red cloth, which had served the man as a belt,
was containing two sealed letters, the superscriptions of which
had been written by Vanity Fair. One was addressed to 'Lafone'
and the other to 'Jean'. We did not wait to read them, for we
wished to bury the body before it was day, and, after a little
discussion, Mansel and Bell took it up and bore it the way we
had come.

We buried the corpse in the circus, scraping a hole in the bed
of the stream that was dry. The only tools we had were the
Spaniard's knife and the two tire-levers which Bell had brought
from the Rolls, but the bed was of stones and sand, so that,
though we could have done with a shovel, the grave grew very
much faster than if we had been digging earth. And, what was
still more to the point, when the grisly business was over, no
one could ever have told that the channel had been disturbed.
We laid the man's knife beside him and buried my useless
glasses a hundred yards off.

As the dawn came up, the three of us stripped and bathed in the mist of the fall, and, though the water was icy, since I had a piece of soap, we did very well. This cost us full half an hour, for whilst one was making his toilet, the others were keeping watch upon either side: but it made a world of difference, and the delicate spray did more than wash the sweat from our skins. Then we set out, all three, to reconnoitre the park.

Though the letters burned his pocket, Mansel would not read them 'because,' he said, 'we need every moment we've got. In less than an hour, this park will be full of light, and by then we must be hiding, if we are to do any good.'

(Here I may say that I dare say many will wonder why Mansel had not read the letters while Bell and I were bathing in the mist of the fall: but that was not Mansel's way. He had set himself to play sentry, and, though he was always the captain of every enterprise, he did his share of duty with all his might.)

In single file we moved at the foot of the mountains confining the park, for so, of course, we were less easy to see, and if we had trodden the meadows, the print of our steps would have stayed till the sun was high. As we went, I began to see that the pleasance had the way of a river that bends and widens and narrows for no apparent cause, and when we had covered about three hundred paces, I saw the edge of some building that stood in a bay on our right.

Mansel had stopped, and I made my way on to his side.

From where he stood I could see a broad, grey house, some five hundred yards away. It was plainly very old and had, I judged, been built when worse than thieves broke in, to do worse than steal, for the windows were small and set high and there was no door, but an archway that gave to a court within. It must have looked grim, when new: but wind and rain and sun had softened its ancient face, and the chestnuts that crowded about it – and especially one that was growing within its court – gave it that air of security which only Nature can give.

Away to the left stood farm buildings, and around and beyond these were pastures, decently fenced.

Sign of life there was none, except for some sheep that were feeding a long way off.

Mansel took out his glasses and pointed across the park.

'D'you see a strip of green there? Halfway up the mountain. It looks like the edge of a plateau. I may be wrong.'

'It might be,' said I, gazing. 'I think it is.'

'It's a dell, I think. I can't see. It looks as if there's a path…' He put his glasses away. 'Come on. We must try and make it. So far as the manor's concerned, it's a natural belvedere.'

At once we turned about and retraced our steps. Always skirting the mountains, we hastened round the pleasance, past the cleft and presently over the water that was feeding my lady's pool. So we came to the bay to which the manor belonged.

The sun was up now and was touching the mountain-tops, so Mansel entered the forest which grew on the mountain-sides. Not to do so would have been folly, for we were now close to the house; but so steep was the slope that, though we held on our course, we were climbing, rather than walking, from that time on. I know no progress more trying than working across a mountain by scrambling from tree to tree, and nearly an hour had gone by before, to our great relief, we encountered a rising path. One glance at the house showed us that this was indeed the path which Mansel had thought that he saw, and five minutes later we stumbled into the dell.

No place could have suited our purpose one half so well.

We could look clean over the house, which was only two hundred yards off, we could watch the farm and the pastures, we could see the bushes that grew at the mouth of the cleft: only the pool was hidden, for that was masked by the point that made one horn of the bay. But we could not be observed. Had we stood close to the edge, we could, of course, have been seen, but, lying there prone, only the birds could see us, for the ground sloped down a little into the dell. Add to this that the coign was as charming as was the pleasance below. The turf was soft and blowing, and, when the sun grew hot, we could, if we pleased, withdraw to the shade of the trees: and there a spring was welling, a very tiny business that lost itself in the forest almost at once, but its water was clear as crystal and meant the world to us, for though we had food and to spare, we had nothing to drink.

There was still no life to be seen about the house, but smoke was now rising from a chimney and cows were leaving a byre which belonged to the farm.

After a careful survey, Mansel gave the glasses to Bell.

'You take the first watch,' he said. 'The moment you see any movement, let me know.'

He pushed himself back from the edge and got to his knees.

'Come and sit by the water, William, and we'll see what my mistress says.'

The notes were in French.

That addressed to 'Lafone' ran as follows.

Lafone,

I am sending you Jean partly because he has made a fool of himself and partly to take Luis' place, when Luis is not with you. I have warned him that if he wishes his food to agree with him, he will do all that you tell him and do it well.

Be very careful just now. Mademoiselle must have less freedom, and either Luis or Jean is to keep a constant lookout. You may be visited. If a visitor comes, he must by no means escape. If he does, you and Mademoiselle will leave for Jezreel within the hour.

The girl from Carlos is dead.

Send Luis to me on Monday. He is not to leave before dusk.

In the note addressed to Jean was a smaller envelope, sealed. For this the note accounted.

Jean,

You will escort Lafone, should she leave for Jezreel. Before you leave, you will give the dog this powder, unknown to Mademoiselle. It is quite tasteless – as so many poisons are.

'Pity Jean can't see that,' mused Mansel. 'He's much too fat.'

We enjoyed a restful day.

By nine o'clock we had all of us eaten and shaved, and though, of course, we took it in turns to watch, this was a lazy duty and pleasant enough to do.

There was little enough to be seen, and in a way we seemed to be wasting time: but, as Mansel said, the pace I had lately set was a great deal too hot to last.

We saw the girl I had seen return from her bathe. As before, the Great Dane was with her. We saw her feed some pigeons and make her way to the farm. The heat of the day she passed within the house. Jean spent the day at the farm: the condition of his clothes suggested that masonry was now his portion: that he found the work uncongenial was very clear, for, when he came in at mid-day, he kept on inspecting his hands and then throwing them up to heaven as if distraught by their state: but by one o'clock he was on his way back to the farm. It was clear that Lafone was a dragon – with poisoned teeth. We saw a man and three women at work on the farm: and a maid came out to hang clothes at the back of the house. But though once or twice we heard scolding we saw no sign of Lafone.

At four o'clock the girl walked into the meadows towards the sheep. When she had passed the farm, she patted the dog on the shoulder and sent him back to the house. Then she made her way up to the sheep, who seemed to be glad at her coming, as well they might, for she looked very fresh and charming and 'grace was in all her steps'. After a while she left them to pass on up the pleasance and out of my sight.

As I lowered the glasses –

'When you're ready, sir,' said Bell. 'It's just gone four.'

'Right-oh,' said I. 'The lady's gone round that shoulder.' I handed over the glasses. 'Did you have a good sleep?'

'Lovely, thank you, sir. This is like the old days, this is. And I'd rather be here than down at the Château Jezreel.'

'By George, you're right,' said I, and got to my knees.

'The Captain's asleep, sir,' said Bell.

'All right.'

Five minutes later I was asleep myself.

Mansel was speaking French.

'Don't be afraid. We're friends.'

As I started up –

'I'm not afraid,' cried the girl, with a stamp of her foot. 'How dare you say such a thing? And what are you doing here? This is my house.'

'We're doing no harm,' said Mansel. 'We were tired and we went to sleep.'

I had not dared dream that the miniature the glasses had framed could be magnified without loss. Yet it was so.

She was standing just clear of some bushes, through which, though we had not seen it, the path we had used went on. Her head and her arms and her legs were, all of them, bare, and I think she wore next to nothing beneath her white linen dress. On her feet she had string-soled slippers, such as the peasants wear. But had she been robed as a princess, she could not have looked more royal or made a more striking picture against the leaves.

Her face and her limbs were not so much brown as glowing and a bloom I had never seen was becoming her exquisite skin as the dew becomes a lawn at the birth of a summer's day. Her shining hair was curly and loosely clubbed, and her great blue eyes had the steady fearless look of a being that knows no wrong. Her features were very fine, and her wrists and ankles were slender beyond compare, and her hands were lovely to look at, because their perfection was virtual and not induced.

To say that her air was natural is to say that the sea is wet. Her beauty and grace were those of some lovely creature which, though it is wild, has not yet discovered fear: but her artless manner – her charm was not so much that of a maiden as that of a child. Though she must have been nineteen or twenty, all the sweetness of girlhood dwelled in her glorious eyes, and I remember thinking that so Eve may have appeared, before she was brought to Adam, to be his wife.

'Why are you tired?' said the girl, using French, as she had before. 'And where is your home?'

'We were up all night,' said Mansel.

My lady opened her eyes.

'That is like Luis,' she said. 'And then he sleeps by day. But now you must go away, because this is my house.'

'It's a very nice house,' said Mansel. 'Did you show it to Julie?'

If he drew a bow at a venture, he brought the light of gladness into the great blue eyes.

'Julie? Is Julie here? I've missed her so much. She was to have come for my birthday.'

'She couldn't,' said Mansel. 'But Julie told us about you, and we're her friends.'

'Then of course you can stay.' She slipped to the turf by his side. 'I'll show you my rabbits, if you like. Ulysse is very tame. He eats out of my hand.'

'I've got a rabbit,' said Mansel, 'that takes food out of my mouth.'

'You haven't! I'd love to see him.' She laughed delightedly. 'What's your name?'

'Jonathan,' said Mansel. 'What's yours?'

'Jenny,' said the girl. 'That's English.'

'Can you speak English?' said Mansel.

The girl shook her head.

'Not now. I did in my dreams, though – before I was born.' In the prettiest way she cupped her chin in her palms and looked up at the sky. *'Pussycat, pussycat, where have you been?'* Triumphantly she lowered her gaze. 'There. That's English.'

My wits were out of their depth, but, quick as a flash, Mansel had picked up the ball.

'I've been to London to see the Queen,' he chanted.

Her precious lips parted, her eyes like stars, one little hand to her temples, the girl regarded him.

Then –

'That's right,' she cried. 'I'd forgotten. How did you know?'

'Perhaps I dreamed, too,' said Mansel.

My lady crowed with delight.

'What fun!' she cried. 'Oh, I am glad you came.'

So far I might not have been there, but now her great blue eyes came to rest upon mine. For a moment she regarded me steadily. Then she turned to Mansel and back to me.

'Who's that?' she said.

'That's a friend of mine. He's called William. He's very nice.'

'If Julie were here, we could play. I've never played. She says you can't play alone, that you want four or five. I told Lafone – she's my nurse: but she only got cross. Julie laughed when I told her I had a nurse. But then she wouldn't believe I was only ten.'

Again my brain staggered, but if the statement shook Mansel, he gave no sign.

'You look more than ten,' he said simply.

'How old are you?'

Before I could think –

'Thirteen,' said Mansel quietly.

My lady was counting upon her pointed fingers.

'You know,' she said gravely, 'I don't think Julie is truthful. She said that she was sixteen, but I'm taller than she.'

'Tell me some more of your dreams,' said Mansel.

The girl looked away.

'I can't remember,' she said. 'I used to, but I've forgotten. There was a room that went up – a little room.'

'*The lift*,' said Mansel.

Jenny clapped her hands with delight. Then she snuggled close up against him, threw an arm over his shoulders and laid her cheek against his.

'I do like you, Jonathan,' she said.

I would have gone, but, when he saw my movement, Mansel made me a sign to stay where I was.

I did not know what to think, but I knew I was near to tears. The girl was, of course, abnormal: that a stone of such quality should be flawed was more than grievous: but the flaw itself was so lovely it rent the heart.

Mansel set an arm about her and picked up her little hand.

'What's your other name, Jenny?'

'I haven't another' – abstractedly. 'Does anyone have two names?'

'Sometimes they do. Never mind. Would you like us to come again?'

'Oh, yes, yes, yes. Tomorrow?'

Her head slid on to his shoulder.

'Perhaps, but listen, my dear. Julie's never come back, has she?'

The girl shook her curls.

'But I don't care now that you've come. I don't want her back.'

'Do you know why she didn't come back?'

With her eyes on the tree-tops –

'Why?'

'Because Lafone knew about her.'

Jenny sat up, wide-eyed.

'Are you sure?' she said.

Mansel nodded.

'Quite sure.'

'She did seem cross,' said Jenny, finger to lip.

'If she knows about us, she won't let us come any more.'

The girl looked from Mansel to me with dismay in her face. Then to my great distress she began to cry.

Mansel's arm was about her and her head was down on his chest. 'Don't cry, my darling. Don't cry. I promise that we'll come back.'

'Promise, promise,' she sobbed.

'I will, indeed: but I can't if you tell Lafone.'

She lifted a tearful face.

'I won't tell her,' she said.

'You must be very careful, Jenny. She mustn't guess.'

'I will. But why? Why wouldn't she let you come back?'

'I don't know. But she stopped Julie. Luis went off to tell her she mustn't come.'

The eyes grew thoughtful.

'That's right. Luis went off the next day, after Julie had gone. She only came twice. I thought he went to see granny. He often does.'

'You see?' said Mansel. 'So if you want us to come – '

'I do, I do.'

'Then keep our secret, *sweetheart*…'

'*Sweetheart*. That's English. Why did you call me *sweetheart*?'

'Didn't anyone call you *sweetheart* in your dreams – before you were born?'

'Yes, yes. They did. Oh, Jonathan, how did you know?'

'I've dreamed, too, *sweetheart*.'

'But not about me?'

'Yes. I have. I'll tell you one day…'

Gravely he dried her tears: like the child that she was, she suffered him: and I sat by and wished that the earth would suddenly open and swallow me up.

Mansel was frowning.

'Lafone mustn't see you've been crying.'

He rose and stepped to the spring to soak his handkerchief.

85

Then he kneeled down and bathed her upturned face...and she smiled...and he smiled back.

'I do like you, Jonathan,' she said, and put up her mouth.

Mansel stooped and kissed the beautiful lips.

Then he surveyed his work.

'No one would know now,' he said. With a sudden movement he turned again to the spring. 'Let's make a cascade, shall we? If we build a little dam there and fill up that pool... Cut me some sticks, William. About six or eight inches long.'

I was glad to go and do as he said.

When I came back the two were kneeling, like children, one on each side of the rill, gravely discussing the form the cascade should take: and when their decision was come to, I shaped the sticks to their liking and then sought pebbles with which they could fill the pool.

If ever there was one, the work was a labour of love. Jenny was radiant: her charm welled out, as the spring. For myself, I would have hauled timber to make her glad. And Mansel looked ten years younger...

He was one of the best-looking men I ever saw. A little grey was stealing into his thick, fair hair, but though he was more than forty, his face was young. His steady, grey eyes were set very far apart, and though his way was most gentle, the set of his chin betokened a strength of purpose which nothing could ever shake. He was tall and well built, but spare, and because of a wound he had had he walked with a limp. Though he had a keen sense of humour, his mien was grave; and he did not smile as quickly as many men. This tale must have shown already how rare was his address, but his gravity was so natural and his manners were so easy and fine that you had a curious feeling that his presence was royal: and, in a sense, I shall always believe that it was, for where he passed by, he was respected, but where he rested, men found him worshipful.

With glistening fingers, Jenny sat back on her heels.

'Isn't this playing?' she said.

Mansel nodded.

'That's right.'

'Then Julie was wrong. You can play two together. William's done nothing but watch.'

'We'll play again tomorrow. Does Luis ever come here?'

She shook her head.

'No one ever comes here, except me. Besides, Luis is away. He's been away ages. Lafone can't understand it – he was to have come with Jean.'

Mansel glanced at his wrist and got to his feet.

'Oughtn't you to be going, Jenny? I mean, what time d'you get in?'

The girl threw a glance at the sunshine which was bathing the heads of the hills on the opposite side of the park.

'About now,' she said.

'Then go, my dear. Remember, Lafone mustn't guess.'

Jenny stood up.

'All right,' she said slowly. 'You'll be here tomorrow, won't you?'

'Yes,' said Mansel. 'I promise.'

'And William, too.'

I felt absurdly proud.

'Yes, Jenny.'

'But do be careful,' said Mansel. 'If Lafone asks what you've been doing…'

'She never asks,' said Jenny. 'Shall I bring Goliath tomorrow? Goliath's my dog.'

'Yes, please. But he mustn't bark when he sees us.'

'I'll tell him not to,' said Jenny. She looked into Mansel's face and caught his hand. 'Come a little way with me. I don't want to say goodbye.'

'I'd better not. They might see me.'

She slipped her arm under his.

'Just to the trees.'

As they crossed the turf, she saw Bell.

Before she could ask –

'That's our nurse,' said Mansel, twinkling.

Jenny threw back her head and laughed.

'Why, he isn't as old as you are. I know. He can play with William tomorrow, and I'll play with you.'

With that, she looked over her shoulder and smiled at me: but before I could make any gesture, her eyes were gone.

I did not watch her going, but turned instead to the spring and the miniature fall of water which she and Mansel had made...

A hand came to rest upon my shoulder.

'Take my watch for me, William. It's long past six.'

'Of course,' said I, and turned.

As I walked to where Bell was lying, something made me look back.

Mansel was lying face downward, with his coat-sleeve across his eyes.

The Great Dane came bounding to meet her, as Jenny approached the house: the maid that had hung out the clothes reappeared to take them in: Jean plodded back from the farm: and, after a little, the cows filed back to the byre. Evening had come to the pleasance, and dusk was at hand.

Overlooking the pretty Georgic, I revolved the entrance of Jenny and the startling role which she had begun to fill.

This lovely, abnormal creature was the grandchild of Vanity Fair. Her existence was a dead secret, to keep which Vanity Fair was ready to go all lengths. Lafone was Jenny's jailer and constable of the park.

That seemed to be all we had learned.

Vanity Fair had had a son – who had died: and that, by her first marriage. Jenny, no doubt, was his child. But her grandmother's blood had prevailed, for she did not look French.

Jenny's brain had never developed. That was most clear. So Vanity Fair had determined to put her away. Nine relatives out of ten would have given her a suite at Jezreel, for, flawed though it was, the stone was too precious to hide. But Vanity Fair could only see the stigma – the brutal, indelible abatement with which a mocking Fate had dishonoured her coat of arms. So Jenny had been immured.

When all was said and done, we seemed to have found out a secret which Vanity Fair, if she pleased, had a right to keep. (She had no right to do murder: but, where her will was in peril, she knew no law.) If she pleased to suppress a grandchild whose little brain had stood still, let it run by the side of Nature and lead this most sheltered life, that was no business of ours or of anyone else. So far as our duty was concerned, the pleasance had become a dead end: and since Jenny's glancing footsteps had made it holy ground, we should have done well to forget it and go our ways.

I say 'we should have'... But it was now too late. Though Jenny did not know it, she had fallen in love with Mansel, *and he with her*.

It was most natural. Both were exceptional beings, 'lovely and pleasant in their lives': and both had been delivered up to that primitive instinct which Convention must always subdue. What had Jenny to do with Convention? She had never eaten of the tree of the knowledge of good and evil. Jenny, obeying her instinct, had just made love. And Mansel, playing a part, had found that he was not acting, but obeying his instinct, too...

A light sprang up in the house, to make the shadows deepen and bring night in. Straining my eyes, I saw somebody clear the chestnuts that dusk had made part of the house, but the darkness so veiled the figure that I could not tell whose it was. I lowered the glasses to wipe them: but when I put them back to my eyes, whoever it was had either returned to the house or entered the deeper shadows of which the meadows were full. With a sigh, I laid down the glasses and got to my knees. Our observation was over, for the night, when no man can watch, had fallen at last.

I was in the act of rising when Mansel sat down by my side.

'I expect you've been thinking,' he said. 'Well, so have I. But I'd like to hear your conclusions before I tell you mine.'

For what they were worth, I told them. He heard me without a word. And when I had done, he spoke: and so far as I can I will set out his very words.

'I'm very much in the dark, but I think that we're on the verge of a very big thing. Nobody knows of this grandchild. Her parents were never married, for Vanity Fair's son was a bachelor when he died. Her mother must have been English or else American. Jenny speaks common French, which suggests that she's been taught by Lafone. But she's an obvious lady – I don't think I need labour that.

'Very well. We have found an illegitimate grandchild, of gentle birth, to conceal whose existence Vanity Fair has not only taken almost incredible pains, but, as you most justly say, is ready to go all lengths. *Why*?... You say, "Because she's abnormal." Well, there you're wrong, for *Jenny's no more abnormal than you or I.* I never yet saw the idiot that didn't wear his badge in his face... And if that doesn't satisfy you, even if she were a maniac, would anyone take the pains *which Vanity Fair is taking* to keep her existence quiet?'

His voice was shaking a little, and a moment or two went by before he went on.

'Have you ever heard of aphasia?'

I shook my head.

'Aphasia is a disorder well known to medical men. As a result of injury to certain brain centres, the victim forgets how to talk: and when the injury is healed, though he be fifty years old, he has to be taught to talk, all over again. Now that's only by way of example, but bear it in mind.

'Jenny must be at least nineteen. Let's say she is. *I believe that when she was nine she was given some drug...to kill her memory...*to do what aphasia does, and more beside. Little fragments of her memory survived: but most of them have faded during the last nine years. To explain them, she was told that before you are born, you dream...

'Well, there you are. According to her, she was born ten years ago. And so she was. *Ten years ago, I believe, Jenny was brought to this pleasance and born again.*'

He paused there, to pass his hands over his eyes.

'Now why was her memory expunged? Possibly because it was inconvenient: certainly because its loss would reconcile her to her captivity. I believe that since she was nine, she's never been out of this park – that since she was "born again", this pleasance has been Jenny's world.

'Now if I'm right, we have an illegitimate grandchild, of gentle birth, perfectly sane and attractive beyond belief, to conceal whose existence Vanity Fair has already done wilful murder. Why?... I confess I can't answer the question. That's what we've got to find out.

'Meanwhile we've got to take action.

'On Monday night Vanity Fair will know that there's something wrong – something very seriously wrong, for she will be waiting for Luis, but Luis will not arrive. What she'll do then I don't know, but, from what she wrote to Lafone, I imagine her one idea will be to get her grandchild down to Jezreel.' He shivered. 'I don't...much like the idea. Jezreel – mayn't – agree with – Jenny. It didn't agree with Julie...

'*We must, therefore, get Jenny away not later than Monday night.*

'Mercifully, we have Anise. That is a most excellent spot for a girl with Jenny's outlook to rest at, while the clock of her understanding is being advanced: it's a sort of half-way house between this pretty pleasance and the world which you and I know. And, mercifully, for her companion we can get the one grown-up child that, if you don't count Jenny, I ever saw. I mean my sister, Jill... I don't think you ever met her. She's married and has two babies, but she has and always will have, the heart of a child. She's over thirty now, but she looks about twenty-two. At the moment she's in Hampshire. If Carson wires tomorrow, she can be at Anise on Monday without any fuss.

'As for the actual abduction, we'll have to work that out. But that should be easy enough, and we've plenty of time.'

He rose to his feet, as I did.

'And now we must go. For one thing, we've got to meet Carson, but what is still more important, we've got to picket that cleft. Jenny said that Lafone was worried because Luis didn't appear. Well, I don't think it's very likely, but if Lafone should take it into her head to send Jean down to Jezreel – '

With a cry I caught at his arm.

'She's done it,' I gasped. 'He's gone. I saw him enter the meadows about twenty minutes ago.'

5

I Attend an Execution

Jonathan Mansel could rise more highly to an occasion than any man with whom I have had to do.

It was not only because his brain was so swift: it was not only because he could see his way clear, where others would have wished for a chart: but whilst he was engaged with the present, the future was in his mind. Hard put to it, he would miss nothing, but seized the chance that was coming before it came. He never did woo fortune, but whilst she was looking him down, he was looking ahead. And though, before now, I had seen him paving his way as he went, I shall always consider the plan which he laid that evening, which *almost before he had started* we had begun to adopt, the very finest achievement I ever saw.

With his eyes on his watch –

'You know the path,' said Mansel. 'How long will it take him to get from here to Jezreel?'

I made a short calculation.

'Five hours at least,' I said. 'It must be quite thirteen miles.'

'And he left twenty minutes ago?'

'I can't swear it was him.'

'It was him all right,' said Mansel. 'No doubt about that. And he's forty minutes' start – it'll take us twenty minutes to get to the fields. Well, we can't pursue him. That's clear. The chance of his hearing us coming's too big to take. If he did, he'd step off the path and let us go by. And so we must intercept him.'

'Intercept him?' I cried.

Mansel nodded.

'Get to Jezreel before him. By the mercy of God, Carson will be where we left him at ten o'clock. And I might have said midnight, easy. But I didn't. I said ten o'clock. We must make for Carson and drive for the Col de Fer. Then we go down to the valley, cross the water and lie in wait on the path. It'll be a pretty close run, but we've got to do it somehow. If that fellow gets down to Jezreel, he'll tear everything up.'

One minute later he and Bell and I were hastening down to the meadows, towards the cleft...

One thing was in our favour, but only one. We did not have to watch as we went, for though I had no doubt we were moving much faster than Jean, he must have crossed the circus by the time we had gained the fields: and once we had crossed the circus, we were to leave the path and bear to the left. So, at least, we had no fear of coming too close to his heels – a very mixed blessing, but better than none at all.

It was when we left the path that our troubles began, for the ground was very broken and the country was very rude: and though this was the way we had found not twenty-four hours before, it had not then been vital that we should make no mistake. For those three heart-break miles, anxiety hung like a millstone about our necks. I will swear that virtue went out of us. It took us all we knew to capture that way again.

And then, at last we saw the roadway below us, and five minutes later we stumbled up to the Rolls.

'Tank full, Carson?' said Mansel.

'Yes, sir.'

'Then in you get.'

As I took my seat by his side, he let in the clutch...

Mansel was speaking.

'I'm going by Lally, of course. It's the only way. Take the map and check our position. In about two miles I think I turn to the left.'

As I did as he said, I stole a glance at my watch.

It was now twenty minutes past ten – not quite two hours since I had seen Jean set out: and, as I afterwards found, we were not quite thirty-nine miles from the point on the Col de Fer at which Vanity Fair had met me five days ago. The roads were not too bad: but they were mountain roads and rose and fell and twisted like so many snakes: and though the way itself was easy to find, the darkness and the bends, between them, were continually forbidding speed. Still, Mansel did all he could, which was more than most men could have done, and when he called on the car, she never once failed to respond.

The two of them should have been proud of that race against time. Into and out of a valley, with the fall and rise of a lift…slow round a very hairpin, and then all out at a hill like the side of a house…round to the left, to find a furlong waiting, straight as a rule…and then a four-tier zigzag, to bring the needle from eighty to seventeen…

Of such was that drive.

After fifty relentless minutes, we snarled through Lally and leaped at the Col de Fer.

The pass is dangerous. Mansel had to reverse on two of the bends. But happily he had driven it twice before. And the night air helped the engine: and I think she liked the breath of the forests on either side.

And then, at last, we were up and had skimmed the flat of the saddle and were floating down in silence upon the opposite side…

It was now for me to recognise the head of the path we sought, and though I record with shame that I twice stopped Mansel before we came to the place, he berthed the Rolls by the boulder at exactly ten minutes to twelve.

'All out,' said Mansel, taking the key from the switch. 'Lock her bonnet, Carson. Have you got that pick and shovel?'

'In the back, sir.'

'You and Bell bring them along.' He turned to me. 'I told him to get them for Luis. They'll do for Jean. I don't like doing murder and I'd spare his life if I could. But I can't afford to spare it, and so he must go. And now you lead, William. Down the path, and straight across the valley to the foot of that fall which you saw from this very place.'

'You can't cross the water there.'

'I know.'

For some reason or other the stars were bright that night and seemed to be fighting for us, to guide our steps. But, though now we made good progress, a full half hour went by before we reached the foot of the slight cascade.

Where this plunged into the torrent, the latter was bristling with rocks, and I saw that a man might have crossed there, if he had not minded a wetting and had had a staff in his hand.

Mansel turned to the servants.

'In not less than forty minutes, dead or alive, a man will come down this fall. He'll die when he meets these rocks, in any event. He is the man who came to kill Mr Chandos, while he was asleep. Now we shall leave you here, and I want you to find a soft spot and start digging his grave. Come back forty minutes from now and keep your eyes on the fall. When you see a torch flash – way up there, you'll know that he's off. Don't let the torrent take him: you must get his body in. When you've got it, say so – by flashing a torch up the fall. Then get on with your digging and wait here till we come back. You're to show no other light, and if you leave any trace, it mustn't be that of a grave. Is all that perfectly clear?'

'Yes, sir.'

A moment later, Mansel and I were hastening towards Jezreel.

'You said that you'd marked two places where the stream could be crossed by night.'

'Yes,' said I. 'I can find them – thanks to these stars.'

'If the first doesn't lead to the path, the second will.'

'You think we're in time?' I panted.

'Yes,' said Mansel. 'It's only just half-past twelve. You said that he'd take five hours. Well, you may be a little out, but I'll bet he hasn't done it in four.'

Neither did he do it in five. Had he lived, he would have done it in five and a half...

We took the last lap quietly. Jezreel was dark: and once we had struck the path, we knew that the race was won. Slowly we climbed to the scaffold – the narrow, railless bridge that was spanning the fall.

This proved to be the trunk of an oak, rudely squared by an adze to receive the sole of the foot. It was roughly nine feet long, and some eighteen inches in width.

'You wait here,' said Mansel. 'I'm going on. I want to know when he's coming, and here we can't possibly hear because of the fall.'

With that, he crossed the bridge, and the heavy dark of the forest swallowed him up.

I must confess that I dreaded the business which we were to do. All the way from the belvedere I had refused to consider the action which we must take if we should be successful in coming first to Jezreel. But the presence of the pick and the shovel had thrust the truth down my throat. I knew that Mansel was right, that we had no choice, that Jean was worthy to die: but Mansel's orders to the servants had set my teeth on edge. I had, of course, killed Luis: but this was an execution: scaffold, drop and grave were all waiting for Jean. Drop...

With my right arm about a fir-tree, I peered down the tresses of foam. The thought of the plunge to come made the palms of my hands grow wet.

A shadow whipped over the bridge, and Mansel spoke in my ear.

'Stand by with that torch. He's coming. You stand directly behind me, and hold the torch under my arm. Wait till he's well on the bridge, and then put the light on his face.'

With that, he took his stand on the oak: and I stood close up against him, with one of my feet on the bridge and the other fast on the gravel from which it sprang.

Staring over his shoulder, I saw Jean leave the shadows and peer at the bridge. For a moment he hesitated. Then he began to cross, with delicate steps.

It was I, after all, and not Mansel that caused his death.

The leap of the light from the darkness took him aback. He started – and lost his balance... For an instant he fought to regain this, frantically working his arms. Then with a scream which rose above the roar of the water, he toppled backwards and outwards into the foam.

Mansel stood like a rock, but I was trembling all over and when I made to pocket the torch, I found he had hold of my wrist.

After what seemed an age, a light leaped out of the darkness at the foot of the fall.

I had, of course, expected that we should now return to Carson and Bell, but when we had regained the valley by crossing the stream, Mansel touched my arm and turned to Jezreel.

'I've a job to do,' he said. 'I want a sheet of notepaper out of Jezreel.'

'Good God,' said I, and stood still. 'You're not going in?'

Mansel nodded.

'I am going,' he said, 'to enter "the corner suite". I know there's some notepaper there. Candle may be there, too, but I'm sure he'll sleep like a log in this mountain air.'

If he spoke lightly, my spirits failed to respond. The sable silhouette of the castle was disquieting enough: the bare idea of returning shocked me: but the thought of a stealthy entry loosened my knees. For me Jezreel was a Newgate, whose holds were all condemned: I had fought with beasts there: and to break and enter such a place against the peace of the beasts...

I moistened my lips.

'Is it vital?' I said. 'I mean – '

'It's vital,' said Mansel, moving. 'But the risk is extremely slight. I only need two keys, and I've got them both. One is the key to my quarters – that I had as chauffeur: the other will admit us to the guard-room – that I had as detective, so that I could report in secret to Vanity Fair. They're both duplicates, of course: I gave the originals up when I went on leave. To be honest, I really don't need you: but I want you to see the system, the secret passage that runs all over the house.'

And something more he wanted, though he did not say so at that time. He wanted to nip in the bud the horror I had of Jezreel. As a child who has been thrown in the riding-school must be made to re-mount at once, lest he lose his nerve, so I must be made to re-enter the house I dreaded and thus outface my repugnance before I became its slave.

Fifteen minutes later we stood in the stable-yard...

Three coach-houses, built together, made up one side of the yard. The middle one of the three was half the size of its fellows and was flanked by a harness-room upon either side: above it lay the flat which Mansel had used. Access to this was obtained by one of the harness-rooms, which had, in fact, been converted into a hall.

Mansel set his lips to my ear.

'Set your back to the wall and watch, while I open the door.' Though I was close against him, I heard no sound except the slam of my heart: but when, a moment later, he touched me, there was the door wide open and the stable-yard seeming light beside the black of the hall.

As two shadows, we passed within, and he shut the door.

'Your torch,' breathed Mansel...

I threw the beam on the floor, but Mansel lifted my arm, and beyond a staircase I saw a door in the wall.

'That's our way,' he whispered. 'That takes us into the guard-room. Once we've passed that door, I shan't open my mouth. If I want any light, I'll touch you: when I want the torch out, I'll nod.'

An instant later he had his key in the lock…

The passage to which the door gave was some thirty paces in length. At its end was another door, the lock of which was the same as that of the one we had used.

Delicately Mansel fitted the key. Then he nodded his head, and I put out the light.

With the door ajar, he waited, straining his ears: then, very gently, he pushed the oak open, and I followed him into the guard-room – the key to Jezreel.

For two full minutes we stood there, as still as death: then Mansel touched my arm and I put a light on the floor.

Like the passage, the room was flagged, and its walls were of stone. A massive chair and table made up its furniture. It had no less than four doors – the one by which we had entered, one that gave to the house, one that was really a postern, opening to a meadow that lay to the west of Jezreel, and one that gave to a stair which rose to the private apartments of Vanity Fair.

We were, therefore, standing at a junction of private ways, reserved for the use of such as Luis and Jean, and if Vanity Fair or one of her creatures was afoot, any moment a door might open and we must be caught.

Before this hideous reflection, I felt the sweat break upon my brow.

But worse was to come.

Mansel was pointing to the fireplace.

This was set in the angle of two of the guard-room's walls. It was old and wide and high: but, instead of dogs bearing wood, a cage of coals stood on the inner hearth. Peering, I saw the coals in the cage were sham. It was an electric grate.

Mansel approached the fireplace. Arrived, he stood listening intently, as though the place were a doorway, instead of a chimney's mouth. Then he signed to me to follow, bent his head and passed beneath the mantel, between the cage of coals and the left-hand jamb.

As he disappeared, I followed – to find the truth.

Though few, I think, would have marked it, the fireplace was wider than its mouth, and within and behind the jamb a very narrow opening gave to a flight of steps.

The opening was so surprising and so well hid that out of ten chimney-sweeps I do not believe that one would have found it out, for, the fireplace being set in a corner and the steps, which ran down, being built in the wall of the room, the vomitory was not on the left of the cage but actually side by side with the fireplace's mouth.

Such was the entrance to a system which truly deserved that name.

Twelve steps led down to a cellar, some twenty feet square, from which rose three winding stairways, sunk in the depths of the walls. Each stairway served four passages, one upon every floor. These corridors were most narrow and, since they were in the walls, they were not winding, but straight: and when one turned, it turned with the wall, at right-angles, to right or left. The doors in the passages were legion, and though I cannot be sure, I believe that the system gave access to every room in the house.

I am told that similar systems are not unknown and that castles, still standing, have passages running in their walls: but, as I have said, Jezreel had been raised to its being by more than one hand, and I find it strange that such as enlarged the castle from time to time should have been at such pains not only to preserve but to extend a feature which smacked so strongly of darker days.

Every door was numbered, but by no means all were bolted, although the great bolts were there: instead, they were held fast shut by means of great counterweights, the cords of which passed overhead, ran through staples and hung down beside the wall. It was clear that doors so fitted could be opened without a sound. Of such was the door which gave to 'the corner suite'...

This I was thankful to enter, Candle or no, for I could not be blind to the fact that so long as we moved in the system, we moved in the worst of traps. Any instant the beam of a torch might leap from some direction which had been black and empty a second before: the place was rife with ambush, and had we been argus-eyed, it would have made no difference because we could not escape.

The suite was unoccupied.

The lovely bed was covered and the windows were shut. Candle lay somewhere else.

I sat down upon the edge of a table and wiped the sweat from my face: but before this toilet was over, Mansel had the paper he wanted and was standing with a hand on the mirror, ready to leave.

Six minutes later we re-entered the stable-yard...

As we made our way back through the meadows –

'It wasn't so bad coming back, was it?' said Mansel quietly.

'No,' said I, 'frankly, it wasn't. And I don't quite know what I'm afraid of. The damned woman's flesh and blood.'

'It's not fear,' said Mansel: 'it's repugnance. The atmosphere she has created is repugnant to you and me. More than repugnant – monstrous. And monstrous things try the nerves. But I'm glad you came tonight. Strip a monster of mystery, and she ought to lose half her bulk.'

'She has, I think,' I said slowly. 'The illusion dies if you're taken behind the scenes.'

Mansel had gained his end. From that time on I had no dread of Jezreel. For the first time since I had known her, my feeling for Vanity Fair was tinged with contempt.

The dawn came up as we drove the way we had come, and we berthed the car by Carlos exactly at five o'clock.

'I've a plan in my head,' said Mansel. 'But as it entails immediate action, I cannot spare the time to lay it before you now. Carson and I are going back to the park, and I want you and Bell to leave at once for Bayonne. From there you will wire to my sister. Then you will go on to Burgos – that's a hundred and eighty-five miles. At Burgos you'll write a postcard and post it to Vanity Fair and you'll buy a pair of boots and send them off to Below. You will also buy a guide to Burgos and visit the cathedral. Then you will return to Bayonne. The roads are good, and you ought to be back at Bayonne by nine o'clock. There you will purchase food for us all for two days and pick up my sister's reply to the wire you sent. Then you will come back here.

'It's going to be a very hard day. You must take it in turns to drive. But once you're back you shall sleep as long as you please.' His chin went on to his shoulder. 'Give me my writing things, Carson.'

Carson gave him a wallet which was kept in the back of the car, and he wrote out the telegram which I was to send from Bayonne.

Two minutes later he and Carson were climbing the wayside bank, Bell was sitting beside me, and the Rolls was again under way.

By the roads we used, from Carlos to Burgos and back was nearly six hundred miles.

Bayonne – San Sebastian – Burgos...

At Burgos I wasted no time. Half-an-hour I gave to luncheon, half-an-hour to the great cathedral, half-an-hour to the city itself. By a quarter past three our flying visit was over and we were hastening back.

No adventure befell us, but I never drove so far and so fast to post a picture-postcard and purchase a pair of boots. Still, alibis cannot be made except in the sweat of the brow.

Mansel's estimate was sound. We reached Bayonne once more at twenty minutes to nine that Saturday night. There I sent Bell off to buy the food we required, whilst I drove to the Post Office to claim the reply to my wire. This was awaiting me.

Will arrive Bordeaux Monday 4.50 a.m. Jill.

I made my way to the café at which I had arranged to meet Bell. As I sat there, waiting, a man came by, selling papers – among them, the *Daily Mail*. I called him and bought a copy. Idly I glanced at the news. Then a sudden paragraph brought my wits up with a jerk.

Mr Elvin Candle, the well-known RA, who was taken ill in Paris on Thursday on his way to the South of France, was successfully operated on for appendicitis yesterday morning. Mrs Candle reached Paris by air in the afternoon and drove at once to the nursing-home. She later stated that her husband was going on very well.

More than twelve hours had gone by.

I opened my eyes, to stare at the clear blue heaven which I had come to expect. Then I propped myself on an elbow and sought to pick up the reins of understanding which heaviness more than fatigue had made me lay down.

I remembered meeting Mansel by Carlos at dead of night: Bell had been fast asleep in the seat by my side, and we had left him sleeping, with Carson standing, smiling, by the side of the Rolls. The rest was a very nightmare. With Mansel's arms beneath mine, I had stumbled and staggered an endless way that I knew – up to and across the circus, through the cleft, over the dewy meadows and up to the belvedere. And there I had fallen down, more dead than alive... I suppose that I could have gone further: but nothing that I can think of would have got me another yard. My desire to sleep was raging: there was nothing else in my world.

Mansel strolled out of the bushes and up to my side.

'Eleven o'clock,' he said, smiling. 'And how do you feel?'

'Not too bad,' said I. 'Did I show you that bit about Candle?'

'Indeed you did,' said Mansel. 'You showed it to me by Carlos. And on the way here you stopped five times and asked if you'd shown me "that bit about Candle in the paper I bought at Bayonne".'

'It was on my mind,' said I, laughing.

'You went to sleep walking,' said Mansel. 'And every time you woke up, you asked me again. You're a faithful officer, William. That's why I drive you so hard.'

'And the wire?'

'Yes, you gave me that. Everything in the garden is lovely: and, except for receiving a lady, you'll have nothing whatever to do for thirty-six hours. And now you get up and breakfast: and then we'll talk.'

I shaved and bathed and ate. Then we sat by the lip of the dell, and Mansel unfolded his plan.

'Before I begin,' he said, 'I want to make two points clear.

'One is that my job – and yours – is to take an active interest in Vanity Fair. That we're doing the right thing by Jenny, I have no doubt. But Jenny is really a side-show. It's like exploring a river. Thanks almost entirely to you, we have traced one tributary to its source: and now we must return to the stream. Virginia's engagement to de Rachel is a riddle which must be solved.

'The second point is that the news of Candle's sudden illness has altered and simplified everything beyond belief.

'Now what is the present position?

'Though Vanity Fair does not know it, Luis and Jean are both dead. Luis was ordered to report tomorrow, Monday, night.

When Luis fails to appear, then and not till then will Vanity Fair be aware that something is wrong.

'Now for Lafone.

'Lafone knows more than her mistress. When Luis did not arrive, Lafone at once suspected that something was wrong. She, therefore, sent Jean to Jezreel on Friday night. She had every right to expect that he would return with a message at dawn today…

'It seemed to me important not to disappoint Lafone. And as, owing to a recent bereavement, Jean was prevented from appearing at dawn today, *Carson has taken his place.* That's why I wanted the notepaper.' He put a sheet into my hand. 'That is an accurate copy of the letter he bore. Not a facsimile, of course. I think you would have approved the original. The words were Mansel's words: but I pride myself that the hand was the hand of Vanity Fair.'

I read the note carefully.

Lafone.

I send you Wright in place of Jean because I wish to see you and I do not wish Mademoiselle left in Jean's charge. You will come to Jezreel on Monday night. Wright is English and wholly reliable. He knows nothing. I have told him that he will answer for Mademoiselle with his life. Tell Mademoiselle that she is to do as he says while you are away.

I am very uneasy about Luis. He should have arrived on Thursday, half-an-hour after Jean.

Mansel continued quietly.

'Carson fetched up this morning – I saw him arrive. And two hours ago he signalled that all was extremely well. Lafone has swallowed the lie.

'That, then, is the present position. Vanity Fair knows nothing: Lafone's suspicions are laid. But the hour of reckoning is coming: somewhere about midnight on Monday Lafone will reach Jezreel – *and the mine will be sprung.*

'Now if we are to continue to deal with Vanity Fair, she must be satisfied that neither you nor I were concerned in springing that mine. And it's no child's play, as you know, to satisfy Vanity Fair.

'First, as to you. Your alibi's pretty good. On Monday morning Vanity Fair will receive your postcard. This will go far to suggest that on Saturday afternoon, only twelve hours before Carson arrived with his note, you were nearly three hundred miles off, at Burgos in Spain. Well, that's not too bad: but mine must be better still. And so it will be, for on Monday afternoon about six o'clock *I shall report for duty at the Château Jezreel.* I shall, therefore, be asleep in my quarters at the moment the mine is sprung.

'Now this is the tale I shall tell her on my return. That when I arrived at my home, I found that my little girl was in perfect health and that those who have her in charge knew nothing whatever about the wire that was sent: that the police are now trying to find out who sent the wire: and that, realising that I had been decoyed, I turned straight round and came back as fast as I could.

'I hope that my devotion will please her, and I'm perfectly sure that when Lafone arrives, forged letter in hand, Vanity Fair will assume that the person who wrote that letter was the person who wired to say that my daughter was ill. Between you and me, she won't be very far out: but she won't think it's me… John Wright…a most dependable man.

'So much for our alibis. Now to return to action. This evening Bell and I shall leave for Bordeaux. At four-fifty tomorrow morning my sister has to be met. I shall drive her straight to Anise and put her wise. Together we shall make the arrangements for Jenny's reception. Then I shall leave for Jezreel. And now for you. Half-an-hour after Lafone has left for Jezreel tomorrow night, you and Carson will escort Jenny to the car. This, with Bell at the wheel, will be waiting by Carlos. You will drive direct to Anise and hand her over to Jill.

'And there you are. Any further instructions later. Although I say it, I can't find a hole in that plan. If you can, for God's sake tell me. I'm anxious not to slip up.'

So far from finding fault, I was overwhelmed. Indeed, I shall always hold that only a master brain could have conceived so brilliant a piece of work. But, though I did not say so, I did not like the idea of Mansel's return to Jezreel.

The charm of Jenny's greeting brought the tears into my eyes.

A rustle…a parting of leaves…then a nymph danced out of the greenwood into the sweet of the dell.

'Why,' says she, 'here's William.'

She slid an arm round my neck and held her cheek close to mine: then she turned abruptly to Mansel and flung herself into his arms.

'You make me so happy,' she said. 'And William, too.'

The words were the words and the way was the way of nature – of a lovely instinct, the nonesuch of paradise lost.

'That's why we're here,' said Mansel, smoothing her beautiful hair.

My voice would have been unsteady, but his was as easy and gentle as if she had been a child. In my defence I will say that, while I am not easily moved, I think that emotion would rule most people today if Eve were to step out of Eden and speak them so fair.

Something touched my hand, and I turned to see Goliath standing quietly beside me, moving his tail. Naturally enough, I encouraged such valuable goodwill.

Jenny sat down by the rill and let the sparkling water play with a delicate hand.

'What d'you think?' she said. 'Granny's sent such a nice new man instead of Jean. Lafone is so pleased. She tries not to show it, of course: but she keeps on rubbing her chin. And that always means she's pleased. He's very quiet, and he goes and gets the water without being told. He's got such a funny name – Rah-eet. Goliath likes him, too: but he doesn't like Jean.'

'He doesn't like Jean.'

My thoughts whipped back to a circle, cut in the blowing turf, perhaps two hundred yards from the foot of an elegant fall. Very soon it would have the look of a fairy ring... I wondered who had liked Jean. Not Lafone, or Jenny: neither Mansel nor I nor his fellows: not Vanity Fair. It seemed I had been the death of a friendless man. Even the dogs were against him...

'And your dreams, my sweet?'

'Oh, yes,' cried Jenny, 'I've remembered some more – a funny noise that went up and then started again. *Gears* it was called in English.'

'That's right,' said Mansel. 'And it always came when you started out in *the car.*'

The great blue eyes were full of the strangest light, and a little, dripping hand went up to the golden hair.

'*In the car,*' breathed Jenny. 'That's right. A great, red *car.*' She caught at Mansel's arm. 'Oh, Jonathan, how do you know?'

'I'll tell you one day, my beauty.' He picked up the little hand and put it up to his lips. 'And now let's forget the dreams and I'll tell you a fairy-tale.'

'Yes, yes. I'll love it. Why do you kiss my hand?'

'Don't you like me to, Jenny?'

'I simply love it. I love everything you do. Please kiss it again.' Mansel did so. With the air of a queen, she put out the hand to me. 'And now, William.'

Smiling, I did her pleasure – and mine.

She cosseted her hand contentedly. After a moment she put it up to her lips.

'You're Nature's darling,' said Mansel.

'I'm not. I'm yours. I love you. I'd like to kill the devil that made you lame.' Quickly, she looked at me. 'I like William very much, too.'

Mansel was speaking very quietly.

'I wish you could have seen William's lady. She was a great princess. And at her coming, although the day was grey, it seemed as though the sun had come out. But the gods loved her so much that they took her away. One day I'll show you her picture, and you'll fall down on your knees.'

Jenny's arms were about me and my head was against her breast.

'Don't cry, dear William. I can't bear to see you cry. I'll always love you – I promise. I always will. And one day you'll go to heaven and find her there. Like my canary. He used to come on to my hand. And one day he died...' I felt her tears on my temples. 'But I know he's happy in heaven – and one day I'll find him there.'

'That's right,' said I, somehow. 'One day.'

There was a telling silence, and after a little we let each other go...

The fairy-tale Mansel told shall speak for itself.

'There was once a princess,' he said, 'who lived all alone in the hills. Although she was lovely and charming, no one had heard of her: nobody knew of her existence, except her duenna and the servants who kept her house.'

'What's a duenna?' said Jenny.

'A sort of nurse,' said Mansel. 'Lafone might be called your duenna. Well, as I say, the princess lived all alone: but the time was coming when she, like all princesses, would have to go out and take her place in the world.'

'Like going to Carlos?' said Jenny. 'Where Julie lives?'

'That's right,' said Mansel. 'Carlos is out in the world. Well, sometimes she felt she wanted to go, and sometimes she felt she didn't. She wanted to see it all, but she had no friends outside her little kingdom, because nobody knew of her existence: so when she went out, she would have no one to play with or talk to, who would know the things she wanted and care for her as she was served and cared for in her kingdom up in the hills.'

'But couldn't her servants go with her?'

Mansel shook his head.

'Only her dog could go with her. In fact, so far from going with her, her duenna and servants would try to prevent her going – not because they loved her, but because, though they knew it was right, they just didn't want her to go out into the world. So that, when she went, she would have to go in secret – and all alone. And sometimes she felt rather frightened… And then one day a man appeared.'

'A prince?'

'No, an ordinary man. But he was quite nice, and she liked him – and he liked her. And when she asked where he came from, he said he'd come out of the world. Then the princess was very excited and asked him all sorts of questions about the world, but the more he told her, the more uneasy she got and at last she told him her trouble and asked him what she should do.

'The man smiled very kindly. Then he took her pretty fingers and put them up to his lips.

' "I shall care for you," he said, "when you go into the world."

' "You?" cried the princess. "You?"

' "That's right," said the man. "My friends and I between us will help you to make the journey and will be your friends for ever – out in the world."

'Well, the princess was so delighted that she flung her arms round his neck, and all her fear fell away and she simply longed for the time for her going to come.

' "When will it be?" she asked, with stars in her eyes.

'The man took out a little picture and put it into her hand. It was a pretty picture, a portrait, very cleverly painted and covered with glass: it showed the head and shoulders of a beautiful girl.

' "When everything's ready," he said, "one of my friends will come to take you away. And the sign they will give will be to show you this picture. When you see that, you will know that they come from me: and that you must do as they say and go with them where they will."

'The princess stared at the portrait of the beautiful girl.

' "But who is this?" she said.

' "She's to be your duenna, when you go into the world."

'Now when he said this, the princess could hardly believe her ears, for her duenna was old and was often cross: but the girl in the picture was young and had the look of a playmate, and the princess longed to see her and be in her charge.

'Well, the man went off with the picture, and time went on, and the princess waited and wished for her day to come.

'And then one night, when the princess was fast asleep, she felt a touch on her arm. This woke her, and when she sat up, there was a man by her side, with a light in his hand.

' "What is it?" she said. "What d'you want?"

' "Look," he said.

'And when she looked, she saw that he was holding the picture, the portrait the man had shown her of her duenna-to-be.

' "Do you trust me?" he said.

'The princess nodded.

' "Then get up quickly," he said, "and make no noise. No one must hear you, or else they won't let you go."

'So the princess did as he told her and was quiet as a mouse. When she was ready, he helped her out of a window on to a ladder leaning against the wall: and when they were down, there was a manservant standing, holding her dog.

'When the princess saw the servant, she thought that her flight had been discovered and nearly cried out with dismay.

'But the man only smiled.

' "It's quite all right," he said. "That's one of my men."

' "But he's one of the servants," cried the princess.

' "He's pretended to be," said the man. "He's one of my servants, really: or rather one of my friend's: he sent him to enter your service against this night."

'Then they wasted no more time, and she and the men and the dog stole out of her sleeping kingdom into the world. All night they travelled like the wind, and just as the sun was rising, they came to a little white house. And there in the doorway was standing the girl of the portrait, but looking even more lovely because she was really alive.'

The quiet voice stopped, and Mansel's eyes left the heaven to rest upon Jenny's face.

'Oh, that's not all?' she cried quickly.

'That's all for the moment, sweetheart.'

'Oh, I want to know so much more. The picture-girl sounds lovely. What was she like?'

Mansel's hand went into his pocket and brought a miniature out.

'She was something like that,' he said. 'That's my sister, Jill.'

Jenny stared and stared.

'And the glass and all,' she said slowly. 'I wish that I was a princess.'

'Let's pretend you are,' said Mansel, and got to his feet. 'This is your pretty kingdom, and you're sitting there, wondering what you will do when you have to set out all alone and go into the world. And then I'll be the man and appear. William, you go over there. You're not on in this scene.'

So the little play was enacted, to Jenny's delight. Mansel appeared from the bushes, to tell her pretty fortune and show her the miniature: then she went to sleep and I roused her and spoke my lines, while Mansel stood for the servant and Goliath was there in the flesh. Twice over we played the two scenes, because she liked them so well, and when, for the second time, the four of us had stolen to the edge of the dell –

'Oh, why isn't it true?' she breathed. 'I want to go on, like the wind, till we come to the little white house: and I do so want to see Jill.'

'We'll play it out one day,' said Mansel: 'right up to where you meet Jill.'

An eager child caught at his arm.

'Oh, Jonathan darling, when?'

Mansel picked her up and held her high in the air.

'I'm not going to tell you when. I want it to be a surprise.'

The sun was going down, and Jenny was gone. Lying on the lip of the belvedere, we watched her crossing the meadows to come to the grey, old house. Obedient to Mansel's counsel, she never looked back.

Mansel sighed.

'*Sic transit*,' he said. 'And by this time tomorrow I shall have already reported to Vanity Fair.' He glanced at his watch. 'I needn't leave before nine, so we've plenty of time to go over the ground to be covered and settle what details we can. After those two rehearsals I think the actual abduction should go all right. Which reminds me...' His hand went into a pocket. 'Before I forget it, William, I'll give you this.'

The miniature passed.

6

A Spoke is Put into My Wheel

Twenty-five hours had gone by, and I was lying alone on the lip of the belvedere, watching and waiting for Lafone to set out for Jezreel.

I had spent a lonely day, for though I had sometimes seen Carson moving below, an attempt by him to meet me might have been remarked by the woman and so have aroused the suspicions we had been at such pains to lull. Three hours of the afternoon I had spent in the woods high up on the mountainside, for though Mansel had told my lady not to expect us that day, he could hardly request her not to visit the dell – and to the dell she repaired about four o'clock. I make no doubt that she was disconsolate, but offer her comfort I dared not, for if I had made my appearance that afternoon, I must have marred the entrance which I was to make that night. Then she and Goliath had gone, and I had returned.

The shadows were falling, but I should be able to see for half an hour yet. If Lafone had not left before dark, I must wait for a signal from Carson to say she was out of the way.

For a moment I lowered my glasses: as I put them back to my eyes, the woman appeared.

She was tall and gaunt and upright, and looked the wardress she was: though her face was set from me, I could see that her hair was grey and could mark the jut of her chin. Her head was bare and she was dressed all in black, and she made a sinister figure as she entered the fading meadows with the stride of a man.

I put my glasses away and got to my feet, and before half-an-hour had gone by I was standing beneath the chestnuts that softened the face of the house.

Dusk had yielded to darkness when a shadow stole out of the archway and Carson came up to my side.

'Everything all right?' I whispered.

'Perfect, sir,' says Carson. 'You can't go wrong. Miss Jenny's asleep, and her room looks over the farm: the servants are all on the courtyard, so, even if they're awake, they can't possibly see or hear. There's a ladder behind the byre that I'm going to fetch: I measured it up this morning, and it'll do us a treat. But first I'll get Goliath and bring him to you: we don't want him giving tongue before he can see who you are.'

'Good for you,' said I. 'Are you sure Miss Jenny's asleep?'

'She was just now, sir. I listened outside her door.'

Two minutes later Goliath was licking my hand and Carson was gone to the farm.

I left the grove of chestnuts and, moving wide of the archway, strolled the way Carson had gone. The thing was too easy. We might have had the park to ourselves.

Indeed, though from first to last we showed no light, except within Jenny's room, I believe we might have flood-lit the pleasance without any let or hindrance of the business which we were to do, for the staff belonged to Nature, and Nature had gone off duty until the dawn. Carson told me later that, while Lafone was 'a caution', the servants were very simple and their understanding was low.

The ladder was roughly made, but seemed very strong. Together we reared it against the side of the house... One minute later I was astride of the sill of the casement of Jenny's room.

I listened carefully. Then I took my torch from my pocket and threw its beam on the floor.

The chamber was clear and bare as the cell of a nun. No curtains hung by the windows, no carpet lay on the floor. The chest of drawers and the washstand were of unpainted deal: a tiny, tin-framed mirror hung on the wall, and the clothes which Jenny had been weaning lay on a rude, oak bench. In a corner, on a cheap, iron bedstead, 'the princess' lay fast asleep…

I swung myself into the room and stole to her side. There I went down on my knees, as well I might. Indeed, to wake her seemed monstrous: the spell was too lovely to shatter, and Jenny's shoulder too precious for me to touch. Jenny awake, was all glorious: asleep, she was worshipful.

Her slim left arm was lying without the sheet. After a long moment, I put my lips to her wrist…

She started up and brushed the hair from her eyes.

'Jenny,' I breathed, 'it's William. See what I've brought.'

With parted lips, she stared at the miniature: then she caught my hand in hers and held it close to her breast.

'Oh, William! Tonight? Is it true?'

'Quite true,' said I. 'I've come to take you to Jill.'

Before I could get to my feet, she was out of her bed.

'Give me some light, please. What a wonderful lamp.'

I could hardly disobey such an order, for Jenny knew no wrong: and I hope I may be forgiven for finding her simple toilet a precious thing. Wild though she was to be gone, she must wash and plume herself first: and clean clothes must come out of the chest to go on to her back.

One final glance at the mirror, while I lighted her glowing face, and then we were at the window and I was handing her out…

I descended to find her dancing.

'I'm so glad it's you and Rah-eet. I never dreamed that Rah-eet was Jonathan's man.'

To take away the ladder seemed idle…

At a quarter-past nine by my wrist-watch we started across the fields.

It was when we were approaching the bushes that hid the mouth of the cleft that Jenny seemed to falter and then stood still in her tracks.

'I mayn't go there,' she said, pointing. 'That's the way to the castle where Granny lives.'

The check was disconcerting. I had not Mansel's gift for dealing with Jenny's beliefs.

'My dear,' I said, 'you must trust me. This is the way to the world and the little white house and Jill.'

'No, no. It's the way to the castle.'

'Perhaps. But we're not going there. We came out of the world, and this is the way we came. Yesterday evening Jonathan went this way.'

Jenny's finger flew to her lip.

'You oughtn't to use this way. You see, it belongs to Granny, and Granny will punish you if you use it without her leave.'

'I don't think she minds,' said I.

'Oh, yes, she does,' said Jenny. 'You see…'

I did what I could to argue, but Jenny stood firm. Indeed, I was very soon desperate, for so surely as I told her a lie which did not agree with some lie I had told her before, she had found me out in a moment and I had to tell her another to save my face. At the end of five minutes, therefore, I had my back to the wall and feared to open my mouth lest she should lose faith in me and seek to return to the house. Then at last I had an idea.

'All right,' I said. 'We must go by the other way. But if we do, you'll have to be blindfolded, Jenny, because it's a secret path.'

The poor child agreed delightedly.

I covered her eyes and took her small hand in mind. Then I led her through the fields for a furlong before I brought her round and up to the mouth of the cleft…

So we escaped from the pleasance into the *Cirque des Morts*.

As I unbound her eyes –

'Is this the world?' said Jenny.

'Yes, my darling.'

'Is it far to the little white house?'

'Quite a long way: we're going to travel all night.'

'Which way? I want to get there. I wish it was day.'

To be honest, I blessed the darkness, because it hid a great deal that I did not wish Jenny to see. It would, I was sure, have been better if we had taken her blindfold from door to door. But it was too late now. My one idea was to get her to Anise as swiftly as ever I could.

If Mansel's theory was good, when Jenny had entered the pleasance her brain had been affected and she had been 'born again'. And now once more she was to be 'born again'. But I was no *accoucheur*. Her body, yes: I could take her beautiful fingers and hand her out of her prison and into Jill's arms: I simply was not able to deliver her eager mind. More. The brain is fragile. I began to be frightened lest this should receive some shock, lest the veil of her memory should be rent by some encounter which I had had no cause to suspect.

We hastened across the circus and took to the horrid country that lay between us and the car. Jenny chattered away about Mansel, laughed at me when I stumbled and moved like a deer herself. Goliath scouted beside us and Carson brought up the rear.

It was just eleven o'clock when I saw before us the spur which masked the bend of the road at which we had made it our practice to berth the Rolls.

I stopped to wipe the sweat from my face.

'Listen, Jenny,' I said. 'You remember how in your dream you used to go out *in the car*?'

I saw her nod.

'That dream's coming true, my darling. *The car* is waiting for us on the other side of that spur.'

Jenny put a hand to her head.

'*The car*. I can't remember…'

'It's a kind of carriage,' I said. 'Jonathan's sent it for you, to bring you to Jill.'

'A carriage? Oh, William, how lovely. *Can I sit in front?*'

The last words were spoken in English.

If they made me start, they frightened Jenny herself.

'What have I said?' she cried. '*Can I sit in front? That's English. That's out of my dreams.*' She was clinging fast to my shoulder. 'Oh, William, don't say I'm dreaming. I don't want to wake up and find that it isn't true.'

'You shan't. I promise. You see, I'm flesh and blood. And there's Goliath besides you, as large as life. And now we'll go over the spur and down to *the car*.'

The shoulder was steep and wooded: we scrambled up it in silence with Carson panting behind. At the top I rested a moment. Dark as it was I could make out the curve of the road. It occurred to me how contrary a dame was Fortune. On Friday, when time was against us, it had taken us all we knew to discover the way: but now, with the night before us, we had found it without a thought. And now for Anise...

The descent was easy enough. When I came to the bank I leaped down into the dust: then I stretched out my hands to Jenny and she leaped into my arms. And both of us laughed and she kissed me, and Goliath began to bark.

'Where is *the car*, William?'

'Somewhere just here,' said I, and began to go down the road...

Two frightful minutes went by before I could believe I was wrong. But the bend of the road was empty. The Rolls was not there, Bell, who never was late, was more than three hours overdue.

The quarter of an hour that followed taught me something which Mansel already knew – that Jenny at heart was a woman and by no means a child.

You can, no doubt, if you are so evilly disposed, to some extent bend to your will another's body or mind: but with instinct you cannot tamper: that sense is out of your reach. For this I shall always thank God, for the fact that the car was missing had thrown me upon my beam ends and my heart, like that of the Psalmist, was melted in the midst of my bowels: but if to this dismay had been added the instant duty of soothing a disappointed child, either my wits must have left me or I must have committed some folly which could not have been repaired.

But it was not so.

I certainly made no secret of my distress. Mansel's plan was in ruins. Without the Rolls we were stranded, and that in desolate country, with a strikingly beautiful creature who must neither see nor be seen. Take her back to the pleasance we could not, for Lafone was nearing Jezreel and the mine was about to be sprung: to walk to the nearest townlet would take us at least four hours: that there they would sell me a car was most improbable. (To hire a car with a driver was not to be thought of. Abduction is a business in which witnesses have no part.) And the dawn was coming, to wake a work-a-day world – a world Jenny must not inspect, save through the peephole of Anise: and Anise, and waiting Jill, were two hundred miles off... It must be remembered that I had a brain in my charge – a highly delicate member that must not be overwhelmed.

A child could have seen that I was troubled: but only a woman could have comforted me.

For a mile we had searched the road, in a hope which we knew was vain, and I was sitting down with my head in my hands, when an arm came to rest upon my shoulders and I felt Jenny's breath upon my cheek.

'Don't worry, please, dear William. It's sure to come right. Don't think I mind about *the car* not being here. I know it isn't your fault. And please tell me how to help you. I can't bear to see you sad.'

I turned to look into her eyes.

'You pretty darling,' said I, 'you've made me well.' I stood up, with her hand in mine. 'Let's walk down the road, shall we? If *the car* doesn't come to us, we must go to *the car*.'

Brave words, if you please. For all I knew, the car was two hundred miles off. But Jenny's understanding had lifted up my heart.

The nearest townlet was Gobbo, the something slovenly servant of the villages round about, sprawling at the head of a valley fifteen miles off. Gobbo commanded cross roads: of these the east led to Lally, the north to Bayonne, the west to Spain and the south to the rugged country in which we stood. It follows that, going or coming, we always had threaded Gobbo: and though, I believe, we might have avoided the place and passed through Carlos instead, that way would have been far longer and much more rough. It was, therefore, a hundred to one that by setting our course for Gobbo, we were setting our course for Bell.

What had happened I could not divine and feared to surmise. Bell was no fool. If the Rolls had failed, by hook or by crook Bell would have contrived to replace her: he carried plenty of money against any such mishap. One thing only I knew – that whatever had happened had happened since Bell had left Mansel, for, cost what it might, Mansel would have had a car waiting at the bend of the road.

I thrust speculation aside, and tried to think what to do...

To my great relief, Jenny seemed more than content. She stepped by my side, exultant – a lovely creature enlarged. She found the world brave and spacious, the countless company of heaven a glorious thing. She revelled in the magic of the darkness: she drew deep breaths, commending the sweet, cool air. She had never before been abroad on a summer night.

We had covered a mile and a half when Goliath let out a growl and we all stopped dead.

Then I heard what the dog had heard – the steps of a man in haste.

Someone was coming towards us, pelting…

I picked Jenny up and left the road for a gully that rose to the right: with his hand on Goliath's collar, Carson stood back to the bank.

I heard the man trip and stumble and smother a groan. Then –

'It's Bell all right, sir,' said Carson, and stepped out into the road.

Bell was so much exhausted that he had to sit down by the roadside to tell his tale. He had come from Gobbo on foot in a little less than two hours.

'It's the police, sir,' he panted. 'The gendarmes. We've run through Gobbo too often. They stopped me at seven o'clock. I believe they think we're smuggling, though they didn't let on. They've been watching us all the time, and our numbers have torn it up.'

'Our numbers?' I cried.

'Our numbers, sir. A cart at Bordeaux hit our wing, so I've got our own car tonight. Well, you know, she's the spit of the Captain's – same colour and all. Well, they think we've changed our numbers. They simply won't believe there's another car.'

'Good God,' said I.

'They're civil enough, sir,' said Bell. 'But they've got the car. If you can satisfy them, they'll let her go. But they've got to be made to believe there's another car. They wouldn't let me go at first. Two solid hours they kept me, and when at last I'd bluffed them, d'you think I could raise a car? There's a fête at Lally, or something: and the only car in Gobbo is short of a steering-wheel.'

'What did you tell the gendarmes?'

'Nothing worth hearing, sir. I haven't done any harm. When they asked me what you were doing, my French broke down.'

'And Captain Mansel?'

'I put him down, sir, at Maleton at four o'clock. From there he'd take the train to Perin and be at Jezreel at six.'

A little hand touched my arm.

'He's talking English, William. I know. I can understand. The car didn't come because the police have got it. They talked like that in my dream. Are you sure I'm not dreaming now?'

'Sure, my beauty. Dreams come true sometimes, and so do fairy tales. Jill can talk French and English, and so very soon will you. So long as you trust me, Jenny…'

'Oh, I do, I do.'

'Then come, my dear. We've a long way to walk, I'm afraid, but it can't be helped.'

'I don't mind a bit. I love it. I love the stars.'

As we went, I considered our case.

The action of the police was natural. In the last seven days we had passed through Gobbo ten times, mostly by night: first with my car, then with Mansel's, and now again with mine. And the two were exactly alike. That the police should have marked our passage was sheer bad luck: but, once they had done so, their action was natural enough. They believed they had seen but one car: they knew they had seen two number-plates. This was out of all order and must be explained. And it could be explained – the production of Mansel's Rolls would settle the matter forthwith. Unhappily that explanation was one which I could not give.

We had gone a little more than three miles, when I saw that, come what might, I must split our party in two. Bell could go no further: the man was dead beat. After a little reflection, I decided to go on alone.

At this point the road was a shelf, cut out of the mountainside. Though the work was the work of men's hands, it had not been hard to do, for the slope of the mountain was not precipitous. God knows it was steep enough, but a man could have gone up or down without breaking his neck. Here and there a spur went jutting, as though to buttress the road, but now and again a gully would call for a culvert and a mass of rubble above it to fill up the dip.

On one such spur I left Jenny, by the side of the road. Though now the prospect was veiled, I knew it to be very fine, for the world fell down in great leaps for mile after lovely mile and, the mountains standing back, she could view such a waste of stars as she had not viewed for ten years, if ever before. Since she was looking east, the sun would rise in his splendour before her eyes, and the world of which we had spoken would seem but a larger pleasance than that she had known so long. That men would pass was unlikely. At the most, some shepherd or peasant would go by that way. And I should be back by sunrise. So much I swore. My resolution was that of a desperate man. Somehow or other I meant to regain the Rolls.

To do this should not be hard. A little tact... And I had the keys of both cars. But, hard or no, I was resolved to achieve it. Good God, it had to be done.

So I left the three with Goliath by the side of the way.

'A little while, Jenny. Go to sleep if you will.'

'No, no. I love it all so. I'm glad the car wasn't there. But you will be back by sunrise?'

I passed my word.

The police-station was easy to see: no other building in Gobbo was showing a light.

I walked to the office, knocked, and then opened the door.

A grey-haired gendarme looked over the top of a desk.

'Good evening,' said I. 'I've come to you because all the other houses are dark: but what I want is a garage. I must get a car somewhere – my own's broken down. At least, I suppose it has. My servant was coming from Maleton to pick me up, but he's never appeared and I've had to walk fifteen miles.' I stepped to a chair and sank down. Then I pushed back my hat. 'I've had to leave my sister by the side of the road. She simply can't walk any further. And we've got to meet a friend at Bordeaux at a quarter to nine.'

The gendarme regarded a clock that hung on the white-washed wall.

'Monsieur will never do it. It is now a quarter to four.'

I started up.

'I must do it somehow. If only I had my car... My servant's between here and Maleton. I suppose you can't telephone there and ask if your people have seen him. He's a very sensible man, and if he had met with trouble I daresay he'd go to the police.' I leaned forward eagerly. 'D'you think you could do that? Of course I'd pay for the call.'

The gendarme frowned.

'Of what make is Monsieur's car?'

'It's a Rolls,' said I. 'I should think you've probably seen it – it's been through Gobbo before. If you haven't, you've seen my cousin's, and that's as good. They're both exactly alike.'

With his eyes on the desk –

'I think I have seen it,' said the man. 'It has a black leather hood and a trunk at the back.'

'They both have,' said I.

At that moment I heard a car.

In a flash I was out in the street. But the car was bound for Lally and did not come by.

As I re-entered the office –

'No good,' I said. 'I hoped that might have been him. D'you think you could ring up Maleton? I mean, my sister's dead beat, and it's dreadful to leave a young girl by the side of the road. I wish to God I'd never brought her: but she wanted to see our work. We're experimenting, you know. Long distance photography. We get up as high as we can and photograph the country all round. But it's fearful labour. Means so much running about. I went to Burgos and back on Saturday last.'

The gendarme was plainly impressed. He asked me to wait a moment and entered an inner room. Though he shut the door behind him, I could hear him speaking at length to somebody else.

As he returned with a sergeant, I got to my feet.

'Look here,' I said, 'I'm sorry to give all this trouble, but it isn't my fault. Can you telephone for me to Maleton? If you can't, then show me a garage where I can hire a car. I mean, the matter's urgent. My sister's not strong, and to leave her – '

The sergeant broke in.

'Can you tell me the number of your car, sir?'

I took out my letter-case and read the number aloud.

'And that of your cousin's car?'

I stared.

'My cousin's?' I cried. 'Good Lord, no. I haven't the faintest idea.'

The sergeant recited the number – with his eyes on my face.

'That may be it,' said I. 'But I really can't possibly tell you. But for this card, I couldn't have told you my own. But I don't see what it matters. My car's the one that's lost. And now can you telephone to Maleton? If not, for God's sake say so and tell me where there's a garage at which I can hire a good car. I've told you my sister's not strong, yet there she's sitting, benighted, ten miles from here – a beautiful girl, unprotected, in country like this. She wept with fear when I left her, but her feet were sore with walking and she couldn't go on. And you keep me standing here…'

Visibly unsettled, the sergeant fingered his chin. The reflection that: if evil befell 'my sister', he would be most deeply involved, was not at all to his taste. I needed my car – and he had it. Authority can be exceeded – even in France.

'You declare that there are two cars, sir?'

I looked from the man to his fellow, as though I mistrusted my ears.

'But of course there are two cars,' I said. 'We have to have two. You must have seen them. We've been through here time and again, my cousin and I. It was his that I drove to Burgos on

Saturday last, and sometimes he uses mine. Wait a minute. I've got the keys of his on me – a duplicate set.' I took out my own and laid them down on the desk. 'Now those are mine.' Beside them I laid down Mansel's.

'And those are his. They look exactly the same, but they wouldn't fit.'

The police regarded the keys. Then they glanced at each other. I had shown them what to do to be saved – a way, with honour, out of a delicate pass.

The sergeant moistened his lips.

'You will understand, sir,' he said, 'that we have to be very careful. We are here to see that the law is observed. Certainly your movements have been seen – and your numbers remarked. But it seemed to us that, though the numbers were different, the car was one and the same. If you please, we will try these keys, which certainly look much alike.'

'Try them? But – '

The sergeant held up a hand.

'If only one set fits, your car will be at your disposal.'

I started forward.

'Then my car – '

'Is here,' said the sergeant, majestically. 'We detained it upon suspicion. Your servant went on to meet you, but you must have passed in the night. Have no fear for mademoiselle. She is, no doubt, at this moment safe in his charge.'

His air had become imperious. I had set the sceptre of Solomon in his hand – and now was to be given judgment.

Humbly I followed my surveyors into a yard. And there I was weighed in the balances and found honest.

It seemed best to laugh – with relief.

Two minutes later the engine of the Rolls was running, and I was making ready to back her into the street.

It was light now: very soon the sun would be up.

Though I could see, the gateway was none too wide.

The sergeant sent his subordinate into the street: himself he followed my bonnet, waving me on.

I was halfway out, when I saw the gendarme behind me hold up his hand. At once I set a foot on the brake. It was then that I heard a car coming, travelling south.

It went by like a squall – I saw it.

Mansel was driving, and framed in the window's mouth was the unforgettable profile of Vanity Fair.

It has been said that, when one is faced with two perils, it is the more evident danger which one is less likely to see.

My one idea had been to spare Jenny's mind. I never saw that unless we were clear of the district before the dawn, her mind, her body and the whole of our enterprise would be put in deadly peril by the action of Vanity Fair.

I have no excuse to offer: a child would have shown more sense. It was not a question of deduction. Vanity Fair was doing the obvious thing.

The moment she knew the truth, she had ordered a car and had taken the road for Carlos with all her main. As her trusty servant, Mansel was abetting her efforts, himself secure in the knowledge that Jenny was nearing Anise. Her hope was, of course, forlorn: but something might have happened to hold the abduction up. *And so it had.* Fate and a fool had played clean into her hands.

As one shrinks from a nightmare, my brain recoiled from the truth.

Jenny was sitting, waiting, by the side of the Carlos road...waiting for a car to arrive. I had said it would come at sunrise...and at sunrise it would appear. As if that were not enough, *Jenny was going to hail Mansel* – as like as not, to throw herself into his arms. And Mansel knew nothing. He would not so much as see her, till he rounded the last of the bends.

I can see the spot now. I think I shall always see it. You swung round the bend to see the gully before you, perhaps twenty paces away. On your left was rising the mountain: on your right, beyond the gully, was jutting the spur. Between this and the opposing mountains was fixed a great gulf of beauty, of pasture and grove and chanting water – three vested celebrants, served with unfailing devotion by acolyte rills. It was a spot from which to hail the dayspring, not to cry 'Havoc!' and prove the power of the dog.

As I left Gobbo, I remember that I felt rather sick…

Jenny was ten miles off. It would take Mansel half an hour to come to her resting place. With the Rolls I could do it more quickly, but Mansel had a start of a mile and even if I could come up with him, what could I do? I supposed, frantically, that it would be better to pass.

Hardly knowing what I did, I put down my foot…

Nearly four miles had gone by when I sighted the car. This was climbing well, but not as the Rolls.

The next moment it swept round a bend and out of my sight.

When I saw it next, it was less than two furlongs ahead, and since those within could not hear me and since they were hardly likely to look behind, I decided to close upon them as fast as I could.

It was at that moment, I think, that I made up my mind to go by. If I demanded passage, Mansel was sure to give way: and I would pass and leave them – to think what they pleased. Once out of their sight I would stop, leave the Rolls broadside on, and take to my heels. So at least I should save something, for I should have blocked the road, and long before even Mansel could come within sight of the spur, Jenny would be gone down the mountain and so out of range.

The bends hereabouts were legion and, though I was sure I was gaining, two minutes or more went by before I whipped round a corner *to see the car I was chasing at rest in the midst of the way*. It was perhaps a hundred and fifty yards off, and Mansel was down in the road and seemed to be sharing a map with Vanity Fair.

Pass them I could not, for the road was very narrow and the car was not to one side. Stop where I was, I dared not: any moment they might look back. But, happily, the gradient was steep. In a flash I had thrown out the clutch and was sliding back round the corner, out of their view.

I applied my brakes and wiped the sweat from my eyes.

The thing was plain. Vanity Fair was uncertain which was the way she sought. Lafone knew only the footpath. Mansel, posing as Wright, knew nothing at all. What I could not understand was what had occurred to unsettle Vanity Fair. There was but one road she could take, and that was the road she was on. Six miles ahead there was a turning, but that was the only one.

It was then that I noticed the track beside which I had stopped.

At once I guessed what I afterwards learned was the truth. Though Vanity Fair had made this journey before, hitherto she had made it by night, and Jean, who had been her chauffeur, had known the road: since now she must find for herself a way which though she had travelled, she never had seen, her heart was all ready to misgive her and the sudden sight of the track had made her mistrust the road.

This was not surprising, for the track, though now it was grass-grown, had once been a road. And, in fact, her sense of direction was very sound, for the track led straight to Carlos, but the road ran round in a loop. I knew this, because I had seen it – I had travelled this way by day. And something else I knew – *that the spur on which Jenny was resting was in the loop, between the track and the road.*

An instant later the Rolls was descending the track with the rush of a lift…

As I say, I had marked the track and the way it ran. At first, I knew, it fell down to the foot of the mountain-side: then for a while it ran level: and then it toiled up to Carlos in a series of bitter zigzags too steep for a car to use. But I was not bound for

Carlos. Somewhere on the track I must stop – and climb up to the road.

It was, of course, a chance in a million: but if I could climb up to Jenny before Vanity Fair and Mansel had rounded the last of the bends which hid her from view… The point was where to climb up.

I was down on the level now and could venture to raise my eyes.

To the left, far above me, I made out the line of the road: between this and the track, the mountain-side was grassy, but otherwise bare. If only –

Here a sturdy fellowship of box bushes obscured my view. As I cleared them, I glanced up again. From below, the spurs looked different: there didn't seem to be spurs. Surely I –

The Rolls was half off the track. I wrenched her back to safety, tore round a horse-shoe bend and looked up again.

And then I saw the white of her frock…three hundred feet above me…by the side of the road.

As I hoped and prayed, I had cut off the ragged corner and had gained at least a mile on Vanity Fair. But I still had to get to Jenny, three hundred feet up.

In a flash I was out of the car and had flung myself at that smiling mountain-side…

I might have done better to shout or to sound the horn, but I was afraid to do either, lest I should attract the attention of Vanity Fair. In such surroundings a cry can be heard for miles. So I put forth all my strength to beat the car that was coming, that Mansel himself was urging, that had for its load the ruin of all his hopes.

I do not know what was the gradient. I only know that before I had gone ten paces, I was helping my feet with my hands. I will not say that I was climbing – when I slipped, I never fell more than two or three feet: but the pace at which I was mounting exceeded the limit which Nature has set for man. My offence was instantly punished: gravity hung like a mill-stone about my neck.

Three hundred feet up.

The beauty about me seemed to have lost its charm: the shining grass had grown shiny: the smile of the mountain-side had changed to a grin: the sky above me was brazen: the gulf below was gaping: the gaze of the new-risen sun had become a glare. And a pack of flies rose with me, bold and merciless insects, disputing my face and my head and driving me half-way to madness because I had no time to put them to flight.

Three hundred feet up.

My eyes were dim with sweat, my muscles seemed to be failing, a stitch was like a sword in my side. My heart was slamming and pounding, as though it were not my heart, but some big drum-stick within me beating on the wall of my chest: my chest was a heaving drum, tight and stretched and strained beyond bursting point: my one idea was to breathe, yet every breath that I drew was a separate agony: I was sobbing rather than breathing – there seemed to be no air left, and the sunlight was black about me and the tops of the mountains seemed to be closing in.

Jenny was fifty yards off. Her lovely head was up and her eyes were fixed on the road. Goliath was lying beside her, and Carson and Bell were sitting a little behind. I tried to shout, and could not. My voice was gone.

Somehow or other I covered another ten yards. Such progress was frightful, belonging to hideous dreams. I was achieving the hopeless, doing what could not be done. I could not, *and yet I had to...* My brain reeled into reminiscence. Once when I was a child and was seriously ill, I had been similarly placed. And then I had waked, to find my mother beside me and a nurse with dry pyjamas at the foot of the bed. I could see the room and their faces and the comfortable flicker of the fire which Wheatley's *Cries of London* were giving back. And then –

The mountain was tilting. The steep was assuming an angle that no man could climb. I began to slip back...

There I dislodged some pebble, and Jenny and Bell looked round.

I raised an arm and beckoned and tried to say 'Come'.

Then I let myself go to the left – and slipped and rolled and tumbled into the gully that yawned by the side of the spur.

Thirty seconds, perhaps, had gone by.

The four were gathered about me.

Jenny was down on her knees with my head in her lap: Bell was kneeling beside me, using his hat to fan the flies from my face: and Carson was holding Goliath, who seemed very pleased to see me and would, I think, have been happy to do what he could to help Bell.

Nobody spoke, for I was far past speaking and the others had only a question upon their lips.

And then the question was answered.

As I lay there, heaving and sobbing, I heard the snarl of a car that had rounded a corner up on the road above.

For a moment it rose steadily.

Then the car passed over the culvert and its uproar began to fade.

And before it had faded, it died – as abruptly as it had begun. Another bend had been rounded, and the danger was past.

I saw the servants' eyes meet.

Then –

'By God, sir,' said Carson, quietly, 'I give you best.'

'Might have broken your heart, sir,' said Bell, and wiped the foam from my lips.

But Jenny knitted her brows.

'You know,' she said gravely, 'you oughtn't to run so fast.'

Then she laid a cool hand on my forehead and pushed back my wringing-wet hair.

That day we passed in the forest south-east of Bordeaux. It seemed better so. Jenny had seen quite enough of a waking world. And I slept and told her stories and slept again. All this with an easy mind. I might be without the law. But Vanity Fair could hardly go to the police.

And at half-past eleven that night I made over my charge to Jill, a dainty, grey-eyed goddess, with the way of a maid.

7

Virginia Shows Her Teeth

Nearly five days had gone by, and I was en route for Jezreel. I did not look forward to my visit, but I could not sleep at Anise, while Mansel was fighting with beasts two hundred miles off.

Bell was not with me. I had left him to play armed guard to Jenny and Jill. Carson was in touch with his master – 'somewhere in France'.

If Mansel knew of my coming, he had not heard it from me: but Vanity Fair might have told him – I had telegraphed from Bayonne.

For my return to Jezreel I had good excuse.

First, I had been invited: at my hotel at Bayonne I had found a week-old letter from Vanity Fair.

…Jezreel is more dull than before, so please repeat your visit, as soon as you tire of Spain…

Secondly, I had heard from Titus – a letter very much to the point.

Dear Bill,

I remember Gaston de Rachel, and so does Blanche. His looks were dead against him, but he proved to be a debonair cove whom everyone liked. He was going abroad to seek a valuable wife. He was the sort of fellow who never has any money, but never sinks lower than the Ritz. You know what I mean. He knew how to behave, and certainly used his knowledge so far as we were concerned. I've no idea what became of him, once we'd berthed.

Yours ever,
Titus.

P.S. ~ Blanche has just remembered the best thing of all ~ if you want a good idea of the Count. He had a double on board, in the shape of a table-steward ~ of all unfortunate things. I give you my word you couldn't tell them apart. It might have been most embarrassing: but de Rachel took the bull by the horns and made it the joke of the voyage. One night he actually took the fellow's place ~ put on his kit, you know: and nobody knew the difference till de Rachel burnt his hand with a plate and said what he thought. He declared he'd take the man as his servant when we got to Galveston. He may have, for all I know.

It seemed right for Virginia's sake, that Vanity Fair should know that her future son-in-law was using his master's name – for that that was the truth I had not a shadow of doubt. The Count of Rachel was dead. He had died, unwept and unknown, in a foreign land. And his servant had seen his chance and stepped into the dead man's shoes.

And that brings me to Virginia.

So far as she was concerned, I felt ill-at-ease. Virginia had asked me not to come back to Jezreel. She had so framed her request that not to grant it would be the act of a cad. And I was not going to grant it…

My action, of course, was not so bad as it seemed. In fact, it was not bad at all. Virginia wished to befriend me – no more than that. She knew it, and so did I. But I could not tell her I knew it. There was the rub.

I remembered David Garrick and how he had feigned to be drunk, to disgust the maiden he loved. The comparison brought me cold comfort. I did not love Virginia; but she had gone out of her way to do me, as she believed, a very good turn. I had no desire to disgust her or anyone else.

Of such were my thoughts as I drove from Bayonne to Jezreel.

For Vanity Fair I was ready. Thanks to the guide I had purchased, I knew the city of Burgos inside out. To explain Bell's absence was easy – the heat in Spain had been furious, and when he had ailed for two days I had sent him home. (His sister was to post me a letter in two days' time, reporting her brother's progress, to bear out the lie.)

I was not obeying orders, as I had promised to do. My coming might even confound some plan that Mansel had set. But that was a risk I had made up my mind to take. Mansel was my very good friend, and though he was playing the hand, it was right that I should be within call. Because he was in her service, he was to a great extent at the mercy of Vanity Fair. Any moment she might give him an order which, though he did not know it, might cost him his life. And though he might suspect it, unless he was to throw in his hand, he was bound to obey. And Mansel, I knew, would never throw in his hand.

Then there was Jenny. For her sake alone, it was right I should go to Jezreel. The child was mad about Mansel. Had anything happened, I could not have faced her eyes.

I was not needed at Anise. There I had left an idyll straight out of Theocritus – one nymph teaching another how to govern the fountain over which she was born to preside. The relation of charge and duenna had never begun to exist. From the first the two were co-equal, for Jill was a playmate born. Though she was, in fact, the Duchess of Padua and was, I was sure, most happy in that estate, she took to the life at Anise as the lizard takes to the rocks. So far as I saw, she never 'handled' Jenny: she was herself too natural to make pretence: but she had command of a language that Jenny could understand. Set a child to teach a child… Within thirty-six hours Jenny's memory was playing like a fountain, while the years she had passed in the pleasance bade fair to take the place of her 'dreams'. I will swear that you could see her mind grow. But her heart, like the spots of the leopard, was not to be changed, and Jill had wired for her babies, 'to make up a four'.

So much for the sonnet: now for the satire to come.

At half-past three I slipped into and out of Perin, and twenty minutes later stole into the dim courtyard of the Château Jezreel.

Vanity Fair was changed.

Her manner was as easy as ever, her dignity was as compelling, the flash of her smile as swift. Of her soul she was still the mistress: but her unslaked thirst for vengeance had set its mark on her flesh. She, Vanity Fair, had been bearded – as never before…*and those that had done it went free*. The reflection fed upon her vitals: it burned in her steel-grey eyes, and sat, stiff and square, in her face. There was no doubt about it. Behind her lips, her teeth were continually clenched.

Perhaps, because of my guilt, I imagined vain things. Be that as it may, I read in her aspect the judgment which she was impatient to give. I confess that it shook me.

'And so you've come back, Mr Chandos.'

I bowed.

'For a day or two, if you please. I'm afraid I'm rather restless. I can't stay long in one place.'

'You must make a great effort this time. I'm uncommonly glad to see you, and that's the truth.'

I bowed again.

'Candle disappointed you, madam.'

'The light that failed,' said Vanity Fair. 'But I'm thankful he failed in Paris, and not in Jezreel. That would have been too much. Would you like "the corner suite", or will it revive distasteful memories?'

'Not in my head,' said I.

Vanity Fair laughed.

'And Spain,' she said. 'Did you go any further than Burgos?'

'So far was too far,' said I. 'The heat was violent. My servant went down, and I had to send him home.'

I saw her brain pounce upon the statement: the suspicion with which she was quick, leaped into and out of her eyes. Then she touched the bell by her side.

When the butler appeared –

'Marc will valet Mr Chandos.' She turned to me. 'Will you give him your keys?'

In silence I gave up my keys: there was nothing else to be done.

I should, of course, have foreseen that this was bound to occur, but it was so long since I had gone without Bell that I had not perceived that his absence would fairly fling open a door to Vanity Fair. I had no objection to Marc's unpacking my clothes: but to have him 'attached to me for duty' was not at all to my taste. Once again I was being treated exactly as I deserved.

As the appointment depressed me, so it cheered Vanity Fair. As though she had sipped some cordial, the muscles of her jaw had relaxed.

For a quarter of an hour we chatted of unimportant things. Then I took out Titus' letter…

'Madam,' I said, 'this letter is an answer to a letter I ventured to write to a friend. It is, I think, my duty to give it to you to read.'

Vanity Fair raised her eyebrows. Then she took the letter and read it without a word.

At last –

'Was this why you came?' she said.

I shook my head.

'I should have come anyway, madam.'

She folded the letter thoughtfully.

'I'm glad of that. Otherwise you would have wasted your time. I never met his late master, but Gaston seems what he is. Did you really think that I took him for anything else?'

I felt rather dazed.

'Then – then you know?' I stammered.

'Of course I know.' She handed the letter back. 'So, let me say, does Virginia. Don't look so surprised. She's not my daughter for nothing. Living dogs have their uses, you know – especially when they're mistaken for lions that are dead. Don't think that I'm not obliged – you've done very well. And I'm rather relieved that you know. But I'm sure that you'll keep your counsel – if for no other reason, because it is also mine. And I have a weakness for having my counsel kept. Gaston believes that he has imposed upon me. I should hate him to be disabused – before his time.'

'Of course,' I said somehow. I stuffed the letter away. 'I'm sorry. I had no idea.'

'That's a good fault. Ideas are dangerous. And now go and change. Nobody knows you're here, so your entrance at tea should be effective. Gaston's nose, for instance, will assume a remarkable hue. A sort of dusky violet. And Below will gobble with emotion. It takes people different ways.'

I drove the Rolls round to the garage before I went to my room.

Mansel came out of a coach-house, as I came into the yard.

He was at my side in an instant. I thought that he looked rather tired.

'Very glad to see you back, sir. Your servant with you again?'

'No,' said I. 'The heat in Spain got him down and he's had to go home.'

'I'm sorry for that, sir. I hope you're all right yourself.'

'Couldn't be better, thanks.' I dropped my voice to a murmur. 'There's a letter behind my cushion. I've shown it to her, but she said that the news was stale.'

'Just there, if you please sir,' said Mansel. 'No. Up the line... That'll do, sir. I'll see that she's carefully washed.'

With that, he opened my door.

As I stepped out, he spoke in a very low voice.

'Don't say any more, but look out for a servant called Marc. He's a dangerous man.'

I strove to look unconcerned.

'Good day, Wright.'

'Good day, sir.'

I made my way back to the courtyard and entered the vestibule. From this a flight of giant steps rose up to the hall. As I came to their foot, Virginia appeared at their head.

She started and stood stock still, with her eyes upon mine and one of her hands to her throat.

'Well, Virginia,' I said awkwardly.

Without a word, she turned on her heel and left me.

When I came to the head of the flight, she had disappeared.

Marc was an excellent valet. He was also a heavyweight and stood about six feet two. Yet his movements were never clumsy. His tread was light, his eye was swift, and his touch was steady and sure. He had about him the grace of a man in training. I had no doubt at all that he knew how to fight. As I afterwards learned, he had been a mental nurse.

'You needn't wait,' I told him. 'If I should want you, I'll ring.'

He bowed and was gone – not before I had seen in his eyes that this was not according to plan.

One thing was in my favour. My pistol was in my dispatch-case, of which I had kept the key. And the lock was a very good lock.

Neither Virginia nor Gaston was present at tea – to Vanity Fair's annoyance and my relief.

She made no bones about it.

'Still, there's always dinner,' she murmured. 'He can't miss that.'

There was doom in her tone.

Even Acorn looked down his nose, and Below choked over his tea. I there and then decided to drink two cocktails that evening, instead of one.

Be sure I needed them.

Gaston's greeting was meant to be casual.

As he turned away, Vanity Fair's clear voice seemed to cut the air.

'I once saw a vulgar, rich man extend two fingers – a supererogatory act: that he was a cad was already obvious enough. Learn of him, Gaston. Condescension must be bred in the bone.'

'Do you say I am vulgar?' blurted Gaston.

'Intensely,' said Vanity Fair. 'There's a fan in the Actaeon salon. When you've done with it, I should like it. It's rather hot.'

As Gaston lurched out of the chamber, Virginia came in.

Her welcome was one of abandon. Almost it made me believe that it was not she I had seen at the head of the steps. I returned it thankfully – while Vanity Fair sat smiling, with a hand to her mouth.

'With a hand to her mouth.'

That is a tiny detail: but if I am to present her picture, a duty of which I am sometimes inclined to despair – that detail is eloquent. Her facial control was absolute. No one had ever less need to cover her mouth. But the gesture was made to be seen by Virginia and me. We knew that we were play-acting. Vanity Fair knew it, too – and she meant us to know that she knew.

In fact, though I saw the gesture, Virginia did not. Her back was half turned. But that I had seen it was enough for Vanity Fair. At least, she believed it enough. But she was not among the prophets. Had Virginia seen that gesture, I doubt that I should have lived to tell this tale.

Dinner was served.

'Now that he's back, the question is how to keep him,' said Vanity Fair.

'I believe he went,' said Virginia, 'because there was nothing to do.'

'Don't be a fool,' said her mother. 'If that were so, Mr Chandos would not have returned.'

'The truth is I'm restless,' said I.

'I know. I heard you say so. Do you shoot at all?'

I saw Below shift in his stall and lay hold of his glass.

I shook my head.

'I've never cared about shooting.'

'That's a pity,' said Vanity Fair. 'You might have gone out with Gaston. He haunts some woods hereabouts in shooting-boots and an unbecoming confection of Harris tweed. He takes a gun with him.'

Again the chaplain shifted. I heard him begin to blow.

Gaston was fool enough to pick up the glove.

'I do not care for just walking. I must have sport. I am born like that, I suppose. It is not my fault.'

Quem deus vult perdere…

Unconsciously I stepped on the trap.

'But what do you shoot?' I asked him. 'I thought – '

'Gaston stalks singing-birds,' said Vanity Fair.

Below made a rattling noise.

'I do not see,' began Gaston…

'How should you? You're born like that. It isn't your fault.'

I began to perceive how it was that Gaston fell so foul of Vanity Fair. The thing was vain. He simply had to establish that he was a man of parts. So Sisyphus simply had to roll his stone up the hill.

Dinner became a coconut-shy, and Vanity Fair had the sticks. I suffered least of all, but she knocked me down more than once.

'Be as frank as your face, Richard Chandos. I hate a simple serpent. Your servant's as well as you are. Why didn't you bring him back?'

'He was taken ill – '

'I know. As the clock chimed the quarter – the castle clock at Jezreel.'

Before the laughter had died, she was aiming at somebody else.

'Virginia, don't bounce. This isn't a Sunday-school treat. I shouldn't be here if it was. No more would Below: he is "too lovely and too temperate". Acorn, Gaston complains that his new chambermaid will not compare with his old. That was, of course, why we chose her. But tell her to be more attentive. She's nothing to fear – with that squint. Which reminds me – your eyes need attention – three mistakes this evening in the letters you sent me to sign. If you read them through – and missed them, you ought to be flogged: if you didn't read them through, you ought to be sacked. Virginia, Suzanne reports that you're putting on weight. That is the normal result of eating and drinking too much. If you don't believe me, ask Below. He's a leading case.'

'Madame, I protest – '

'Why should you? We can't all have the digestion of John the Baptist. Besides, he appealed to the ear: but you fill the eye. He is the Authorised Version: you are the Illustrated Edition. I often say to myself, "It is easier for a camel to go through the eye of a needle than for Below".'

Never have I subscribed to so electric and mordant a flow of soul. She certainly whetted our wits, but the play which she made with her tongue would have made a Juvenal gasp. I had found her brilliant before, but never like this – an expert swordsman at work on a body of clowns. But the brilliance was sinister. I had an uneasy feeling that the vials of wrath were brimming and this was their overflow. It was like a display of sheet lightning – that distant, restless magic that teases sight. The storm was to come.

'Then I am a liar?' mouthed Gaston.

'Of sort,' said Vanity Fair. 'But you do it very badly, like everything else.'

Gaston attempted a sneer.

'I am afraid that you see through me – as through Chandos: I hope – '

'You don't resemble the lanterns, if that's what you mean. They're very valuable things.'

'But I am worthless?'

The man was trembling with rage.

'Not at all,' said Vanity Fair. ' "The toad, ugly and venomous, bears nevertheless a precious jewel in its head." The truth is you've missed your vocation – as nine out of ten of us have. I ought to have been a gangster – a really big one, I mean. Virginia ought to have been a music-hall star. Acorn could have managed a night-club extremely well. Below should have been wine-steward at some very old-fashioned club. And you should have been a shepherd.'

'A shepherd?' cried Gaston.

'A shepherd…attached to some casino…guiding the steps of massive Cleopatras, whom age has withered, but whose custom will never fail.'

Below was shaking like a jelly: the singing-birds were avenged.

I emptied my glass.

'Madam,' I said, 'I'll buy it. What should I have been?'

Her eyes came to rest upon mine.

'A professional poker-player,' said Vanity Fair.

Sitting on the edge of my bed, I wished very much for Mansel and tried to fit into the puzzle the curious fact which I had been handed that day – that Vanity Fair and Virginia were fully aware that Gaston had been the servant of the Count he was pretending to be.

That explained the contempt which they showed him: it also explained why he suffered their whips and scorns: but it made Virginia's engagement more than ever incomprehensible. 'Living dogs have their uses.' Perhaps. But you do not use them as husbands or sons-in-law, nor do you present them with incomes beyond the dreams of greed.

I left the bed and fell to pacing the room.

My standing with Vanity Fair was very much what it had been ten days ago. She had then suspected me – deeply. By leaving Jezreel, I had sent her suspicions packing; but Jenny's abduction had brought them back in full force – only to be disconcerted by the intimate knowledge of Burgos which I had taken care to display. All the same…

For the hundredth time I wondered what was to come. Things could not go on like this. A child could have felt the tension. The waters of vengeance were swollen beyond belief. Unless they were offered some outlet, the dam would burst.

In a way I felt sorry for the woman, ruthless and evil as she was. For years her whim had been law. For years she had kept her palace, so that her goods were in peace. And now in the twinkling of an eye a stronger than she had come upon her, had taken away her armour and was dividing his spoils. Luis gone, Jean gone, Jenny gone. And all without trace. Three desolating blows. Yet whence they had come she had not the faintest idea. Little wonder that she was raging.

For the first time for nearly three weeks the night was close; and when I leaned out of the window I saw that the west of the heaven was blotted out. Plainly a storm was approaching. Thunder was in the air.

I left the casement, more than half-minded to bathe. Though the air could not refresh me, the water would.

As I crossed the room, I stopped to regard the mirror – the pier-glass which gave to the system pervading the house. If

Mansel thought it safe, he would certainly visit me: that anyone else would come was unlikely enough: if they did...

I had made myself a bed – *beneath* the sumptuous bedstead on which I had lain before. The valance would hide me, and, though the quarters were close, I should do very well. So I could take my rest without any fear. Any search of the bed above me was certain to wake me at once and would put at my mercy the man who was making the search. My pistol, of course, lay ready, by the side of my lowly couch.

I was just about to return to the bathroom, when something moved.

For an instant I thought it was the pier-glass. And then I saw that the glass itself was not moving, but was reflecting the movement of something else.

The door behind me was moving – the door of my bedroom that opened into the hall.

With my eyes on the mirror, I waited, as still as death.

The door stopped moving. It was little more than ajar. I began to wonder if the latch and some draught between them were playing an ancient trick.

Then a slight figure, swathed in silk, slid into the room. Virginia.

She did not see me at once, for, though a lamp was burning, the chamber was dim: but when she had shut the door, she turned to find me before her, two paces away.

She caught her breath and lay back against the door.

I can see her there now, with her fair head against the oak. She was dressed in powder blue – a dressing-gown over pyjamas. The colour matched her eyes and suited her very well. But the droop of her mouth was tragic and her palms were planted on the woodwork as though, in soul as in body, she had her back to the wall.

That she knew something was clear. And she was risking her honour to save me from Vanity Fair.

'What is it, Virginia?' I whispered. 'Why have you come?'

A hand went up to her brow.

'Because I'm mad, I suppose. I don't care. Any answer you like.' For a moment she hung her head. Then she looked up and clasped her hands and held them up to her breast.

'Oh Richard, why did you come back? I asked you not to. I told you to go away.'

I braced myself to play the difficult game.

'I know you did, Virginia. And I didn't mean to come back. But after I'd gone I received some information which I felt that your mother should know.'

She turned her head and laid her cheek to the oak.

'You could have written,' she said. 'Why did you have to come? I told you not to. I told you…'

'I know,' I said. 'I know. But please believe – '

'I told you you'd make me unhappy. I went as far as I could. To save my soul I stripped it – I tore up my self-respect. I made you free of the secret no woman can ever tell. I told you I – liked you, Richard. And I asked you to pocket that knowledge and go away…' She looked me full in the face. 'And because you've some news for my mother, you come straight back.'

She threw up an arm and laid it across her eyes.

It occurred to me that her mother was perfectly right. Virginia had missed her vocation. She would have made her mark on the stage. And something else I saw – with a sinking heart. And that was that the game was beyond me. No one – not even Mansel could stand up to bowling like this. *If I was to stay at Jezreel, I must lift the edge of my mask.*

Although I was sure that I could trust her, this seemed a most desperate move. Still, in order to do me a service, she was playing a desperate part.

'Virginia,' I said, 'now listen. I'm older than you. I haven't forgotten what happened the other day. I never shall forget what has happened tonight. You've done me extraordinary honour – God only knows why. But fancy's not fact, my dear, and – '

'It isn't fancy, Richard. I know what I know. And I asked such a little thing of you, to leave me in peace. You're rich and independent: you've got the world to wander, but I'm tied here. And so I asked you to choose another – hotel. What was it to you? Nothing. And I told you why, Richard… What if it had been fancy? What would it have cost you to humour that pitiful fancy and let me come to my senses by keeping away from Jezreel? Fancy!' She let fall her arms, and I saw that her eyes were shut. 'What stuff d'you think I'm made of? D'you think it was fancy tonight that brought me here?'

I moistened my lips.

'Virginia,' I said, 'you're making it frightfully hard.'

'I want to make it frightfully hard. I came tonight to – to force you to leave Jezreel. I – I…' She bowed her head and clapped her hands to her face. 'I've told you right out that I – I love you. I'm under no illusions – I know that I'm nothing to you. But I'm weak – the weaker vessel. And you're so terribly strong. D'you mean to stay and break me? Does that sort of thing amuse you? To watch a girl writhe and – '

'Virginia, listen to me.' I set a hand on her shoulder. 'This play has gone far enough.'

She dropped her hands and stared up into my eyes.

'This play?' she repeated.

'This play,' said I, and gave her back look for look. 'Why you should have done as you have, I've no idea. But I'll never forget it, Virginia, as long as I live.'

'What's that to me? Can't you see – '

'Please listen to me. There's something I want to tell you, that you ought to know. That day when you showed me the lanterns and – and spoke as you did. Your mother was present, Virginia.'

She started violently. Then she knitted her brows.

'Mother? But that's absurd. She was – '

'She was in the sedan-chair, Virginia.'

I saw the blood leave her face, but she did not speak. For a moment she stood, swaying. Then a hand went up to her head and her knees gave way.

I was just in time to catch her, before she fell.

I laid her in the great bed, which was, of course, open and ready for me to use. Then I ran for water, fell on my knees beside her and bathed her temples and wrists. After what seemed an age, she put up a hand for mine and, when she had caught it, she carried it down to the sheet. But her eyes were still shut. So we stayed for some moments. Then –

'Thank you,' she said quietly. 'I'm better now.'

'I'll make you still better, my dear. It's true that your mother was there and heard what you said. But she doesn't suspect you, Virginia. She thinks you were speaking the truth when you said that, unless I went, you might come to like me too well.'

There was a long silence.

At length –

'What makes you think that I wasn't speaking the truth?'

Her eyes were open now and were fast on the silken canopy, hanging above.

I shrugged my shoulders.

'I'm not like Gaston,' I said.

'You're not like anyone. A thousand men out of a thousand would have – taken me at my word.'

'I've – no illusions, Virginia. In fact I can't conceive why you should have gone such lengths to save an odd stranger's life. As I say, your mother believed you – I'm sure of that. But if she had dreamed that you were trying to save me...'

I stopped.

Virginia was trembling. I took her hand in mine and held it tight.

'Don't have any fear, Virginia. It's quite all right. Believe me, I know what I'm doing. And I'm not going to ask any questions. But I simply had to show you that I knew what your object was. Otherwise I'd have had to go. And I don't want to go, Virginia.'

'Why…don't you want…to go?'

The words came stiffly – as though her tongue were reluctant to handle the naked truth. Her hesitation seemed to give me address.

'I'm rather curious,' I said. 'I want to know why Jean, the chauffeur, attempted to take my life.'

Virginia lay still as death. Then, very slowly, she turned her head to look me full in the eyes.

'To – take – your – life?'

'In this bed,' said I. 'While I slept. The night before you showed me the lanterns. You knew that I was in danger. Didn't you know an attempt had already been made?'

The strangest gleam was lighting Virginia's eyes.

'Was that why Jean went?'

I shrugged my shoulders.

'Well, she had to pretend to sack him. I mean, I caught him red-handed and tied him up.'

'Pretend?' breathed Virginia. 'Pretend? D'you mean she didn't sack him?'

'Why should she?' said I. 'It wasn't his fault that he failed.'

'My God,' said Virginia, quietly. And then again, 'My God.'

It was clear that I had gone far enough.

'Listen, Virginia. I've said enough to show you that I can look after myself. And now the matter's closed, and you must go back to your room. Because you saw no other way, you pledged your honour, Virginia, to force me out of this house.' I put her hand to my lips. 'On my knees, Virginia, I give you that honour back. I can't tell you how much I respect you, how much I – '

'Don't Richard, don't. I can't bear it.'

'My dear, it's true.'

'It isn't.' She snatched her hand away to cover her eyes. 'And she tried to kill you…YOU!'

She wailed the words rather than spoke them.

Then she buried her face in the pillow and burst into tears.

If I had made her suffer, in the next ten minutes I paid a part of my debt. Her last words had opened my eyes, and I saw the length and the breadth of the folly which I had committed and the damage which I had done.

The spectacle made me feel faint.

I had used Virginia barbarously. She had thrown herself on my mercy: and I had shown her no mercy, but had chastised with scorpions her poor, susceptible heart. I felt as though I had been thrashing a wounded dog. As if that were not enough, I had as good as told her my business and had made her free of a secret which her manner towards her mother was sure to betray.

With my head in my hands, I tried to think what to do...

A hand came to rest on my shoulder.

'I want you to help me, Richard.'

Virginia was sitting upright, staring ahead.

'My dear Virginia, I'll do anything that I can.'

'I'll hold you to that. I want you to take me away. I haven't got any money. Perhaps you'll lend me a little until I can get some work. If I could get to England, she wouldn't come after me there.'

So soon as I could speak –

'You must sleep on this, Virginia. You're speaking on impulse now. And I'll think it over, too. I couldn't promise off-hand to help you to that. After all, she is your mother.'

'No, she isn't,' said Virginia, quietly. 'She's no relation at all.'

Twice I tried to answer, and twice I failed.

At the third attempt –

'She's – not – your – mother?' I said.

'No,' said Virginia, 'thank God.'

'Do you know what you're saying, Virginia?'

'More. I know what I'm doing,' she said. 'But you don't know that, so I'll tell you. I'm betraying the innermost secret of the wickedest, cold-blooded butcher that ever wore woman's clothes. I wish she was here...to hear me give her away.'

I can never describe the hatred with which she spoke. Her face was a mask: her eyes were narrowed to slits: her teeth were clenched: and her breath whistled in her nostrils, as though indeed the very spirit of vengeance had entered into her soul.

Before I could make any answer –

'You want to know,' she said, 'why Jean, the chauffeur, was sent here, to take your life. I'll tell why. Because she thought it possible – only possible, mark you – that you had come to pry into her affairs. That was enough – *for her*. So YOU, in your power and splendour, were to be just wiped out.' She threw back her head. 'My God, I could spit upon her... Never mind. When she knows I'm gone, that'll shake her. When she guesses that her confederate has let her down. And that filthy Hebrew, Gaston. He's in it, too. I tell you, Richard, we're not a sweet-smelling bunch. But I'm not so vile as the others. You'll take my word for that.'

'I can think no ill of you, Virginia.'

'Can't you? I'll put you wise. She laid the truth before me two years ago. "You think you're my daughter, don't you? Virginia Brooch? Well, take a good look at that paper – and try again." That paper was a birth-certificate... And attached to it was a statement, with a photograph signed and sealed. I came out of an orphanage, Richard. I was born in prison, at Utah, just twenty-one years ago.'

'I see nothing in that, Virginia. I'm only rather prouder to be your friend.'

She turned and looked at me.

'You know,' she said slowly, 'there's something the matter with you. I've broken every rule that your class observes. And yet you – you show me respect.'

'I behave as I feel, Virginia. And for that you must thank yourself. I don't care what you've done – I can't help honouring you, because you compel respect.'

She seemed to think that over, and then she laughed.

'I guess you'll swallow that saying before I'm through.' She drew up her knees and laced her fingers about them. 'All the same I'm so thankful to tell you. I want you to know.

'The disclosure hit me hard – as she meant it to do. Ever since I could remember, I'd been Virginia Brooch, and if life had been a bit lonely, it hadn't been rough. And the future, of course, had been dazzling – half a million a year, when I'd found the right man. The press used to ram it home whenever I showed my face. "The guarded heiress" they called me, last time I was in New York.

'Then she laid her cards on the cloth.

'I had been changed with her daughter when we were both eight years old. Very well. If I cared to do her will, I could go right on as I was and stick to the name I bore. I must marry the man of her choice on five thousand a year. Otherwise, I could go back to Utah. She'd give me my third-class fare.

'I suppose you can call it blackmail, but what could I do? For ten years I'd lived like a princess, and a third-class fare to the workhouse looked pretty grim. Sticky business or no, I didn't take long to decide…

'Then she got Gaston.

'He's not the Comte de Rachel. But he was de Rachel's servant, and the two were exactly alike. One night in Buenos Aires the Count fell ill: the next morning he was all right, but his servant was dead. She's got it all down – and a statement from one of the maids, who'd noticed the ring Gaston wears on the hand of the dying man. You ought to have seen Gaston's face when she brought it all out.

'Well, he came in on the deal. It wasn't what he had hoped for, but he liked the idea of exposure a good deal less. Blackmail again, you see. She'd got us both tight. And she thinks of everything, Richard. She's most frightfully, damnably clever. Once put a foot wrong, and as far as she's concerned you'll go lame for life. And if you don't do it she'll lame you. When I asked how it was I didn't remember Utah, "I saw to that," she said. "At the age of eight the two of you had brain-fever: at least, when I asked the doctors they gave it that name."

'And that's my – biography. I was born in prison, and prison is where I belong. Both Gaston and I are impostors: but I'm a far worse one than he. The Comte de Rachel is dead, and the dead have nothing to lose. But Virginia Brooch is living – under restraint. *And I've signed away half her fortune during the last two years*. False pretences, forgery, theft – though I haven't touched a centime. Why she's not dead, I don't know. Her mother's obvious course was to bump her off. But for some reason or other she couldn't: so she had to go round this way.'

There was a little silence.

I wanted to comfort Virginia: but my mind, like some naughty dog, refused to obey my call. The bone was too big. The truth which we had been seeking was here, in my hands. It only remained to secure it, to establish it so fast that it could not be moved. Somehow, I must see Mansel…

'I say "she couldn't",' said Virginia, 'because if she could have, she would. Murder's nothing to her. I can't prove she did in her son, but I know she did. And so do Below and Acorn. And six other deaths I know of. I can't prove a single one – nor can anyone else. She's too damned slim. But the poor devils got in her way – and she got them out. I tell you, Richard, we're hardened. When somebody dies at Jezreel, we talk about something else. You see, she's got us all cold. Acorn's real name is Omer. He's wanted down in Kentucky for cutting a woman's throat.'

I put out my hand for hers, and after a little she laid her fingers in mine.

'I've an aunt in Wiltshire,' I said. 'She's looking after my home. I think you'd like her, Virginia – she's very gentle and charming: and I know that she'd take to you. Would you like to stay with her there? There are nice people round about, and if you care for riding, the horses need exercise. And cub-hunting's coming on… And later on we can talk about the future. When I say "later on", I mean it. As late as you please. You'll be under no obligation in eating my salt. If you ate it for the rest of your life, I couldn't repay the service you've done me tonight.'

Virginia stared.

'I've done you a service?'

I nodded.

'Beyond all price, Virginia. Please leave it there for the moment. As soon as ever I can, I'll take you away. Tomorrow, perhaps, I can't say. But till then you must go straight on. Behave as you did this evening. Play up for all you're worth. Until the moment comes – and it's very near now – your mother must never dream that you've opened your mouth.' I rose to my feet. 'And now, my dear, I'll see you back to your room. Pray God, there's no one about, but you've got to get back.'

'You needn't see me back. Let me go as I came.'

She slipped out of bed, and I fitted her small, blue slippers on to her feet.

As she steadied herself by my shoulder –

'Did you mean what you said about Wiltshire? You'll have to tell your aunt who I am.'

'You shall tell her yourself,' said I. 'But I don't know that she'll believe you. Anyone can run themselves down: but over there we go by the stuff they're made of – not where it was made.'

The clasp on my shoulder tightened.

'Why are you so good to me, Richard?'

'My dear,' said I, 'the boot's on the other leg. You know that as well as I do. That I'm a fool in a million is no excuse, but you know I didn't mean it, Virginia: if I'd dreamed how things stood, I'd have cut my hand off before I came back to Jezreel.'

She nodded.

'Yes, I know that. You're forgiven. Knave forgives fool. Never mind. I'm thankful you came.' She cupped her face in her hands and closed her eyes. 'From this house of hell to your home.

Perhaps tomorrow! Oh, Richard... And I'll play up, I promise: but don't keep me waiting long.'

The words seemed to set her thinking, for she took her hands from her face and opened her eyes. Then, with a sudden movement, she caught my arm.

'Are you out to get her?' she breathed.

I shrugged my shoulders.

'If I am, I think I've the right.'

Her eyes aflame, she caught her lip in her teeth.

Then –

'By God, I'm glad. And I've helped you... See that she knows that, Richard. I'd like her to know that I helped to bring her down... But for God's sake watch your step. They say "clever as sin", don't they? Well, she is sin. And she'll stick at nothing, I warn you. My dear, are you armed?'

I nodded.

'That's right. But you must get in first. If you don't, you'll never get her – because she'll get you.'

'She won't do that. You sit tight, Virginia, and we'll take the road for Wiltshire any day now. And now you must go.' I shot a glance at the door. 'You're sure the hall will be empty? My God, if she knew you'd been here...'

Virginia frowned.

Then –

'The hall's always empty,' she said. 'Besides, I took jolly good care. Still, put out your light, if you like, before I open the door.'

I stepped to the oak.

'You put it out,' I said. 'I'll open the door.'

'All right.'

The next second the lamp went out.

Using the greatest caution, I turned the handle about.

But the door would not move.

Virginia was there. I could feel her breath on my cheek.

'What is it, Richard?'

'The door's jammed. You didn't lock it?'

She pulled me away.

'It isn't jammed. It's bolted.'

'Bolted? But how?'

'I don't know. But someone has done it. Every one of these doors has a bolt – *on the other side.*'

As though to attest the saying, a sullen grumble of thunder came rolling over the hills.

The storm had begun.

8

Behind the Scenes

For what it was worth I tried the door of the salon, and when I had found that fast I led the way back to the bedroom and made Virginia sit down.

If the poor girl was pale and trembling, I confess I was shaken myself, but what held me up was the knowledge that, though I had lost this trick, I had the game in my hand.

I patted her shoulder.

'Don't worry, Virginia. It's going to be quite all right. I'll get you back to your room.'

'But, Richard – '

'In five minutes' time. I promise. But I want to think for a moment. You see, I hold all the cards – now: if I play them right, I must win.'

I think it will be clear that I spoke no more than the truth.

Mansel and I were not policemen. Our instructions were to discover what was toward at Jezreel – and to act, if what we discovered should give us good cause. That being so, with the taking away of Virginia our work would come to an end. We had found out the truth and had acted on what we had found. Jenny was escaped out of prison and we were to rescue Virginia from something worse.

If only I could see Mansel...

That Virginia had been trapped in my room was highly disconcerting, but nothing more. Vanity Fair would require an explanation – which neither Virginia nor I could possibly give. And yet we should give it – a very full explanation...*by leaving Jezreel.*

There was no doubt about it. I had the cards in my hand. If only I could see Mansel...

'Listen, Virginia. In a moment now I'll take you back to your room by a secret way. You must go to bed and to sleep. In the morning we shall be found in our proper rooms – a hell of a jolt for "your mother". She will hold such an inquisition as never was seen.' Virginia shuddered. 'But we shan't attend it, my dear. As soon as I'm dressed, I shall see Acorn. I shall tell him that I am going because I do not stay at houses where guests are locked into their rooms. And with that, I shall go. You will come round to the garage to see me off. And so you shall. Off the map. You won't be seen, if you sit well back in the Rolls. But you mustn't bring any luggage or even put on a hat. You must play right up, Virginia. Be absolutely natural in all you do. If she sends for you, stick her out that you never entered this room. She won't believe you, but that doesn't matter at all. You've only to play out time, and it won't be long.'

'As soon as you're dressed, you say. What time will that be?'

I pointed to the flowers on a table.

'When I leave this room for the garage, I'll stick a rose in one of the open shutters against the wall. Directly you see it there, go round to the yard. I'll wait till you come, of course: it's a show that mustn't be rushed: if you're with her, for instance... But the sooner we're off, the better – and that's the truth. And now I must put on some clothes...'

This took but a moment. I slipped a coat and trousers over my sleeping-suit, and changed my slippers for a pair of rubber-soled shoes. Then I took my torch and my pistol and put out the light.

The storm was fast approaching. I could see the flicker of the lightning, and the heavy roll of the thunder was louder with every flash. As I glanced at the open window, I heard the forests shiver at the touch of the running footman that goes before: and the air was definitely cooler – I could smell the rain that was falling some two miles off.

I lighted the torch and kept its beam on the floor.

'Give me your hand, Virginia.' Her fingers caught mine. 'Once we're out of this room I shan't show a light. Tread as softly as ever you can. Your room looks on to the terrace and it's the fourth from this. Am I right?'

'Yes, Richard.'

'Then, come, my dear,' and, with that, I stepped to the pier-glass and put out the torch.

The passage was black and silent as any tomb. We moved like shadows, I with a hand on the wall to count the doors. Arrived at the fourth, I stood listening and glancing to right and to left. If Virginia had left lights burning, their glow would illumine the passage the moment I opened the door. But my ears at least reported that we had the place to ourselves…

An instant later we were standing within her room.

This was as she had left it, more or less illumined by a heavily shaded lamp.

'Put out the light,' I whispered. 'I daren't shut this door: it's got no handle inside.'

The door was backed with the beautiful linen-fold panels that lined the room, but its counterweight was so heavy that I could not have pulled the door open by what purchase the carving gave.

I imagine her fingers were trembling, or else, maybe, the switch of the lamp was stiff: but at last the light went out and I breathed again.

As she moved to my side –

'Virginia, I'm going now. Try and sleep, and mind you play up in the morning for all you're worth.'

A groping hand brushed my face and came down to my arm.

'I wish – you weren't going, Richard. It's all right with you, but I don't want to be alone.'

I found and held her fingers.

'Buck up, Virginia. This is the last of the fences. Early tomorrow morning we'll be in the straight.'

'You – you won't go without me, Richard?'

'Need you ask me that, Virginia?'

'I suppose not,' she said slowly. 'But you've fixed all this on impulse. Supposing tomorrow morning you change your mind.'

'I shan't do that,' I said quietly.

'It'd be the end of me, Richard.'

'Now you go to bed,' said I, 'and don't imagine vain things.'

'I'll try not to,' she faltered. 'But, you see, you've promised me something that seems too good to be true.' With a sudden movement she caught my hand to her lips. Then, 'Good night, my dear, and God bless you – all your days.'

'And you, Virginia. Good night.'

The next instant I was back in the passage and the door of her room was shut.

I listened carefully. Then I went gently back the way we had come. I remember that I counted three doors, so it must have been close to that which gave to my room that someone who knew how to hit put me down and out.

When at last I came to my senses, the daylight was broad. But as I made to start up, an agony flared in my temples to make me forget all else.

Then –

'Drink this,' said a voice in French. 'It will make you well.'

Lafone. I knew her at once. Gaunt and harsh and bitter, she seemed to embody the unkindness of Shakespeare's winter wind. Charity ill became her. Her grudging manner assured me there was no death in the cup.

With an effort I drank the potion which tasted and smelled of herbs. Then I lay back on my pallet and fell asleep.

I have an idea that I slept for about two hours, but when I awoke the pain in my head was gone. My wits were at my service, for what they were worth.

I found that my head was bandaged, that my temple was very much swollen and tender beyond belief. And I knew that no fist had done that. A life-preserver or truncheon had been employed.

I found that my bed was a pallet, laid in a slight recess in a chamber of stone. I found that I was chained to the wall – chained by the leg. And I found that the chain would allow me to reach a wash-stand which stood between my bed and a window, sunk in the wall. But the window was out of my reach.

I made what toilet I could…

In shape the chamber resembled a very thick slice of cake, and since the window was set in the curving side, I had no doubt that I was lodged in the tower. The window boasted a seat, but except for my bed and the wash-stand the chamber was bare.

Again well out of my reach was a massive door. This was of oak and iron and plainly opened outwards, for the doorway was smaller than the door. Chin-high in the oak was a grill, through which a man, standing outside, could look into the cell. The place was a proper prison and had, of course, been made to that end.

I glanced at my watch.

The hour was a quarter to ten.

At once I remembered Virginia and wondered what she would do. I hoped very much that she would give nothing away. If she kept her head and possessed her soul for a little… After all I could scarcely be held here for more than another few hours. Though Vanity Fair might dare, Mansel would take some action to spoil her game. When he learned of my disappearance – as learn he must – he would guess at once that I was confined in the tower. And he would have me out in a twinkling, cost what it might. *And in fact it would cost him nothing*, for I had the truth in my hands. Once I was free, we had only to take Virginia and go our ways. Vanity Fair had struck: but though she did not know it, her blow had fallen too late. The game was ours, and what had befallen me now was no more than a hitch.

The clack of wood made me look up.

At once I saw that someone had drawn the shutter that masked the grill: between the bars of the lattice I could see the white of a face.

Then the wards of a heavy lock clashed, and Lafone came into the room.

Without a word she set a small tray beside me, on which were some tea and toast: then she turned to the wash-stand, to empty and wipe the basin and make all clean.

Once she left the room for fresh water, which she drew from some tap outside, but because, I suppose, she knew the length of my chain, she showed no fear of my trying to follow her out. For all that, she did not ignore me, but rather took care to insist that all that she was doing was done in enmity. Had she known what I knew, she could not have been more hostile. Once again it occurred to me that Vanity Fair had a flair for obtaining the very service which she required. Her unconscionable treatment of Jenny would have melted most jailers' hearts: but this woman was stony-hearted: inhumanity inhabited her face.

Tea and toast was the fare which I would have chosen and I knew, without being told, that this provision was due to Vanity Fair. As her enemy, I was condemned: as her guest, my desires must be honoured up to the hilt. That was her way.

I made an excellent breakfast – and waited for Vanity Fair.

Whilst I waited, I examined my chain. This was of steel. The links were carefully made and looked very strong. They hung from an iron staple, thick as my little finger, sunk in the wall. The cuff about my ankle was of fine steel.

Lafone returned, with bed-linen over her arm. This she laid down on the window-seat. Then she took up the tray and carried it off. It seemed she proposed to come back, for she did not relock the door: but when this was opened again, there was Vanity Fair.

I rose to my feet.

She smiled and nodded and passed to the window-seat.

As she sat down –

'You know I did warn you,' she said.

'Madam,' said I stiffly, 'if a guest in my house offends me, I ask him to leave.'

'With your spoons in his pocket? I think you'd get them back first.'

I raised my eyebrows.

'At least,' I said, 'that's downright. At least you've made a clear charge. And that gives me the right to demand that you call in the police.'

'Your "demand" is refused.'

I took my seat on the pallet and crossed my legs.

'Madam,' said I, 'I was plainly a fool to come back.'

'That,' said Vanity Fair, 'is indisputable. But you were a much bigger fool to try to stand up to me.'

I shrugged my shoulders.

'Let's get down to facts,' said I, 'and leave fancies alone. Last night I heard a sound in the hall outside my room. I rose and went to my door – to find it locked. As a guest, I have a distaste for being locked into my room. I, therefore, left by the passage which Jean, your ex-chauffeur, employed.'

'Why didn't you tell me that you had seen him come in?'

'Because I suspected that he visited me by your orders. If I was right, it was idle to tell you how much I knew.'

'I see. Go on – with your tale.'

'I found several doors in the passage, and the one which I ventured to open led into Virginia's room. Her light was burning, but she herself was asleep. I must have made some sound, for whilst I was there she awoke. But she didn't see me and presently put out her light. When I judged her asleep again, I left her room for the passage, proposing to return to my room: but before I had time to get there, somebody laid me out.'

'That was Marc,' said Vanity Fair. 'He's a great improvement on Jean.'

I drew in my breath.

'It seems,' I said, 'that my suspicion was just. For some reason best known to yourself you mean me ill. Well, that's your affair: but – ' I picked up my chain and looked her full in the eyes ' – you can't do this sort of thing to people like me... Please have me released at once.'

'And then?'

I shrugged my shoulders.

'I shall leave Jezreel, madam: and I shall never come back.'

'Taking my spoons with you?'

I sighed.

'Do I look like a thief?' I said.

'No,' said Vanity Fair. 'That's why you're not dead.'

'I'm not easily frightened,' said I.

'I know. Neither am I. It makes life much easier.'

'Madam,' said I, 'if you suspect me of theft, you have your remedy. You can telephone for the police and give me in charge. Until they arrive – but no longer – you have the right to detain me against my will.'

'I suspect,' said Vanity Fair, 'that you made that up. I do not believe that you know the law of this land. But it sounds common sense.'

There was a little silence.

At length –

'I suppose you mean,' said I, 'that you are not concerned with the law of the land.'

Vanity Fair raised her eyebrows.

'I would hardly say that. I look on the law as I look on the fire brigade. I should summon the fire brigade – if I couldn't cope with a fire.'

'In other words you propose to deal with me yourself.'

'Don't you think I'm capable of doing so?'

'Madam,' said I, 'I think you are capable of anything.'

Vanity Fair vouchsafed me a dazzling smile.

'Good for you, Richard Chandos. You're perfectly right.'

Strange to say, I smiled back. I simply could not help it. Her personality beat me, as it had done before. Then –

'In that case, madam, there is little more to be said.'

'Don't you want to know what you're charged with?'

'You've told me I'm charged with theft. Such a charge is so fantastic that its details would worry me, madam. I am not in the mood to listen to fairy-tales. I mean, we both of us know the thing's absurd. You might as well charge me with murder.'

'Perhaps I do.'

'There you are,' said I.

There was another silence.

Presently –

'I wish I didn't like you so much,' said Vanity Fair.

I touched my chain.

'Is this a sign of your favour?'

'Yes.' Her change of tone made me look up. She proceeded slowly, her grey eyes feeding on mine. 'In the next room to this the chain is very much shorter. And it ends in a collar – not a cuff. Whoever wears it can neither sit nor lie down.'

It was not a pleasant saying, but her rendering made it hideous. I can only hope that I did not appear to flinch.

'I see,' I said. 'How very – uncomfortable.'

Vanity Fair nodded.

'That's the idea,' she said. 'But, as I say, I like you: and I'm not at all surprised that Virginia fell flat. Which reminds me – tell me one thing. *In view of the confession she made, how could*

168

you come back to Jezreel? I mean, it was the way of a cad. And you're not a cad.'

With a hammering heart, I looked at her very hard.

'Your secret service,' I said, 'is extremely good.'

Vanity Fair was pleased.

'It might be worse,' she purred. 'Why did you come back?'

I made a most desperate effort to keep my head.

'If you must know,' said I, 'I didn't take her seriously. I simply couldn't believe that she meant what she said. And so I decided to ignore it.'

'That's not like Richard Chandos,' said Vanity Fair.

'We all make mistakes,' said I, somehow.

Quick as a flash –

'How d'you know you made a mistake?'

'She told me as much...in the hall...as I entered the house.'

Vanity Fair raised her eyebrows.

'D'you deny that she came to your bedroom...last night...at a quarter to twelve?'

I opened my eyes.

'To my bedroom?'

'That,' said Vanity Fair, 'was the phrase I used.'

I shrugged my shoulders.

'For all I know,' said I, 'she may have come to the door. Perhaps it was she that made the noise that I heard.'

'She was seen to enter your bedroom,' said Vanity Fair.

'Which is why my door was locked. Madam, your secret service is not so good as I thought.'

'In other words...'

'Nobody saw Virginia enter my room.'

Vanity Fair nodded.

'That's better,' she said. 'But I'd love to know why you came back.'

'I've told you I made a mistake. I simply – '

'I know. I heard you say so. The trouble is – you're not Gaston. Yet you made the one mistake which no gentleman ever makes.'

There was another silence, which I sought to carry off as well as I could. But the round was Vanity Fair's: and she knew it as well as I. More than the round – much more…

The writing had been there – on the wall: I can only think that some Fate had bandaged my eyes. I had fretted all the way to Jezreel, because I feared that Virginia would think me a cad. *But never once had I seen that Vanity Fair would know that, in view of Virginia's confession, only some bounden duty could ever have brought me back.* The thing was so glaringly obvious… And that is why I think that some Fate had bandaged my eyes – for if I had seen it, I should have turned back to Anise though I was at the gates of Jezreel.

As though she could read my thoughts –

'I seem to have confirmed your opinion – that you were a fool to come back.'

'I came at your invitation.'

'Naturally. If there weren't any flies, fish wouldn't rise, would they?'

The contempt in her voice annoyed me.

'Madam,' said I, 'I've never been very much good at playing with words.'

'No one on earth would know it,' said Vanity Fair.

'Well, it's not my forte,' said I. 'But that's neither here nor there. The point is this. You suspect me of theft and murder and God knows what. Because I accept your invitation to repeat my visit to Jezreel, you consider these charges proved. You, therefore, have me laid out and chained to a wall. You decline to go to the police or to let me go. Well, I can only repeat that you cannot do this sort of thing to people like me – *with impunity*. If I don't walk out today, when I do walk out, I'm going straight to the police: and if I…never walk out – well, my servant knows where I am…and will know where I was.'

Vanity Fair regarded her elegant hands.

'Is Chandos also among the prophets?' she said.

I made no reply, and presently she lifted her eyes.

'I have,' she said, 'an infinite variety of failings. I'm sure you'll agree with me there. But when I am dead and the tale of my shortcomings is whispered by those who stand by my bier, no one will ever say, "She was improvident." I look ahead, Mr Chandos: and I never do things by halves.

'One of my windows commands the stable-yard. At half-past seven this morning I saw some movement below. Marc was there, with your luggage, and under his direction your car was being pushed from its coach-house into the yard. At once I dispatched a servant, to ask what this meant. For this particular mission I chose a talkative maid...

'Now this was the report which she brought me.

'Mr Chandos was leaving Jezreel. He had rung for Marc at seven and had told him to pack his things. When this was done, he had given Marc the keys of his car, told him to take them to Wright and ask the latter to bring the Rolls round to the door. As it happened, Wright wasn't there. He had left, on my business, for Perin, ten minutes before. (He's an excellent man – John Wright: but I didn't want him on in this scene.) So Marc, who knows how to drive, was proposing to do Wright's duty and drive the Rolls round himself. And so he did. I saw him drive out of the yard.

'Well, I waited for half an hour. Then I sent for the sergeant-footman and asked him if it was true that Mr Chandos had left. He replied that you had been gone a quarter of an hour. When I seemed incredulous, he declared he had seen you go – that so had all the servants that happened to be about.

'This was his report – in detail.

'That just after half-past seven Marc brought your car into the courtyard and went upstairs to your room. That ten minutes later you yourself came down, gave the sergeant-footman two hundred and fifty francs, entered your car in silence and drove away.

'That was his report – in detail. And you can't say the man was lying, because he firmly believed he was telling the truth.

'Now what was the truth? I'll tell you…

'Marc is almost exactly your height and build. When he went upstairs to your room, he whipped off his clothes and put on those you were wearing yesterday afternoon. Then he put on your hat *and the sun-glasses which you were wearing when you arrived*. Then he hid his own clothes in the passage of which you know: and then he went down to your car and drove it away.

'And there you are,' she concluded. 'By nine o'clock this morning the whole of Jezreel was aware that Mr Chandos had gone without taking his leave.'

In the silence which followed her statement I kept my eyes on the floor. To be honest, I dared not look up, lest Vanity Fair should read the utter dismay in my face. She knew that her news would hit me – and hit me hard: but she did not know that it had laid in ruins the smiling prospects I had. Mansel fooled…the game I had won, thrown away… Virginia left in the lurch – to find me the cheapest blackguard that ever let a girl down. I could hear her pitiful sayings – *You won't go without me, Richard?… It'd be the end of me*. As for myself, I was now a pawn on the board – a pawn about to be taken and pitched to one side.

With an effort, I pulled myself together. At least I was not yet taken. I could put up a fight, so long as I was still on the board.

'You don't stick at much, madam, do you? *My* clothes, *my* car – '

'*My* spoons,' said Vanity Fair.

I rose to my feet.

'I cannot leave you, madam: but you can leave me.'

Vanity Fair frowned.

'Pray sit down, Mr Chandos. When I rise you will know that this interview is at an end.'

With a sigh of resignation, I did as she said.

'Be sure that that air won't help you,' said Vanity Fair. 'You can fight me as much as you like, but you'll only annoy me by kicking against the pricks. You have been arrested and charged. Well, you quarrelled with your arrest, as I knew you would. I, therefore, took pains to show you that any hopes you might harbour of righting that particular wrong would be disappointed. Now if my demonstration had been less convincing, you would, I think, have been wise to decline to discuss the charge. In fact, to be perfectly frank, that is what I should have done in your place. But now that it's clear that your future depends entirely on me and that, however I may use you, the shadow of retribution can never fall on my path, to decline to discuss the charge would be, I think, the act of a fool. I mean, you've nothing to lose.'

'Oh, I see that all right,' said I. 'But, frankly, it irritates me when you talk about theft.'

'D'you prefer the word "abduction"?'

' "Abduction"?' said I, staring.

'An idiot child was abducted a week ago. I associate you with the crime.'

'An idiot child.' A wave of fury swept through me and left me cold.

'Am I to be downright?' I said.

'I advise you to be.'

'Then one of us, madam, is mad. But I don't think it's me.'

There was another silence, of which I was very glad, for so far I had kept my temper, but now, for the moment, it had the upper hand.

'An idiot child.'

The offensive phrase had provoked me as had nothing else: and the mother's contemptuous tone had made still more outrageous the outrage her tongue had done. I knew that beneath my tan I was white with rage.

Virginia's words came to my mind. *They say 'clever as sin', don't they? Well, she is sin.* It was true. Sin was ensconced before me – in the shape of a beast of a woman, a ghoul that dishonoured its dead. In her lust for gold, she had seized her daughter's birthright, ravished her understanding and put her away. And now she was blowing upon her, defaming the very nonsuch that she had debauched.

I had pitied the woman, and feared her: I had admired and despised her: at times I had felt a liking for Vanity. But now these emotions were gone: and only a deadly hatred possessed my heart. In the window-seat was crouching a hag.

My thoughts whipped back to Jenny – that blessed, gentle darling that knew no wrong. I remembered the light in her eyes and the breath of her parted lips. I saw her grave face above me, as I lay with my head in her lap and I felt the touch of her fingers, disposing my dripping hair. I remembered her arrival at Anise and how, when Jill had come running, Jenny, all shy for an instant, had hidden her face in my coat. I saw her sleeping and walking and 'sitting in front' in the car. I could hear her cries of pleasure and watch the grace of her steps. I saw her at my feet in the greenwood, hanging upon my efforts to tell her of *The Wind in the Willows* and the folly of *Mr Toad*, and I saw – a tiny nosegay, that might have been made by a child and a fairy, between them, lying on the seat of the Rolls...

She had not bade me goodbye, when I had left for Jezreel. She was, I think, upset at my going, which indeed was natural enough. First, Jonathan, her beloved, from whom she had heard no word: and now her faithful William... She might have been forgiven for wondering who would go next and whether her precious dream was not coming about her ears. And so she was not there, when I went: and my going had been the darker – for want of the flash of her smile and the light in her eyes. And then I had noticed her nosegay – a little posy of harebells, because I had found them so pretty the day before... Little wonder that I worshipped a nature that knew how to make a gesture so lovely as that. Worshipped? *Loved!*

It was there in that cell at Jezreel, chained to the wall and bayed by Vanity Fair, that for the first time *I knew that I was in love with Jenny... Jenny who was mad about Mansel... Mansel who was mad about her.*

'Are you quite sure you went to Burgos?' said Vanity Fair.

I put a hand to my head.

'Yes, I went to Burgos,' I said. 'I – I sent some boots from Burgos – some boots to Below.'

The woman regarded me curiously.

'Think again,' she said.

'All right,' I said. 'I don't mind.'

And I thought again of Jenny and how neither she nor Mansel must ever suspect that she could have filled the void which was for ever insisting that there was no object in life.

Vanity Fair was frowning. My demeanour was disconcerting: of that there can be no doubt.

'A postmark tells no tales. Some boots were dispatched from Burgos, and the label the parcel bore was written by you. Are you still sure you went to Burgos?'

'Yes, I went to Burgos all right. I said so just now.'

'Kindly pull yourself together,' said Vanity Fair.

I looked up angrily. Then, all of a sudden, my wits fell back into line. The past and the future faded, and the present took savage shape. I was up against Sin, sitting there, in the guise of a hag. And Sin was out to get Jenny... I moistened my lips.

'I went to Burgos,' I said.

'By car?'

'Of course.'

'This morning I inspected your *triptique*. According to that, your car has never left France.'

This was, of course, correct. When I had visited Burgos, I did so in Mansel's Rolls.

There was nothing to do but lie.

'I didn't use my *triptique*. I went into Spain on a pass.'

'What a singular thing to do. Your *triptique* is ready and waiting: but rather than use it, you go off and purchase a pass.'

'I rather imagine,' said I, 'you'd have done the same. Half Biarritz was crossing the frontier that afternoon. There was a queue before me of fifty or sixty cars. And those that were touring on *triptiques* were being turned aside and made to wait to the last, while those on passes went through. I didn't take long to decide. I left my man with the car, crossed the road to a garage and paid them to make out a pass.'

'How long did you stay at Burgos?'

I touched my head.

'I don't feel like addition this morning, so perhaps you will work it out. I stayed two nights at Bayonne, but I haven't been anywhere else.'

'I suggest that you have.'

'I daresay you do,' said I. 'But I can't help that.'

'This manner won't help you, Mr Chandos.'

'It is perfectly clear that nothing will help me, madam – except a full confession of something I haven't done.'

I am glad to record that that shook her. With the tail of my eye I could see the knit of her brows, and, after a little, a hand stole up to her chin.

Then –

'Do you know the country about here?'

'I know the country,' said I, 'which lies between here and Bayonne.'

'More to the south.'

'I've been over the Col de Fer.'

'I know. And so to Gobbo, and there turned north for Bayonne. What I – '

'As a matter of fact, I turned at Lally,' I said.

'Why at Lally, instead of Gobbo? Most people turn at Gobbo, if they're *en route* for Bayonne.'

I shrugged my shoulders.

'It's of no importance,' I said, 'but I think you've got the towns mixed. Gobbo lies west of Lally, about five miles.'

'Would you like to bet, Mr Chandos?'

I shook my head.

'That's as well,' said Vanity Fair. 'You see, I know you're right. *But if you turned north at Lally, how do you know?*'

I had walked clean into the trap. The only thing to do was to brazen it out.

'I can only suppose,' said I, 'that I know from the map.'

'Haven't you been to Gobbo?'

'No.'

'Yet you know its name: and you know it's five miles from Lally, travelling west. Can you tell me as much of any other town – that does not lie on the road from here to Bayonne?'

'I don't know that I can,' said I. 'But Gobbo's a curious name. I suppose it stuck in my mind.'

'Like the distance and the direction? Well, well…' She rose to her feet. 'I suppose you didn't notice that Gobbo would have lain on your road, if you had been travelling south.'

I stood up straight.

'Madam,' said I, 'I am sick of supposition. For all I knew you can go to hell through Gobbo. Well…what if you can?'

'Only this,' said Vanity Fair. 'You'd be going out of your way. You don't have to go by Gobbo…to get to hell…from Jezreel.'

With that, she turned and left me: and the door of the chamber was shut.

I think I could fill up a book with the many meditations to which I gave myself up for the next two hours: but since they may be imagined, I will do no more than report that one and all pointed to misfortune and some to catastrophe.

That my days were numbered was clear: so far as I was concerned, Vanity Fair had stepped over the safety line: though she were to find me guiltless, she simply could not afford to let me live. Virginia would go to pieces: the shock of her brutal betrayal would break her down. Mansel was presently doomed: when he learned that I was not at Anise, he would instantly seek to unearth me – at any cost: his attempt must needs unmask him, and Vanity Fair would award him a traitor's end. And Jenny would be left high and dry, to make what she could of life – and to find it a broken dream, that no one could ever mend. But one thing, at least, I was spared, and that was the contemplation of heart-ache to come. *What is love? 'Tis not hereafter...* Jenny might have come into my life, but her tenancy did not matter – because the head lease was up.

Soon after noon Lafone appeared with some luncheon, and when I had eaten, I made up my mind to rest: in spite of all my troubles I slept very well for four hours: and I think I might have slept longer, but for the slam of my door: but that, no doubt, was Lafone's idea of attention, for when I sat up I saw some tea by my side.

No doubt my sleep refreshed me, for whilst I was taking my tea the thought came into my head that though things were desperate enough, something might be saved from the wreck if only I could escape. *Something? All* could be saved...

At once I began to consider this most forlorn of all hopes and, for what it is worth, I will say how I went to work.

I remembered the famous Jack Sheppard and how that great-hearted man had escaped from 'the Castle' in Newgate, the strongest ward in the jail. Five doors had barred his passage, and he had reduced them all – and that, with irons on his legs...

Again I inspected my bonds. They might, I thought, be broken: but that I dared not attempt until it was dark. I then regarded my prison, inch by inch. Fireplace there was none. The ceiling, like the walls, was of stone. The door looked immensely strong, and the plate which accepted its lock was clearly outside the chamber – an ugly thought. The window remained – the window I could not reach.

The afternoon sunshine showed me that the window faced south by east, and that meant that a man, leaning out, would find the terrace below him, perhaps some sixty feet down. Had the window faced north, a man, leaning out, would have found the roof below him – the steep-pitched roof of Jezreel. And the roof would be twenty feet down – perhaps twenty-five. And then there were dormer windows... But the window did not face north.

I asked myself what I should do if the tower was afire...

Then and there I decided that, once I had burst my bonds, I should let myself down by my sheets and do my best to swing myself on to the roof. I doubted that this would receive me, because the pitch was so steep: but, if it did, I should try to reach one of the dormers and so climb into a room.

And there I let my exercise go, for the thought of such a venture made the palms of my hands grow wet. For all that, I knew in my heart that Jack Sheppard would have escaped – and have gone that way.

It was not until seven o'clock that once more the shutter was drawn and Lafone looked into the cell. I supposed she had come with my dinner, but when the door was opened, it was Vanity Fair who appeared.

I shall always remember that moment – against my will.

She stood still as death in the doorway, while the door behind her was shut, and she made me think of some effigy, set in a niche in the wall. She was dressed, as always, in black and was holding one hand to her breast, while the other hung down by her side: since the oak behind her was dark and her little hood of black silk was hiding her hair, her face and her hands stood out in most sharp relief and might indeed have been waxen, they looked so pale. There was no denying her beauty, which, thus presented, seemed to have flouted age, and a smile that might have been Jenny's hung on her parted lips. But the light in her eyes was not Jenny's... I can only describe it as lazy – a lazy light. But a child could have read its meaning. The moment I saw it, I knew that the game was up.

'I knew I was right,' she said quietly. 'The very first moment I saw you, I knew I was right.'

I made no answer, but only got to my feet.

'Forgery, murder, abduction. If I chain you up, Mr Chandos, I don't think you can complain.'

'Have it your own way,' said I.

'I think that goes without saying,' said Vanity Fair.

There was a little silence.

Then –

'I've not come to ask questions,' she said: 'but I gave you some news this morning, and now I've come to give you some further news. It's not very good news, Mr Chandos – from your point of view: but somehow or other I don't think you'll find it dull.

'Marc left Jezreel in your car at a quarter to eight. His orders were to drive south, to berth the car near Carlos and leave her there. So he went by way of Gobbo – I think, though you've never been there, you know where that is. It was market-day in Gobbo, and Marc had to stop at the crossroads to let some cattle go by: and whilst he was sitting, waiting, *a gendarme touched his hat and gave him good day.*'

She paused, but I dared say nothing. I could not trust my voice.

'Now Marc is no fool: and so he improved the acquaintance so unexpectedly made. "Out of the eater," you know…

' "You don't know me," said the gendarme, "but I know you."

' "Who am I?" said Marc, for he thought he might as well know.

' "You're the cousin of Mr Chandos and you're driving his car."

' "Quite right," said Marc, "but how on earth did you know?"

'The gendarme told him, Mr Chandos…told Marc how he knew. And then – he – asked – after – *Miss* Chandos…the

180

beautiful, delicate girl…who was sitting by the road to Carlos at four o'clock in the morning on Tuesday last…'

Though I knew her consumed with fury, her voice was gentle and steady as never before: and because it was so unnatural, I found this self-possession most hard to bear. Some string within me was taut: and every sentence she uttered strained it a little tighter… I almost prayed for an explosion. Such tension clawed at the nerves.

'Well, Marc went on. And left the car by Carlos, as he had been told to do. But before he left her, he searched her – I told you the man was no fool. He found a document… Yes, I thought that that would surprise you. You left no document there. *But the garage did*, Mr Chandos. The *Garage Central* at Anise – a little village, I think, some seventy miles from Bordeaux…

'It was a bill for work done. If the bill is honest, they drained the oil from your engine and put in new. And they did it on Wednesday last…the day after you ran through Gobbo…you and your beautiful sister… And it gives your address, Mr Chandos. *The Black Lamb Hotel*, Anise…'

That I stood like a rock was natural. I was petrified with horror. The expression is literally true. Had the heaven itself fallen down, I could not have moved.

Vanity Fair nodded.

'You have my sympathy. It must be extremely galling to see your achievement demolished because some clerk was too lazy to cross the road. Never mind. I've nearly done now. And I've no more surprises to spring, for the action I've taken is the action which you would have taken if you had been in my place.

'Marc telephoned from Carlos. In view of his news, I told him to take your car and meet me at Maleton at four this afternoon. There he changed into clothes which I brought him, and at five o'clock he left in your car for Anise, bearing a note to your servant – *as a few days ago a note was borne to my servant…up in the hills.*

181

'The note was written by Acorn – with the postcard you sent me from Burgos, he couldn't go wrong. All the same he did it so well that I asked him to make me a copy. To tell you the truth, when he'd done so, I didn't know which to send. I mean, they were both perfect – and if you'll allow me to say so, much better than yours.'

She took the hand from her breast and I saw that it held a paper, folded again and again. She opened it carefully. Then she stepped forward and gave it into my hand.

I stared at my own handwriting.

Bell,

Bring Miss Jenny at once to Bayonne. Drop the bearer of this note at Bordeaux.

R C

Vanity Fair was speaking.

'In a sense it's a bow at a venture. But if Bell is at Anise, I think he'll do as you say. At least, he'll set out to do so – and, you know, it's the effort that counts.

'And now I must go. I'm afraid you'll have to dine early, for Lafone has a journey to take and she wants to be off. She – has – to – get – a – room – ready…ready by dawn, Mr Chandos…a room at a house in the hills…

'And so, good night. I will report progress tomorrow. If you try very hard I think you might break your chain. But I don't think you'll open that door. Of course, there's always the window. But if you lean out, I think you'll reject that way. And I shouldn't call for assistance. The last man who called for assistance suffered terribly before he died.'

She turned and left me standing: and almost at once Lafone came in with my meal. And then she left me, still standing: and I had the cell to myself.

9

I Take My Life in My Hands

The castle clock roused me by chiming a quarter to eight, and I found myself still standing and still regarding the doorway where Vanity Fair had stood.

I sat down on my pallet and put my head in my hands.

'She has to get a room ready…a room at a house in the hills.'

I could see that room – that hold. I could see the strength of its walls, its inaccessible window, the weight of its ponderous door. And the vision tore at my heart. The beautiful singing-bird had had a fine cage – of which we had opened the door, to let it go free: and now that it had tasted freedom, it was to be taken again and kept in a box. 'And the last state of that man was worse than the first.'

I can think of no office more dreadful than to condemn to misery someone to gladden whom you are ready to sell your soul: and I think in the next ten minutes I aged ten months.

At last I looked up, to see on the stone before me the paper which I had let fall.

Bring Miss Jenny at once to Bayonne. Drop the bearer of this note at Bordeaux.

The hag was damnably clever. Suspicious as Bell would be, he would see slight danger in taking his charge to Bayonne; while

183

the order to drop Marc at Bordeaux would make him dissociate Marc from the Château Jezreel. He had, of course, never seen him. When first I had stayed at the castle, Marc was not there.

The castle clock struck again.

Idly I regarded my watch.

Marc was not yet at Anise. He could hardly be there before ten. If they left at half-past ten, the Rolls could be at Carlos by four tomorrow morning, but not before. And now it was eight.

Instinctively I turned to the window.

The light was failing. Any moment dusk would come in. To attempt to escape by that way might well be hopeless: but it would be hopeless, unless I could determine by daylight the line I must take in the dark. If night were to fall before I had made my survey, the chance which might be there would pass out of my reach and would only return with the daylight – *at four tomorrow morning...when Marc was nearing Carlos*, with the singing-bird in his hand.

With trembling fingers I put my tray aside and turned to the instant business of breaking my chain.

Though the cuff lay close to my ankle, it was not tight, and by turning up the leg of my trousers I was able to lay a second thickness of flannel between the steel and my flesh. In other words, I turned up one leg of my trousers four inches instead of two, taking care to keep all the flannel within the cuff. I then took the slices of beef which lay on a dish on the tray and stuffed them into the 'turn-up', to make a still thicker cushion between the steel and my flesh. Then I sat down on my pallet and slowly turned head over heels.

By the time I had completed six somersaults, the chain, which could not turn with me, had shrunk to one half of its length: and when I had turned four more, its links were so locked together that it was almost rigid and less resembled a chain than a strangely distorted bar. I set out to turn my last somersault.

This I could not complete, for the chain was now too short to allow my leg to descend, and I lay on my back on the pallet with my right leg perhaps ten inches up in the air. Luck, of course, had been with me: by contracting so far, but no further, the chain had played into my hands.

I swung my right leg forward, well over my head. Then I brought it back like a flail, as hard as ever I could.

For an instant I thought that I had broken the bone, for I heard a snap, and a stab of pain, like a flame, ran up to my knee. Then I knew that the chain was broken, and when I got to my feet, my leg felt stiff and sore, but no more than that.

Swiftly I stepped to the window, pushed the casement open and put out my head...

The sill of the window was low, and I do not like heights. I recoiled instinctively. Then I took a firm grip of the stone-work and looked out again.

I was at least eighty feet up: directly below me the balustrade of the terrace was joining the wall of the tower: since the terrace was twenty feet wide, I was exactly that distance from the edge of the roof of the house: this edge was well below me – I made out, about forty feet: though this did not appear from within, the tower was octagonal, and my window was in the third face, if you count from the wall of the house: the sill of my window projected a short two inches beyond the face of the tower, and I saw no other projection of any kind.

I sat back on my heels and wiped the sweat from my face.

Vanity Fair was right, and I was wrong. I had thought the tower less high and my outlook more to the east. Sheets or trapese, only an ape could have leaped to the roof from my window. The bare thought of such a venture made me feel weak at the knees.

I lifted my head.

The shadows were falling now. I could see a long slice of the valley, but after a little its lovely detail was blurred. And the hanging forests beside it were losing their dainty colours and melting into a bulwark that served to make up a skyline, but nothing more. Very soon there would be nothing to see but the folds in the curtains of darkness made by the topless hills.

I remembered the night when out of my tribulation I stumbled upon the pathway which led to the *Cirque des Morts*: I saw Jean plodding before me and the rugged face of the country slowly shaping beneath the pencil of dawn: I saw the smile of the pleasance and the immemorial magic of sun and dew: and I saw a straight, girlish figure, standing ready to plunge, by the side of a pool...

With a groan of desperation, I put my head out of the casement, to measure once more a chance too slight to be measured, because it did not exist.

I shall never forget the masonry of that tower. Inch by inch I scanned it with hungry eyes – for anything that a desperate man could lay hold on, for anything that could raise a hope that was dead. And I scanned it in vain. It presented no handhold at all, within or out of my reach.

Frantically, I tried to look upward, craning my neck.

And then I saw the drip-course...

I drew in my head, turned on to my back and put out my head again.

I give it the name of drip-course, for that was what it appeared: but it may have been just decoration intended to please the eye. In fact it was a stone ledge, protruding at least two inches from the face of the tower. That it ran right round the tower, there could be no doubt. The tower was roofed with a conical cap of slates, and there were no eaves and no gutter that I could see: and the drip-course lay just midway between the first of the slates and my window-sill.

Carefully, I measured the distance – and found it near seven feet up.

I drew myself into my cell and sat up on the window-seat.

I had discovered a handhold which was within my reach. Once my hands were upon it, if I had the strength to hold on, I could shuffle my way round the tower until I hung over the junction of the tower with the roof of Jezreel. (I think I have said before that the tower rose out of the roof, as a chimney-stack which is built half within the house and half without.) The further I could shuffle, because of the pitch of the roof, the less would be the distance which I should have to fall and the safer would be my landing upon the slates. In a word, if Fortune were ready to help me from first to last, the drip-course offered a definite chance of escape.

If Fortune were ready to help me…

The protasis was vital. I could not see the top of the ledge, and a drip-course is sometimes loaded – with a slant of mortar, sloping away from the wall. In that case there was no handhold… Then again, I am no feather-weight, and unless I could make good progress, I could not hold on until I was over the roof. And when I let myself go, even though I fell on the saddle between the tower and the roof, a twenty-feet fall is no joke for a heavy man.

I had found a possible way: but I liked that way so little that there and then I got up and examined the door. But that, of course, was hopeless. Jack Sheppard could never have forced it without his bar.

There was nothing for it but the drip-course. And since it was growing dark, and since the peril was such that the longer one stared upon it the fouler it seemed, I made my preparations to brave it at once.

Not to make any bones about it, my case was this. If I stayed where I was in my cell, the game was lost. Jenny, Virginia, Mansel – all three were doomed. And I should very soon die at the hands of Vanity Fair. If I could make good my escape, the four of us might be saved. If I sought to escape – and failed, we were no worse off than before. In a word, I had nothing to lose – not even my life.

But I must be fair to myself. I have not a head for heights. And had I been free and a beggar, I would not have essayed to reach the roof by that drip-course though my success was to make me a millionaire.

One thing I was spared, and that was any fear of being disturbed. When Lafone had brought my dinner, she had taken up the linen and put it within my reach – a gesture which made it clear that I was to make my own bed, and, as there was no lamp in the room, I had no doubt at all that I was to be left to myself until the next day. There was, of course, always the grill: but though Vanity Fair might think it worth while to make sure that her prisoner was safe, I did not think she would do so till just before she retired.

The chain, as luck would have it, had broken quite close to my cuff, so at least I was not to be plagued by a length of loose links: but before I did anything else, I plucked the beef out of my trousers and slid the cuff into its room.

Then I turned to the wash-stand. This something resembled a tripod and was made of enamelled iron. I stripped it of basin and slop-pail, carried the frame to the window and laid it across the recess. Then I took one of my sheets and fastened one end to the wash-stand, drawing the knots as tight as ever I could.

Except that I drank some water, I made no more preparation – because there was none I could make: it is, of course, the unhappy lot of a captive who means to break out, that however shocking the risks his escape will entail, his precautions must be so makeshift as scarce to deserve that name.

For the twentieth time I wiped the sweat from my hands: then I took my seat on the wash-stand, now on its side, and leaned back slowly on to the window-seat.

Holding fast to the sheet, I worked my way gradually forward until my head and shoulders were out in the air. And there I rested a moment, to measure once more my distance and judge as well as I could the movements I had to make.

The casement was three feet high, and my plan was this – to pass backwards out of the casement and then stand up on the sill: still holding the sheet with my left hand, I could then put up my right and take hold of the ledge: and when I had hold of the ledge, I could let the sheet go.

But for the fall of night, to this day I do not believe that I should have made the attempt: but the light was now so dim that the ledge itself was only just to be seen, and since, if I was to go, I must go at once, I sat up without more delay and, bending well forward, began to project myself backwards out of the tower.

(Here, perhaps, I should say that, since I knew where the ledge was, whether or not I could see it was really of no account: for all that, I am perfectly sure that, so foolish and weak is the flesh, nothing on earth would have got me out of that casement, when once it was dark.)

As I thrust myself out of the tower I gradually pulled myself up by means of the sheet, and a moment later I was standing on the sill of the window with all of my body outside and my face to the wall. Holding fast to the sheet with my left hand, I put up my right, but I was trembling so much that I had to bring it back to the sheet and to wait for a moment or two until my nerve had come back.

It goes without saying, of course, that I was streaming with sweat, and I now was beset with a fear that the slippery state of my hands would betray the most resolute grip. And that made me sweat the more... Indeed, my condition was piteous. But at last the attack died down, and again I put up my hand.

I did not look up, for my face was against the wall, but my fingers encountered the ledge and then crept up to its top... With an effort I got them upon it – another inch and it would have been out of my reach... Slowly I pushed them on till their tips were against the tower...and then I took hold.

I shall never forget that moment.

The ledge was not a drip-course. It was a little stone gutter, more or less choked with dirt which the rain of the night before had made into mud.

I have often thought since – and Mansel agrees with me – that had it not been a gutter, but only a ledge, my fingers must have slipped off it before I had reached the roof. Be that as it may, from the moment I found it a gutter, I knew no more fear. Indeed, to be honest, I could have shouted and sung – and laughed at the depths below me because they had lost their sting.

Such jubilation was natural. From the time that I saw the ledge, it had been a question of handhold and nothing else. Any fool can hold on to a gutter... But I had not dreamed of such luck. Who would ever expect a gutter six feet from the top of a wall?

I must have let go the sheet and put up my other hand, but those things I did without thinking, for the next thing that I remember was finding half a slate in the gutter and pitching it into the meadows out of my way.

I think that will show the confidence which I had found. It was out of reason, of course. I was doing a dangerous thing. But it saw me through my gauntlet: and I moved two feet at a time until I judged I was hanging above the saddle – that is to say, the centre of the junction of the tower with the roof of Jezreel.

It was by now so dark that, except for outlines, I could see nothing at all. I could see the shape of the tower where it stood up against the sky, and turning my head, I could see the line of the ridge-pole that held up the roof of Jezreel. But I could not see what was below me. I judged that the saddle was roughly twenty feet down: I assumed that some sort of gully would lie between the tower and the roof: but judgment and assumption alike were really no more than guesswork, and indeed, for all I knew, I was not hanging above the saddle at all.

I moved a few inches further and tried to think what to do.

That the worst of the danger was over was perfectly clear. More. From being as good as hopeless, my position had become very strong; for if I could complete my escape, I should have the game in my hand. *But I had to land on that roof.*

I purposely use the word 'land'. It was no good my meeting that roof to find I was not on the saddle but on the south or west slope – to roll and slide down its pitch and then fall some forty feet to the terrace or meadows below: it was no good my meeting that roof to find myself on the saddle with a broken leg bent beneath me, or something worse: I had to make a good landing: if I was not to make a good landing, for all the good I had done I might as well have stayed in my cell.

Now as I came round the tower, I had passed a window exactly like that of my cell. I had not seen it, of course, but my knees had brushed against it as I went by. And now it came to my mind that, if I went on, I might come to another window. This might be beyond the saddle; but, if it was not too far round, I might be able to use it to help myself down. I confess that how I should use it was not at all clear: I could kick in the glass and rest my feet on the sill: but, without my sheet to take hold of, I did not see how I could let the gutter go. Still, anything was better than hanging thus in mid-air. Besides – it was no good pretending – *my fingers were growing tired.*

I had moved, I suppose, some three feet, when my knees struck against some obstruction, projecting out of the tower. At once I put down a hand, to see what it was. I found a vertical bar.

In that instant I knew the truth.

I had come to another window: and, because it gave to the roof, that window was barred.

With a leaping heart, I left my faithful gutter and took to the bars...

I had now gained some seven feet, but strain my eyes as I would, I could not see what was below me or where I was. This fact, however, worried me very much less, for the window would not have been barred, if the roof below had not offered a chance of escape. All the same, having got so far, I simply was not prepared to take any leap in the dark. With success, so to speak, at my feet, the idea of failure seemed monstrous as never before: and after searching in vain for any sort of excrescence which would let me still further down, I decided to take off my belt and do what I could with that.

It was whilst I was unbuckling my belt that I first became aware that my arms could not much longer support my weight.

The mind so rules the body that, though for at least five minutes I had imposed on my muscles a heavy continuous strain, my relief at finding the gutter, and then the bars, had each time suppressed the protests which they would have normally made. But now they spoke out, themselves demanding relief – which I could not give. Before I had freed my belt, I had to put back my left hand, because my right could no longer hold me alone: and when, after resting a moment, I tried again to drag the belt from its loops, I found that I could not do it, because I had no hand to spare.

In vain I repented my haste in leaving the gutter. If I had not been so quick to take to the bars, by placing my toes on the window-sill I could have rested my arms: but now, though I sought to climb up with some frantic idea of getting one foot on the sill, I had not the strength to do it, and the frenzied effort I made only served to hurry the sands which were fast running out.

I pulled myself together.

To kick and struggle was futile. In another thirty seconds I should simply have to let go. Better to drop quietly and so be ready to make the best of – of whatever lay below me…down in the dark.

For the last time I peered down over my shoulder…

Then –

'Well done, indeed, William,' said Mansel. 'I was coming to look for you. Hold on a second or two. There's a slater's ladder just here.'

'You'll have to be quick,' I said somehow. 'I – I'm damned near through.'

Mansel made no answer, but after what seemed an age I heard and saw a movement beneath me and heard the clack of a ladder against the wall of the tower.

In vain I sought it, feebly waving my feet.

'My God, where is it?' I cried. 'If I can't find it, I'll simply have to let go.'

'Don't do that,' said Mansel. 'Keep your hold somehow. I'll take your weight.'

Then he set my feet on his shoulders and held me up.

Nearly five minutes went by before I was enough rested to take off my belt and make it fast to a bar. Thereafter all was plain sailing, for the length of the belt brought my feet to the second rung. Supported by Mansel's hand, I let the belt go, and a moment later my hands had hold of the ladder, and I was out of the wood.

As I went down to the roof, I counted the rungs, which were roughly twelve inches apart. I found that there were sixteen. Had Mansel not come when he did, and I fallen down, the probability is that I should have stayed on the roof. What is perfectly certain is that I should have broken my back.

Though I wanted to tell him my news, Mansel would not listen, but led me as fast as he could the way he had come.

With the help of the ladder, we gained a slater's hatchway high up in the steep-pitched roof. From the attic to which this led us, we passed to a landing which served the third floor of Jezreel. And there Mansel pulled open a door, which one of six lacquered panels kept to itself.

Once in the system, we made as fast as we could for a winding stair, and two minutes later we were in Mansel's quarters and I was taking my ease upon Mansel's bed.

'And now,' said Mansel...

I told what I had to tell from beginning to end.

When I had done –

'William,' said Mansel, 'you have a remarkable gift. It's almost a conjuring trick. You can make an irreparable blunder – and then repair it. For what you've done tonight, you deserve to be canonised: but for coming back here as you did, you deserve to be shot.

'I meant you to come back all right – but not as a guest. You were to come back in secret, unknown to Vanity Fair. When I saw you drive into that yard, I damned near died. It was no good my taking you up, for the damage was done: but I knew that you would be for it, if I couldn't get in first. And I couldn't get in first – for I couldn't get through the guard-room: there was always somebody there.

'Well, she sent me off this morning to meet a train – and pick up some parcel or other which never arrived. And when I got back, to hear that Mr Chandos had left, I knew at once that the dirty work had begun. From the very first I didn't believe you'd gone: and when I couldn't find Marc, I knew that he'd laid you out and taken your place. That was the chink in her armour – the disappearance of Marc. But it wasn't at all apparent: and, to tell you the truth, I think she did very well.

'Well, I could do nothing till night: but, somehow or other, I meant to do something then. It seemed unpleasantly likely that I should have to throw off my mask... And then she played into my hands – by sending me off to Poly at six o'clock.

'It was perfectly clear that she wanted me out of the way, for Poly's two hundred miles off. I was to stay the night there, leave a note in the morning, and then come back. She doesn't suspect me, you know: but she knows that John Wright wouldn't stand for some of the things she does.

'Well, I left for Poly at six, had a word with Carson, left the car in a thicket and came straight back. I was sure you were up in that tower. But from what I saw this evening, I'm perfectly certain I couldn't have got you out.

'And there we are. As you say, the game's in our hands, and our job is as good as done: and that's all thanks to the only blunder you've made.' He laughed lightly. 'Fate's a contrary lady – you can't get away from that... And now to business. Thank God, we've plenty of time.'

'We've none to spare,' said I. 'It's thirteen miles to the pleasance, and – '

'Carson's standing by with the Rolls. I've only to show a light, and he'll be below the village before I can get there myself. All the same, I'd rather like to get you clear of Jezreel.'

'To be honest,' said I, 'I wouldn't mind it myself.'

Mansel laughed.

'I'm damned if I blame you, William. She – she's not a nice woman, is she? I can see the look in her eyes, when she knew that she'd got you down... And now, as I said, to business. Two maidens have to be rescued. One is the real Virginia, the other the false. To save the first shouldn't be hard: we know where she is – or will be before very long. And I think you'd better do that.'

'I think that's your job,' said I, with a hammering heart.

'I don't agree,' said Mansel. 'And in any event, you can't very well go wandering round Jezreel. Virginia the Second is somewhere within these walls: but where I don't know. I haven't seen her all day, and I'll lay a monkey she isn't within her room. In a word, she's under restraint. Now that she knows of that system, Vanity Fair will keep her under her hand.'

'Good God,' said I. 'And then, well, she can't shut her up. I mean – '

'She's not going to,' said Mansel. 'Unless I'm much mistaken, she's going to marry her off.'

'To Gaston?'

'Of course. From Below's agitation, I'm certain that he has been warned. He knows the truth, of course, and he shrinks from dipping his spoon in such witches' broth. Poor old Below. He was a gentleman once – before he met Vanity Fair.'

'But why is she doing this?'

Mansel fingered his chin.

'D'you remember our first day at Anise – how we sat by the stream in the evening, and I told you of Vanity Fair?'

'Yes,' said I.

'Well, I told you then that when she fixed the date of her daughter's marriage, it would mean she had fixed the date of her daughter's death.'

'You don't mean – '

'I mean this,' said Mansel. 'Vanity Fair is going to take no more risks. She told you Lafone was going to get a room ready. She spoke – euphemistically. *Lafone has gone to the pleasance to dig a grave.*'

I was so much shocked by his words, that, without thinking what I did, I got to my feet and made my way to the door.

'Summon Carson,' I heard myself say. 'I want to be gone.'

Mansel smiled. Then he set a hand on my shoulder and took out a flask.

'When I say there's plenty of time, I mean what I say. Marc is not yet at Anise. Yes, I thought of the telephone, but the exchange at Anise closes at eight o'clock. And so – we've plenty of time. And now have a drink and sit down.'

I did as he said, while Mansel paced the chamber and now and again stood looking into the night.

At length –

'Tell me one thing,' said I. 'You say she's going to…kill her. Why didn't she do it before?'

'I've no idea,' said Mansel. 'And I doubt if anyone has, except Vanity Fair. But one thing is clear – that she dared not part with Virginia, while Jenny was yet alive. And the reason for that is clear. She doesn't trust Virginia – she knows that she's got a good heart. *Vanity Fair was afraid that once Virginia was married and clear of Jezreel she would do what she did last night and give her away.* But with Jenny dead and gone, Virginia can go to the devil and say what she likes. But *prove* what she says, she cannot. And nor can anyone else.'

'Yes, I see that,' said I slowly. 'I suppose she raked up Gaston simply to stop her from marrying anyone else.'

'Exactly,' said Mansel. 'Virginia's celibacy was dangerous. She might have run off and got married to someone whose record was clean.' He threw back his head and expired. 'I'll be glad to be done with this show. I never handled such filth. But it all fits in.'

There was a little silence.

Then –

'Look here,' said I. 'I'd rather you went to Carlos and left me here. I'll find Virginia somehow. But Jenny's show mustn't be bungled.'

'Neither must be bungled,' said Mansel.

'I know,' said I. 'But – well, you're safer than I am, and Jenny must have the best.'

'Why?' said Mansel. 'I think we owe Virginia as much as we can repay.'

'That's very true,' said I, staring, 'but – damn it, if you had to choose, you know you'd put Jenny first.'

'Yes,' said Mansel, 'I frankly admit that I should.'

'Then you go,' said I. 'I – I want to see Virginia. I want to show her I'm not the swine she believes.'

'Don't you want to see Jenny?' said Mansel.

'Look here,' said I, somehow. 'I'd rather you took Jenny on. It's a – a responsibility that – that I'd really rather not take. I've taken it once, you know. And – I don't know if Carson told you, but I devilish near slipped up.'

Mansel raised his eyebrows.

'Are you sure you mean what you say? I mean, five minutes ago you made for that door.'

I put a hand to my head.

'I know I did,' I said slowly. 'I've not got your self-control. When you said what you did, my impulse was to start in. I felt we couldn't get there too soon...to prevent – to make sure of preventing so dreadful a thing.' I raised my head and looked him full in the eyes. 'But you know it's your job, Mansel.'

'To be perfectly honest,' said Mansel, 'I don't agree. But I said that five minutes ago. You have broken prison: as yet, I'm not even suspected, and so I can pass in Jezreel.'

This was so patently true that I threw in my hand.

'All right,' I said. 'I'll do it. I take it you'll give me Carson? Now how shall I go to work?'

'Half-a-minute,' said Mansel. 'I've got a question to ask. Don't answer, if you don't want to. It's nothing to do with me.'

'Go on,' said I. 'What is it?'

'Are you in love with Jenny?'

'Good God, no,' I blurted. But the blood came into my face. Mansel frowned.

'I'm sorry for that,' he said quietly. 'I hoped you were.'

Twenty minutes later he saw me clear of Jezreel.

'Give her my love,' he said gently. 'And that's no figure of speech. She is the most perfect darling I ever saw. And I shall always love her... But I'm not in love with her, William, nor she with me. If I were twenty years younger... But her mind is too young for my mind, her soul too young for my soul. "Men do not put new wine into old bottles, else the bottles break and the wine runneth out." I'm mad to see her, of course. And I hope and believe that she'll throw her arms round my neck. But then I've a weakness for children...that show a weakness for me.'

Still feeling rather dazed, I touched his arm.

'I don't like leaving you,' I said.

'Don't be greedy,' said Mansel. 'You've played a glorious innings: don't grudge me the winning hit.'

'A glorious innings.'

I turned and looked back at the castle – at the dim silhouette of its roof and the sable thrust of its tower.

'You came to find me,' I said. 'And saved my life – and the game.'

Mansel clapped me upon the shoulder.

'See you tomorrow, William. And don't forget what I said. Give Marc a hell of a pasting, but don't do him in.'

Ten minutes later I took my seat beside Carson and told him to drive to the thicket where Mansel had hidden his car.

10

Meadow-Sweet

Mansel would have made a fine general in olden days, if for no other reason because, if he knew the facts, he could predict the action which his opponent would take. Of this talent he always made light. 'It's simple enough,' he would say. 'All you've got to do is to try and put yourself in the other man's place.' Which, of course, sounds easy enough. But, viewed from opposite standpoints, facts do not look the same: and the one, which, seen from the north, seems insignificant, may hit you between the eyes, when seen from the south.

Be that as it may, Vanity Fair had shown me the cards she held. It was Mansel who told me the way she was going to play them – and how he knew she was going to play them that way.

And since I have reason to think he was perfectly right, before I relate what happened that summer morning, I will set down Mansel's prediction, because, of course, it dictated the moves I made.

'Why was John Wright sent to Poly? That he might be out of the way. Why did Vanity Fair want him out of the way? Because no one but Wright ever drives her when she goes out: if, therefore, she did go out with another man, Wright, the detective, would know that she was visiting something which she did not wish Wright to see. What was it, then, that she did not wish Wright to see? Not the bridle-path to the pleasance, because he's driven her there – it's the other side of Carlos and it brings you into the circus quite close to the fall. *She did not wish Wright to see Mr Chandos' car.*

'Very well. Vanity Fair's going out and she's going to meet Marc. Where is she going to meet him?

'Jenny is going to die, and Vanity Fair herself is going to put her to death. But no one knows that but Lafone – and no one must ever know. Of course not Marc. So Jenny must be in good health when Marc puts her out of the car. Now transporting a corpse is no joke. It's very, very hard labour – you know the phrase "dead weight". Then again the day will be breaking and waking a curious world. So Jenny will travel alive to the nearest point to the pleasance to which the car can be got. And there her mother will meet her – at the mouth of the bridle-path.

'It's a mile and a half beyond Carlos – there's only one road. The path's overgrown, and the villagers never use it, for it only runs to the circus and they're all of them frightened stiff of the *Cirque des Morts*.

'A car has gone from the garage: no doubt it has taken Lafone to the bridle-path. From there she will walk to the pleasance, dig a grave close to the cleft and then come back to the road to meet Vanity Fair. She might bring a mule with her.

'I've little doubt that Jenny's to die by poison. Her mother will give her an injection. As like as not, she will use the very syringe we found upon Jean.

'Don't forget that Bell will be there – almost certainly drugged. You'll be saving his life as well. Marc would have done his business – left him inside the car, set the engine running, put her in gear and turned her over the edge.'

That, then, was Mansel's prediction. But when I had asked him how I should go to work, 'As you think proper,' he said. 'I leave it to you.'

With the enemy's plan before me, and plenty of time to spare, I could, indeed, hardly go wrong, and before we had reached the thicket, my plans were laid.

Driving from Carlos to Gobbo, at a point three miles from Carlos you turn to the left. If you do not turn there, but drive on, you will only have to come back, for the road has never been finished, and after a mile and a half it comes to an end.

But a road such as that has its uses. This one made me a siding that summer night.

Almost exactly at midnight I berthed the French car there: then I walked back to the Rolls and Carson drove me up to the bridle-path.

There was no one there, of course. The car which had brought Lafone had gone back for Vanity Fair. It seemed unlikely that she would arrive before three, for Marc could not possibly get there before four o'clock.

I sent Carson back to the siding and walked to the *Cirque des Morts*.

The going was very easy, and twenty minutes later I passed through the dripping vapour that hid the mouth of the cleft.

As I left the bushes which masked its opposite end, I saw a light in the meadows, not very far from the pool which Jenny had used. I made sure that the light was not moving. Then I went slowly towards it, using the greatest care...

Since I am determined to relate without passion the things which I saw and the part which I played that night, I will only say that if Hell is hung with pictures, the scene which I was to witness should have a place on its walls.

The light was shed by a lantern, set on a pile of loose earth at the head of a grave. In the grave a man was working, and on the turf by his side was standing Lafone.

The woman's skirt was kilted, her sleeves were rolled, and her hands and arms and feet were all caked with dirt. She was leaning upon a pickaxe, grimly surveying the work she had helped to do. Uncleanness became her. I found it hard to believe that she had been born of woman and once was a baby child.

The man was using a shovel, and the two must have laboured hard, for when he stood up he was elbow deep in the ground. I had never seen him before, but he looked very dull, and I had no doubt that he belonged to the pleasance and so to Lafone's command.

As I watched, he stopped, to wring the sweat from his brow. 'It is deep,' he said slowly. 'Too deep for a lazy man. You could put two of him here.'

'There would be a mound,' said Lafone.

The man shook his head.

'Never.' He sighed and spat. 'I always say a man should dig his own grave.'

Lafone was bowed with laughter.

With a hand to her side, she laughed till the tears hopped down her cheeks. So perhaps witches laugh. The sight and the sound of her mirth made my blood run cold.

The clown stared up at the woman. Never before, I dare swear, had he seen her smile. Then a grin spread over his features – an eloquent grin. He perceived that a saying of his had made his mistress laugh.

Then –

'Deeper, you fool,' crowed Lafone, and pointed into the grave.

With a gesture of resignation, the fellow put up his shovel, took up a second pickaxe and fell to work.

'Deeper there,' said Lafone and stepped to the head of the grave.

The man stood up to face her.

'Deeper where?'

Lafone pointed down.

'There. Make a hole for his head.'

As he swung his pick, she swung hers...

I shall never forgive myself, but I was still wondering why she should swing her pick, when its head sank into the base of the other's skull.

So I saw bloody murder committed – to cover the crime to come. I confess that I fled from the pleasance – and moved with my chin on my shoulder for half a mile…

I crossed the *Cirque des Morts* and took the way to the road which Jenny and I had taken a week before.

At last I came to the spur which masked the bend of the road: and when I had climbed over this and down to the bank, I sat down with my back to a beech-tree, to take some rest.

And there I sat until Vanity Fair went by – at a quarter past two. I knew it was she, of course: but as she went by, I leaped down, to look at her number-plate. Sure enough, it was that of the car that had taken Lafone.

The eagles were gathering.

I walked down the road to the siding, two miles away.

As Carson rose out of the shadows –

'Bring up the Rolls,' I said. 'I've a job to do.'

'You saw her go by, sir?'

I nodded.

'We've plenty of time.'

Twenty minutes later we ran into sleeping Gobbo and stopped by the only house which was showing a light.

As I got out of the car –

'Turn her round,' said I. 'And if you should hear a car coming, sound your horn.'

'Very good, sir.'

As before, I walked into the office, to see the same grey-haired gendarme behind the desk…

'Will you rouse the sergeant?' I said. 'I've just seen a murder done.'

The sergeant came.

'Now look here,' said I. 'Statements and things can wait. The point is to catch the murderess – whilst you have time.'

The sergeant agreed, and his fellow took a cap from a peg.

'Less than two hours ago a woman murdered a man before my eyes. I will tell you where she did it, and drive you two-thirds of the way. The body lies where it fell – in an open grave. In an hour or two's time the woman will return to the spot, to fill the grave in. If you are there, in hiding, you will, of course, be able to…watch her at work. And later, if you require it, I'll make any statement you like.'

Two minutes later I ushered them into the Rolls.

As I took my seat by Carson –

'This by the way,' I said, 'is my cousin's car. If you'd like to look at her papers…'

But the sergeant waved them away.

'If you please, sir, describe this woman and tell us exactly how the murder was done.'

I did as he asked…

I set them down at the spot where I had rested, at the bend of the road: then I set them on their way to the circus and told them of the fall and the cleft and the pleasance beyond.

Whilst I was doing these things, Carson was turning the Rolls: and five minutes later he backed her into the siding and round a bend out of sight of the Carlos road.

It was now a quarter to four, and since Marc might be expected from four o'clock on, we took the French car from the siding and berthed her a furlong ahead by the side of the way. We chose a place where the road was very narrow, where two cars could barely have passed: *and we berthed her four feet from the edge*, as drivers who know no better will sometimes do. Unless and until she was moved, no car could go by.

I left her key in the switch, but I opened her bonnet and turned the petrol off, letting her engine run till it fainted for lack of fuel. Then I switched it off and left her – for Marc to find.

Ten or twelve paces away, towards the siding, a clump of bushes was clothing the mountain-side. We took our seats behind them, Carson and I, and there I gave him his orders and told him very briefly what was to come.

He was a splendid servant, and because he knew that I did not feel like talking, he never asked a question in all those hours: and I often think that my silence laid upon him a burden he should not have borne, for he had played his part in the drama and had played it uncommonly well.

So we sat behind the bushes, while the sun came up in splendour, to flush the heads of the mountains and kiss the face of the landscape we knew so well.

And then, at last, came Marc…at a quarter past five. His brakes went on, and he stopped directly below us. And I heard him let out a curse as he left the Rolls.

He left her engine running and stepped to the other car. And when he had glanced inside her, he cursed her driver again and flung open a door.

As he took his seat inside her, I opened a door of the Rolls…

As a hare in her form, Jenny was lying asleep in a nest of rugs. Only her face was showing, and her golden hair was all tumbled, and her lashes looked very long against the bloom of her cheeks. I put my face close to hers. Her breathing was steady and even: her breath was sweet. So I knew that her sleep was natural – and thanked my God.

I turned to see Carson slide into the seat Marc had left.

Marc, of course, was attempting to start the French car…

As Carson closed his door, I lifted Bell's head. He was sunk down beside the driver, and might have been dead. His breath reeked of chloroform.

'Carry on,' I said. 'Don't disturb Miss Jenny, but get him out in the air as quick as you can.'

I closed the door, and Carson took the Rolls backwards without a word.

I watched her steal round a bend. Then I stepped to the side of the road, leaned against a boulder and folded my arms…

Hoping, I suppose, against hope, Marc continued to use his self-starter – of course, in vain. But at last he knew it was hopeless and, using excusable language, he erupted into the road.

'Well, Marc,' said I, quietly.

As well he might, the fellow stared upon me, as though I were not of this world. Then he turned his head very slowly, to gaze at the place in the road where the Rolls had stood…

I thought he would never look round, but at last he turned again, to find me standing before him within arm's length.

'You filthy blackguard,' said I, and hit him between the eyes.

I must have hit harder than I thought, for though he was standing four feet from the side of the car, the back of his head hit a window and shattered the glass. To my content, however, he did not fall…

If the man was tired, so was I, and I thrashed him without compunction until he could not stand up. And then I held him up against the side of the car and 'very near knocked his head off', as Bell would have said. And when my arms were weary, I lugged him to the edge of the road and kicked him down the mountain with all my might.

Since he could no longer see, I suppose he thought I was launching him into space, for he let out a scream of terror that warmed my heart. Then he met the ground and pitched headlong… In spite of the frantic efforts which I would not have thought he could make, he rolled and slid and tumbled for a hundred and fifty feet, to fetch up against a boulder, to which he clung like a madman, as though to slide any further must cost him his life.

And that was as much as I saw.

I gave the French car petrol and backed her down to the siding without delay.

Bell was still unconscious, and Carson and I, between us, put him in Mansel's Rolls.

And Jenny, too, was sleeping, with a smile on her lovely lips.

A sudden impulse struck me, and I turned to the side of the road. Some little wild flowers were blowing between the grey of the rocks, and the dew was still painting their beauty and sweetening their faint perfume. Quickly I pulled nine or ten and bound them into a posy as well as I could. Then I laid it in Jenny's lap, and hoped that she would see it as soon as she waked.

As I closed the door upon her –

'Do all you can for her, Carson. But on no account leave the thicket until I come. Tell her I'm bringing some breakfast.'

'Very good, sir.' He put out his hand. 'This is Bell's, sir. I think you ought to be armed.'

'Very well.'

I took the pistol and slid it into my coat.

I entered Mansel's Rolls and took my seat at the wheel.

'Are you all right for petrol, Carson?'

'Yes, sir. The tank's half full.'

'Then you get off now. I want to see you go.'

When Carson, with Jenny behind him, had taken the road to Gobbo, I, with Bell behind me, drove up to the bridle-path.

Some moments before she saw me, I saw Vanity Fair.

The hag was consumed with impatience, for now it was six o'clock.

The car was very silent, and she neither saw nor heard it until it was very close. But, as I say, I saw her. And I saw how she twisted her hands, and savaged her underlip.

And then she looked round – and a hideous light of triumph leaped into her eyes, for though the car was Mansel's, it might have been mine.

So for a long moment…

And then the light faded, and the eyes rounded into a stare.

As I left the car, she stepped back, with a hand to her breast.

With my eyes upon hers –

'Good morning,' I said. I inhaled. 'What beautiful air. You know, I think it's purer than that of Jezreel.'

I could see that her lips were moving, but no sound came.

I leaned against the door of the car and folded my arms.

'Yesterday evening,' I said, 'you were good enough to give me some news. Now I have some to give you. I trust – but without much hope – that it will be as useful to you as yours was to me. *That Marc is not here is my fault. But for me he would have been here forty minutes ago.*'

Somehow she found her voice.

'Who let you out? Acorn?'

I laughed in her face.

'Lafone,' said I.

'*Lafone?*'

'Yes,' said I. 'She left a broom-stick behind, and I flew out of the window and over the Col de Fer.'

The jest seemed to do her good. The strength returned to her face, and the steel to her eyes.

'And my...pretty...spoons?'

'*Will not be melted this morning. The treasure you meant to bury...is not available.*'

By my words I might have unveiled the Gorgon's head. The woman seemed to turn into stone. I saw the flesh freeze upon her face: her eyes took on the sightless look of a statue's: and for more than a minute I swear that she never drew breath.

Then a tremor ran through her, and she shivered back into life.

'I liked you,' she said. 'And because I liked you, Chandos, I let you live.'

'Do you suggest,' said I, 'that I'm in your debt?'

'I never suggest. Because I liked you, I spared you.'

'Did you send Jean – to spare me?'

The woman moistened her lips.

'Because I liked you, I sent him to – warn you off.'

I raised my eyebrows.

'Was Julie another of your favourites?'

She started ever so slightly, and after a moment a hand went up to her mouth. Both hand and mouth were unsteady, and I knew that at last I had shaken her iron control.

At length –

'Are you a policeman?' she said.

I shook my head.

'Then who are you to judge me?'

'I do not judge you,' I said.

'If I break the law, that is the law's affair.'

I shrugged my shoulders.

'It amused me to make it mine.'

The contemptuous phrase stung her. I saw her eyes burn in her head.

'By what authority, Chandos?'

I looked her full in the face.

'By one you should recognise, madam. That of my will.'

There was a little silence.

Then –

'I hope Marc suffered,' she said, 'before he died.'

'When last I saw him,' I said, 'he was still alive.'

She frowned.

'And Jean?' she said. 'And Luis?'

'Have left your service,' I said.

She sighed. Then she lowered her hand and regarded its palm.

'You could have been my grandson, and yet you have brought me down. It's written here, of course – in the lines of my hand. But I would not have it so. I could not believe that Fate would mock me like that – and I twisted another meaning out of the lines. Do you believe in palmistry, Chandos?'

'No more than you do,' I said. 'If you did, you would be afraid to look at the palm of your hand.'

She looked up at that.

'Only a fool,' she said, 'would have spoken like that. And there lies your strength. You not only seem a fool, but you are a fool. That's why I couldn't believe that you were the Jack that was going to kill the giant.'

'For all that, you took certain precautions.'

'I didn't put you to death,' said Vanity Fair.

I had still one card to play: but I did not know how to play it, and so I turned to the car.

As I opened the door –

'Just now,' she said, 'I told you that the lines in my hand declared that a man less than half my age would bring me down. And I told you that I would not believe them – but that was less than the truth. I did not want to believe them: but their declaration made me uneasy, and so – *I had Gaston watched.*'

I looked at the woman sharply, but her eyes were fast on her palm.

'Why Gaston?'

'Because the lines insisted that the man who brought me to ruin would be my son-in-law.'

I shall always believe that she was speaking the truth. There is, I think, no doubt that prophecy is to be found in the lines of the hand: and though it does not follow that she was not making believe, yet *it was in fact to watch Gaston that Mansel had been engaged.*

I regarded her curiously.

True or false, Vanity Fair had some object in making such a statement to me. Yet she was not seeking information. If she had sought information, her eyes would have been upon mine.

'I can't understand it,' she murmured, knitting her brows...

And then an idea seemed to strike her – a happy idea.

In an instant she was transfigured, and all the gifts she had lost or cast or trampled came back for one fleeting moment to take up their shining roles.

Small wonder I stared upon her. Before my eyes she had put on incorruption – *an incorruption I knew.*

The eager lift of her head, the stars in her eyes, the light of her countenance, the way of her parted lips – there was Jenny, standing before me, with her charm welling out like a fountain – to overwhelm all my hate.

Her voice was sweet and breathless.

'Will you...let me look at your hand?... I know what's there – now... But I would just like to see it...before you go out of my life.'

I took my hand from the door and inspected its palm. I knew what was there – now, too. Somewhere there it was written that I was to marry the daughter of Vanity Fair.

The secret, in that strange cipher, had lain there for thirty years. It had lain in her hand far longer. Yet of all the hours of her life, this was the hour appointed for her to read it aright.

Revolving this last and most fantastic trick of Fortune, I almost forgot her request. But when I had thought for a moment, I made up my mind to grant it – because it was Jenny that had made it – not Vanity Fair.

I looked up suddenly.

'Madam,' I said – and stopped dead.

She seemed to be adjusting her sleeve.

In a blinding flash I saw the pit she had digged – and my foot on the edge. Once my hand was before her, a flick of her wrist and I should be dead within two minutes of time.

If her hope was black, the way she had sought to fulfil it was blacker still. She had called back the soul she had lost, to lure me into the shambles: she had called up the spirit of Jenny, to make me lay my head on the block.

White to the lips with fury, I played my last card.

'Your request is refused.'

I saw her stiffen. All her grace fell away. Treachery twisted her lips and the hungry spirit of Murder leaned out of her eyes.

I continued deliberately.

'I extracted a drop from that syringe on the night that you lent it to Jean. I had a wire from the analyst three days ago.' I looked her up and down. 'Just now you had the impertinence to call me a fool. Maybe I am, but those who live in glass houses shouldn't throw bricks. And I'd rather be a fool that can smile than a bloody-minded butcher that's short of a sheep.'

'Billingsgate!' spat Vanity Fair.

'Good enough for Smithfield,' said I, and entered the Rolls.

I went about and drove off.

That I had worn borrowed plumes I most frankly admit. What glory there was was Mansel's. But that I dared not tell her, in case he was still in the field.

Nearly four hours had gone by.

The heat of the day had come in, but the meadow at the back of the thicket was sweet and cool, for the trees, which were tall and thick-leaved, were laying an apron of shadow upon the grass. Now and again I could hear the low of a cow or the drone of a distant car, but the silence was mostly stippled by the pipe and the flutter of birds and the speech of the running water that hemmed the edge of the sward.

Bell, who had come to his senses, was sleeping a natural sleep by the side of the track which came to an end in the thicket some thirty yards off. Carson was ten miles off, sitting up in the mouth of a loft, with Mansel's Rolls beneath him and field-glasses up to his eyes. From where he sat he could watch his master's window – the window of Mansel's room in the Château Jezreel. And Jenny was sitting beside me, remembering Amaryllis and smiling upon a grasshopper who was plainly content with the landing which he had made on her knee.

It was but three days since I had seen her, and yet in that time she had aged. At least, so it seemed to me. When I had left Anise, she might have been seventeen. But today she seemed full-grown and twenty years old.

'I wish,' said Jenny, 'you'd say why you sent for me.'

'I'll tell you one day,' said I.

'Tell me now.'

I shook my head.

'One day, I promise, Jenny.'

My lady tilted her chin.

'I shan't come next time,' she said.

I smiled at her perfect profile – at a nostril no chisel could have rendered and half the bow of a mouth which Shakespeare alone could have sung.

She turned to see me smiling, and looked away.

'Jill doesn't treat me so. She tells me everything.'

'What does Jill tell you?' I said.

Jenny spread out her arms.

'Oh, heaps of things.' She shot me a sudden glance. 'I know I'm grown up, you know.'

'Twenty or twenty-one is not very old.'

'You're only thirty,' said Jenny. 'And Jill says a man of thirty is no more grown up than a girl is at twenty-one.'

'I wish it was true,' said I, and put a hand to my head.

'It *is* true, William.' She hesitated. 'Jill says I haven't missed much by being shut out of the world.'

'That's true all right,' said I. 'It's been the world's loss – but not yours.'

'What d'you mean – it's been the world's loss?'

I looked up to meet her wide eyes.

'You're very sweet and pretty,' said I. 'And all the world feels better when a sweet pretty maid goes by.'

Jenny's eyes fell, and her beautiful visage mantled and a hand went up to her heart.

'Why, Jenny's blushing,' said I.

'Don't tease me. You made me blush.'

'You've learned a lot,' said I, 'since I saw you last.'

'I told you I had. Jill's told me everything.'

I lay back and looked at the sky.

When all was said and done, now that she knew she was adult and that her dreams were no dreams, but worldly memories, Jenny's case was much the same as that of a man who has lain in jail for ten years. Only she had gone in as a child, to come out as a maid: and so she had to be taught that the way of Nature is not always the way of the world – a highly delicate instruction, which had already begun. Of this there could be no doubt, for when I had found her that morning, she had greeted me very shyly, and my lips had but brushed her fingers before she whipped them away.

'What are you thinking of, William?'

'I was thinking how glad I am that you know you're grown up. This time a week ago I was telling you fairy-tales.'

Jenny nodded thoughtfully.

'I'll always like fairy-tales, though. Jill loves them. She says her life is like one – and that my life's more like one than hers.'

'Sleeping Beauty,' said I, sitting up.

'I'm not like her,' said Jenny, 'but I did sort of go to sleep: and then – Jonathan came and woke me… I wish he'd come,' she added, and glanced at the coppice behind.

'So do I,' said I, frowning.

I found her words disquieting.

God knows I wished Mansel would come. God knows I wanted to see him safe and sound. But why did Jenny wish that Mansel would come? That he was in danger she had not the faintest idea. And yet – she wished he would come.

Jonathan came and woke me – like the prince in the fairy-tale…

I considered the revelation which Mansel had made to me some twelve hours ago.

I'm not in love with Jenny, nor she with me.

I was sure that the first half was true. Mansel never pretended. If he said he was not in love, then he was not in love. More. His manner was not the manner of a man who is standing aside. But what of the second half? How could he answer for Jenny? And almost all the evidence pointed the other way. When I said as much to Mansel, he only laughed and compared me to 'the idols of the heathen, the work of men's hands': by which, of course, he meant that I could not see. And though I had taken his word, as that of a wiser man, now Jenny

215

had made me uncertain whether I had not been right, and Mansel wrong.

I determined to try to find out…

'If you watch,' I said, 'he won't come. That's always the way. But if we don't watch, and talk about something else, all of a sudden we shall look up to see him beside us – you know how quietly he moves… What will you do when you see him?'

Jenny was nothing if not downright.

'Do?' she said. 'Why, I'll put my arms round his neck.'

Though the sunlight was just as brilliant, the world went grey.

'That's right,' I heard myself saying. And then, 'He's the best in the world.'

And with that, I got to my feet and began to walk over the meadow, towards the stream.

Now although I did not feel sleepy, I must have been very tired, for, while I had done a great deal, I had not closed my eyes since Lafone had brought me my tea on the day before. Then, again, I felt dazed and shaken and had no idea where I was going or what I was going to do. Because of these things, I suppose, I took no care, and before I had gone twenty paces I stumbled over a molehill and fell on my face.

No doubt because of my state, the fall seemed to buffet my wits, and I sat up very slowly, as a man who must take his time, before he gets to his feet.

'Are you all right?' said Jenny.

I turned to see her kneeling beside me – as once before.

I swallowed before replying.

'Yes, I'm all right,' I said slowly, and looked away. 'I don't know how I came to do such a silly thing.'

Jenny sat back on her heels and clasped her hands in her lap. 'With that bruise on your head and your hands all swollen and cut! You promised to sit still in the shade. You know you did. You said…you wanted nothing better – ten minutes ago.'

'I know,' I said. I put a hand to my head. 'What a damned-fool thing to do!'

'Then why did you do it?' said Jenny.

'Ask me another,' said I. 'I must have tripped.'

'I don't mean that. Why did you get up and leave me – without a word?'

'Oh, that?' I managed to laugh. 'I really don't know. I think I wanted a walk.'

I heard her draw in her breath.

Then –

'That isn't true,' she said quietly. 'I think I made you unhappy by something I said.'

In the knowledge that her eyes were upon me, I dared not look round. Instead, I regarded my palm – in which it was somewhere written that I should love, *but not marry*, the daughter of Vanity Fair.

'What nonsense, Jenny,' I said.

'It isn't nonsense,' said Jenny. 'I'm not a child now. You did what I would have done, if you'd suddenly said something that hurt me. I'd have felt I couldn't sit there. And so I'd have got up and gone.'

Instinct or understanding – God knows which it was. But either was equally embarrassing, as even an 'idol' could tell.

'Jenny,' I said, 'I'm all right. And that's the truth. But I've – got a good deal to think of. And – and I'd like to be alone for a little. I can't explain.'

With my words came the chink of steel...

As I spoke, I had drawn up my leg, to get to my feet: and, with my movement, the cuff, which I was still wearing, had slid down my leg.

Till now I had been very careful to keep this sinister emblem from Jenny's eyes: but my fall had jerked it out of the 'turn-up', into which it had now returned. But what remained of the chain had not so returned: and the six or seven inches of steel were trailing out of the 'turn-up' on to the grass.

I think we saw it together. But when I glanced at Jenny, I knew that the fat was burnt.

Jenny's eyes were starting. The breath was whistling in her nostrils, and the colour was out of her face. That she was acquainted with fetters was hideously clear.

She pointed a shaking finger.

'What's that?'

Before I could make any answer –

'You've been in prison,' she flamed. 'Someone's been chaining you up.' In a flash her arms were about me, and her face was pressed tight against mine. 'Oh, William darling, what devil treated you so?'

I should not, I think, have been human, if I had not held her close: but I did not misconstrue her outburst. Had Goliath come to her limping, he would have been used the same.

There was a moment's silence.

Then she started out of my arms, flung herself down on her face and burst into tears.

This was too much.

I lifted her up, took my seat beside her and held her against my heart. She suffered me gently enough, with her hands to her eyes.

'It's all right, my beauty,' I said. 'What if – '

'No, no. I shouldn't have done it.'

I stared at her golden head.

'Shouldn't have done what, Jenny?'

'Put my arms about you,' she sobbed.

Grimly I supposed she was right. The favour belonged to Mansel. Jill, no doubt, had explained that gestures could be misconstrued, that –

'And all the time I longed to,' she sobbed.

'*What?*'

'Your little posy – I saw it. It's here – all warm on my breast. And I did so long to – to put my arms round your neck.'

'You longed to?' I cried. '*You longed to?*'

She nodded her golden head.

I caught her hands and drew them down from her eyes.

A tearful child regarded me.

'Then why didn't you do it, my darling?' I said unsteadily.

'Jill said I mustn't do it...*till you put yours about mine.*'

I was desperately uneasy.

Flaming noon had driven us into the coppice, the cool of the day had drawn us down to the stream: and now at length it was sundown, but Mansel had never come.

I had visited Carson twice and had ventured into a village to purchase food. Bell was fit for light duty, but nothing more. Jenny bore with me like an angel, accepting my continual abstraction with a patience which was not of this world. And now the day was over, and the hopes to which I was clinging were going down with the sun.

My place was, of course, at Jezreel, but until it was dark, it was hopeless for me to take it. Had Blueskin lain in Newgate, Jack Sheppard would hardly have tried to enter the jail by day. That he would have tried at nightfall, I have no doubt.

Although I still hoped against hope, I had given Carson his orders at three o'clock.

'If you've still no sign by sundown, leave the loft and drive all out for the thicket, to pick me up.'

'Very good, sir,' said Carson, gravely.

He did not ask where we were bound for, because he knew.

I did not like leaving Jenny, but no one, so far as I knew, had discovered our lair and Bell was not fit for the duty which Marc had made him lay down. I proposed that she should stay in the Rolls, with one door locked and Bell on the opposite side...

So much I told her plainly, strolling up from the sparkling water, to the sanctuary of the trees.

'You'll be a good girl, my darling? I think they've got Jonathan down: and I must go and save him – as he saved me.'

Jenny's clasp on my arm tightened.

'That's right, of course. But I'd like to go with you, William.'

'I know, my sweet. But you couldn't do any good.'

'Oh, William, my very darling, you will come back?'

'Bringing Jonathan with me, my beauty. I give you my solemn word.'

A sudden fear brushed against her. She stopped in her tracks and caught the lapel of my coat.

'Supposing they take you again and chain you up!'

I covered her fingers with mine.

'They won't do that twice, my darling. And I was alone then: but now I'll have Carson with me, to watch my back. Before I'm through, I'll bet they're sorry I came.'

There was no mistaking my meaning, and Jenny caught my fire.

'That's right. I hope you kill them.'

I could only laugh.

'You're very bloodthirsty, Jenny.'

'They put a chain on your leg.'

There was a little silence.

Then –

'You know I want to marry you, Jenny. D'you know what marriage means?'

'Yes, yes. Jill's married to Piers. I want you to give me a baby, but no one else.'

Her eyes, it seemed, were open: but there was still one truth which she had to be told.

I put up a hand, to push the hair from her temples. Lifting her chin, she looked me full in the eyes.

'Listen, Jenny. Now there's only you: but there used to be somebody else. Since she was taken from me, I've never mentioned her name. But she was my wife.'

Jenny nodded gravely, and I lowered my gaze.

'I want you to know, my darling – it's only fair – that if she hadn't been taken, I – I couldn't have loved you, Jenny, because she had all my heart.'

'I wouldn't have expected you to.' Her hands came up to my shoulders. 'I'd have hated you, if you had. She was – Jill's told me about her. She saw her once.'

I could not trust my voice, but she took my face in her hands and raised it up. Her fingers were all outspread, and I could feel their pressure from temples to chin.

'I know what she was, William: and I know I can't take her place. Jill told me so. She said there was no one alive that could ever do that. But I'll pray to her, William. I'll pray to her every night – to teach me to make you happy...and I'm sure she'll hear me, my darling, and do as I ask.'

As I wondered then, so I shall always wonder what I had done to deserve a devotion so lively and so supreme. Be that as it may, her excellence left me dumb. But she seemed to fathom my silence, for she drew down my head and kissed me and then slid an arm round my neck.

Ten minutes later the jewel was fast in its case, with Bell, like any detective, sitting with his back to the door: and I was seated by Carson, listening to the brush of our tires and the steady whisper of the engine that was whipping us back to Jezreel.

11

Beyond the Veil

Inaction feeds upon the nerves, and, now that at last we were moving, I felt a new man. I had neither hopes nor fears, but a definite resolution first to reach Mansel's side and then to bring him and Virginia out of Jezreel. Counterfeit, masks and moves had served our turn: but now these things were done with, and the hold had got to be opened by force of arms. I would not declare our presence, for that, of course, would have been the way of a fool: but wait upon obstruction I would not, and the man who sought to withstand me could pay my price. I had not one shadow of doubt that Mansel was in the toils and, knowing those toils as I did, I was out for blood.

Here I should say that I had my own pistol again. Carson had found it that morning, and that in my car. Marc must have taken it with him, when he had set out for Anise: and perhaps because it had galled him, had taken it out of his pocket and thrust it into the pouch on the door by the driver's side. So Carson and I were both armed, and so was Bell.

We left the Rolls in the shadows, ten minutes' walk from the village that clung to the skirts of Jezreel. Then we climbed a path that led through the hanging meadows, over the rim of the valley and into the cobbled lane which stood for the village street. Because it served the castle, the way was pretty well lit, but the folk we met did not belong to Jezreel and what they made of our passage was nothing to us. Two minutes later the gateway was looming before us... It was easy enough to enter the kingdom of Vanity Fair.

The dusk was fast turning to darkness, as we made for the stable-yard. This was not lit, but someone was busy in the coach-house which lay beneath Mansel's room. A light was burning there, and the doors were wide.

It was an under-chauffeur – at work on one of the cars. Beside him, a standard lamp was glaring upon the engine to which he stooped, so that even if he had looked round, his eyes could not have seen us, because they were tuned to the light.

We stole through the coach-house and so up to Mansel's room.

This was empty. The bed had not been lain in, and such disorder as I had left on its surface had been arranged. We left the room to try the door of the passage which led to the guard-room: but this was locked.

In silence I led the way back to the stable-yard.

There was here another door which led to the house. I had never used it and did not know what was behind: but I knew that it would be open, if only for the sake of the workman whom we had seen; for none of the chauffeurs, but Mansel, had rooms on the stable-yard. A moment later we had passed it and stood in an empty passage, not too well lit.

The passage led to swing-doors, in each of which, chin-high, was a square of plate-glass: and since the hall beyond them was brilliantly lit, we were able to take its measure with no fear of being observed.

At once I saw that we were regarding the hub of the household wheel.

The hall before us was round and boasted no less than eight doorways, each shut by swing-doors like those behind which we stood. As I looked, one of these was opened, and a scullion crossed the pavement to enter another department of this remarkable sphere. So brilliant was the light in the hall that, try as I would, I could not see through the panes of the other swing-doors, but those that were opened by the scullion let out the clash of vessels and the clatter of tongues.

Since my object was to enter the system, I sought to make up my mind which of the doorways would lead to the quarters I knew, for though I was ripe for violence, I did not want to squander the element of surprise. And I was still wishing for a footman to give me a lead, when a maid came out of a doorway, letter in hand.

It was the good-looking girl on whom Gaston had sought to impose his sweet-smelling charms.

As she stopped to read her letter, I reached her side.

If she was taken aback, I forced her hand.

'Will you show me the way, please? I want to get to my room in "the corner suite".'

'Certainly, sir. This way.'

She led the way to a doorway, held a swing-door open and followed us into a lobby, less brightly lit. Here was a broad well-staircase, in the well of which was a lift. But the girl was for passing on to a pair of mahogany doors…

I touched her arm, and she stopped.

'I helped you once. Would you like to help me now?'

'Indeed I would, sir. Please tell me what I can do?'

'Where's Miss Virginia?'

She started at that, and the colour went out of her face.

Then –

'She's in her room, sir, I think. She was there half an hour ago.'

'Why d'you think she's still there?'

'Because – she's not very well, sir.'

'D'you mean she's in bed?'

'Oh, no, sir.'

'D'you think she's alone?'

'I don't know, sir. She was alone when I left her but – '

'Are you her maid?'

'For the moment, sir. Suzanne has gone to *Madame*.'

'Who d'you think may be with her?'

'*Monsieur le Comte*.'

'Good God,' said I. 'They're not married?'

'They were married this afternoon. They are to stay here for the present. And the door between has been opened, and he has the room next to hers.'

'And you are her maid,' said I. 'But how nice for you.'

She shrugged her shoulders helplessly.

'It really looks,' said I, 'as if I might help you again.' I glanced at the staircase. 'Can I get to my room that way?'

'Yes, sir. Would you like me to show you?'

I nodded.

'I want to get to the hall. Then I'll know where I am. It's important that no one should see me. Will you go first?'

At my words she started again, and her eyes grew wide. Then she glanced right and left and took to the stairs…

'You wait here, sir,' she whispered, 'while I go into the hall. If I do not return at once, it will mean there is somebody there.'

'All right,' said I. 'And now listen. The moment I'm out of the hall, go to Miss Virginia. Don't knock on her door. Just go straight into her room.'

She looked at me very hard.

'Very well, sir.'

The hall was empty and the girl as good as her word – with the happy result that, before two minutes were past, she and I were both in Virginia's bedroom and Carson was on guard in the system with his back to the panelled door.

Virginia was not very well, because Virginia was drugged. I never saw man or woman in such a pitiful state. Her mind was like a battery that has almost run down. It could work very slowly and feebly, but its output was next to nothing and could not command her will. There was no spirit in her: and her mind was an empty surface *on which she was the only person who could not write*.

She stared from me to the maid and then on the floor. But when I bade her rise, she did so without a word.

That Gaston had dared to go through a form of marriage with a creature so utterly helpless fanned to a flame the anger with which I was ruled, and had he come into his room, I believe I should have broken his neck. But, happily for us both, he did not come, and his chamber was still in darkness when the three of us entered the system and made for a winding stair.

I have shown that the private passage which ran from Mansel's quarters to the guard-room was shut by two doors which were locked. But both the locks were spring-locks, and could be opened by hand from the guard-room side. Once, therefore, we had gained the guard-room, we had a way out of the castle as secret as it was safe.

When we came to the narrow stair which led to the guard-room grate, I turned to the maid.

'From now Miss Virginia's your mistress. I will look after your future, so long as you stay with her.'

The girl glanced over her shoulder: but only Carson was there to hear her reply.

At length –

'It is understood, sir,' she whispered.

A moment later we stood in the guard-room itself.

As I let them into the passage –

'D'you know where you are, Carson?'

'I think so, sir. This leads to the Captain's room.'

'And the stable-yard,' said I. 'Take them down to the Rolls and come back – as quick as you can. I shall wait for you here by this door. When you get back, knock twice, and I'll let you in. The other door you must wedge.'

'Very good, sir.'

I turned to the maid.

'My servant is going to take you down to my car. You will get in and sit there until I come.'

'Very well, sir,' she said obediently.

I watched the three pass down the passage: then I shut the door behind them and set my back to the oak.

So far we had been very lucky. Nobody knew of my presence, and Virginia was out of the wood. But Mansel remained in the tower. I was sure he was there. More. I had an uneasy feeling that he was in the cell next to mine…where the chain was very much shorter and did not end in a cuff… The questions were first how to reach him and then how to set him free.

How many floors the tower had I do not know to this day. But, as I have said before, its ground floor was the guard-room and its first floor part of the suite belonging to Vanity Fair: but the stair which joined these two storeys was shut by a heavy door. When Carson returned, therefore, we must re-enter the system, climb the first winding stair and find some door which gave to the woman's apartments or else, on the second floor, to the tower alone. And that sounds easy enough… The trouble was that I was by no means sure that the system ran into the tower, while I had an unpleasant feeling that though it would show us a door which gave to the woman's suite, that door would be locked.

I afterwards learned that both these suspicions were just, and since, though I did not know it, there was no time to be lost, had we re-entered that system, it would have cost Mansel his life. And we *should* have re-entered that system if Carson had been back to time. But Virginia collapsed in the meadows, and his journey took five minutes longer than we had hoped.

It was now ten minutes to nine, and out of sheer impatience I opened the door to the passage and strained my ears. Carson would be back in five minutes – perhaps in less. With my eyes on the dial of my wrist-watch – the only thing I could see, for I had no torch – I stood there, like any schoolgirl, wringing my nerves for nothing and doubling every minute that whiled away.

It follows that when they were gone, but Carson had not returned, the fever which I had been courting possessed my soul.

I cursed myself for not sending the girls alone: I cursed myself for seeking Virginia first: I cursed myself for waiting for Carson: and I made up my mind that if he did not come before nine, I would wedge the door with my wrist-watch and enter the system alone.

Two haggard minutes limped by.

And then I heard someone stumble…on the farther side of the door which gave to the stairs.

In a flash I had shut my door and had whipped to the jamb of the fireplace and out of view.

The next moment the door was opened and the doorway was full of light.

Esther appeared – Esther, the personal maid of Vanity Fair.

She had a sheet on her arm: and in her hands was the end of another sheet. This seemed to be laid upon the steps, and there she seemed to wish it to stay, for she did not pull on her end, but only laid it down gently upon the flags. Then she shook out her second sheet, laid it end to end with the first and then stepped swiftly backwards, paying it out as she went. It was more than long enough to reach to the postern door – which gave to the meadows west of Jezreel.

And then and there I knew that Esther was laying a train.

The sheets were dry now, but, when she was ready to leave, she would come down those steps with petrol, soaking the sheets as she went. And then she would open the postern… And then she would strike a match… And then she, and whoever was with her, would vanish into the night.

I watched her go back up the stair. Shut the door behind her, she could not, for the sheet lying over the threshold was heavily bunched. And, as her footfalls faded, I heard Carson knock…

Of such are the ways of Fate.

If Virginia had not fallen by the way, then Carson would not have been late. If Carson had not been late, then we should have left the guard-room before Esther came down. And if I had not been there, to see Esther come down, Jonathan Mansel would have been burned alive.

With Carson behind me, I whipped up the steep, stone staircase and into a hall that I knew – the hall that served the apartments of Vanity Fair.

Now, though our goal was the room in which Mansel was lodged, we must first prevent the mischief which Esther was going to do. And if we were to do this, we had not a moment to spare. The suite was reeking of petrol, and the carpet laid in the hall was already wet.

A light was burning in 'the Star Chamber'. Pistol in hand, I thrust in. But the exquisite salon was empty: Esther was somewhere else.

As I swung about, someone exclaimed.

Then –

'Don't go yet, William,' said Mansel. 'I want your help.'

Mansel was in the sedan-chair.

For eleven hours he had sat there, because, though he entered himself, he could not get out.

The chair was especially lovely, and rich without and within. But it was a blind chair: that is to say it had no windows, but only a row of air-holes high up in each of its sides. Its roof was fixed, and the doors could not be opened, except from without. I do not know for whom it was built, but it must have been built for someone who went in fear of his life, for from top to bottom that chair was lined with steel. I cannot think what it weighed, and it must have required four chairmen, instead of two, but the fact remains its work was very well done and, once he was seated within and the doors were shut, only a very Samson could ever have broken out. Had he had room to move, the great strength which Mansel had might have set him free, but, as luck would have it, the chair was smaller than most, and so restricted all movement that he could not bring his strength into play.

Had we not arrived when we did, he was going to use his pistol upon the lock of the door. In fact, he had it drawn ready. But that was the counsel of despair, for his chance of so bursting the lock was certainly very much less than the chance of his being killed by a ricochet, to say nothing of the concussion which must have left him senseless for some considerable time.

I sometimes wonder whether there was not some trick by which the doors could be opened by someone within the chair – some trick which had baffled Mansel, for all his wit: but I am told that chairs that lacked handles inside were not at all uncommon, and I do not find it likely that Vanity Fair ever entered this chair herself. If it was used, it was probably used by a witness whose presence she wished to conceal, for, thanks to the rows of air-holes, anyone in the chair could see and hear what he pleased.

What Mansel had seen and heard, he shall presently tell for himself: at that moment he told me nothing.

As I helped him out of the chair –

'Virginia,' he said. 'She's – '

'Virginia's safe,' said I. 'She's down in the Rolls.'

'Well done,' said Mansel. 'That only leaves old Below.'

As he stepped to the door –

'But what about Esther?' said I. 'She's going to fire the place.'

'Let her,' said Mansel. 'Come on.'

In a flash we were out of the suite.

How Mansel moved so fast, I shall never know: after a day in that chair, I should, I am sure, have been crippled for half an hour: but he afterwards said that he had made it his business not to get stiff, in case, when once he got out, he should have to run. Be that as it may, he led us at break-neck speed – through the mahogany doors, down the stairs to the lobby and up by a tiny staircase into a low-pitched room.

And there he stopped dead, and a hand went up to his mouth.

'Too late,' he breathed: 'it's too late.' And then, 'It can't be helped.'

His words conveyed nothing to me: but that was because of my surroundings – because I could think of nothing but what I saw.

There was no light in the room, which, though it was nearly square, had only three walls. Where the fourth wall should have risen, there was stretched a very thin veil. And beyond the veil were the depths of the dining-room, that very lovely chamber which I have elsewhere described.

And Vanity Fair was at table...

We were, of course, in the musicians' gallery, which hung like a cave high up in the dining-room's wall: and the veil was the Gobelin tapestry with which the dining-room was hung. But while these things are easy enough to write, I despair of conveying the impressions I then received.

Of the four who were sitting at meat, not one had the faintest idea that they were being observed. We could not be seen, and, so very thick was the carpet which lay on the floor and the stairs, we could not be heard. Yet we could see all they did and hear all they said, as they sat in their stalls below us, some twenty feet down. We stood in the dark, while they sat in a blaze of light: and, perhaps because this remarkable picture was framed – for framed it was by the square of the gallery's mouth – I had the feeling that I was seeing some film and that soon the lights would go up and we should go home. I remember turning to Carson and asking him if he could see.

Vanity Fair was at table. Acorn sat on her right and Below on her left. Gaston, as always, faced her. The cloth had been drawn and the servants were out of the room.

One thing at once caught my eye.

A bottle was standing on the table in front of Vanity Fair.

This was out of all order. No bottle ever stood on the table until she had left the room.

Below was speaking. His glass was cupped in his hands.

'Madam,' he said, 'this is brandy. I have never drunk such a liquor for thirty-five years.'

'I'm afraid that's my fault. You've been with me thirty-three.'

'Not your fault, madam, only your whim. You have "kept the good wine until now".'

' "And when men have well drunk".'

'*Touché*,' cried the chaplain, and buried his nose.

His mistress advanced the bottle.

'Have another glass,' she said. 'You'll need it before I've done.'

Below helped himself.

'Do your worst, madam,' he hiccoughed. 'I am forearmed.'

Gaston tossed off his brandy and filled his glass.

'I have tasted worse,' he said.

'Where?' said Vanity Fair. 'On the *Pompadour*?'

Below was consumed with indignation.

'You poisonous bounder,' he belched. 'I was a judge of brandy before your father was jailed.'

Acorn was shaking with laughter: but Vanity Fair only smiled.

'The church militant,' she said. 'You'd better help yourself, Acorn, and see how you feel.'

'And you, madam?' said Acorn, bottle in hand.

'I have no need of courage,' said Vanity Fair.

The only coward present took the slight to himself.

'Do you say that I drink to find courage?'

'I think you'd be well advised to,' said Vanity Fair.

Gaston laughed.

'I am tired of Jezreel,' he said softly. 'I think I will go to Paris. You see, I am married now.'

'To five thousand a year?'

Gaston shrugged his shoulders.

'I have done my part,' he declared. 'I do not choose to rest in this house.'

'I see. And how will you live?'

'I do not think that you will allow me to starve.'

Vanity Fair laughed.

'Optimist,' she said lightly. And then, 'By the way, I ought to have told you, Chandos knows who you are.'

Gaston started violently.

'Chandos? That – that – '

'English gentleman,' said Vanity Fair.

Gaston writhed.

'What does he know?'

'One night in his presence you mentioned the *Pompadour*. And Chandos had friends on board. A Mr and Mrs Cheviot. You may recollect them – by sight.'

'It is not true,' mouthed Gaston.

'As you please,' said Vanity Fair. 'They knew your master quite well. He borrowed your clothes one night and took your place.'

Gaston's face was working.

'What can they prove?'

'Nothing,' said Vanity Fair. 'All his relations are dead, so you're perfectly safe. Chandos merely confirmed the report of his eyes and ears. That you look like a waiter is nothing: so, it seems, did de Rachel himself. But your ways are the ways of a waiter and will never be anything else. You have a waiter's instincts, a waiter's tastes – and if you must know, why, I think that your master cursed you before he died, for the leprosy of Gehazi creeps in your hang-dog eyes.'

This shocking denunciation sobered even Below, for he seemed to forget his brandy and wagged his head and raised his eyes to heaven, as though he were a Judge's Chaplain, accorded a seat on some Bench. For Gaston himself, from being most red, the fellow went white as ashes, and when Acorn passed him the brandy, he emptied his glass and refilled it without a word.

The spirit revived him forthwith.

As he set down the bottle –

'After all, who is Chandos?' he said. Vanity Fair raised her eyebrows.

'If you want to know,' she said, 'I should keep an eye on *The Times*. I think he's going to marry Virginia Brooch.'

For one moment there was dead silence. Then something like uproar arose.

Both Below and Gaston were talking violently, at first demanding information and then each rending the other and bidding him hold his peace. Acorn stared straight before him, with a shadow of a smile on his lips.

'Madam,' boomed Below, 'this is serious – '

'Serious?' screamed Gaston. 'Whom have I married today?'

'I believe her name to be Schmidt,' said Vanity Fair. 'Mabel Schmidt of Utah, a – '

A yelp of rage from Gaston smothered what else she said.

'But, Madam – '

'Silence, drunkard,' howled Gaston. Before the other could counter, he had turned upon Vanity Fair. 'Is this your sense of humour? Or how should you know?'

'He admitted as much this morning.'

'*Before I was married?* Knowing this, you let me marry – '

'If you ask me,' said Vanity Fair, 'I think you've made a very good match.'

'Madam,' insisted Below, 'I am involved in these matters.'

'Up to the neck,' said his mistress. 'If you remember – '

'You have paid my poverty, madam, but not my will. Be that as it may, I am most deeply involved: and I have a right to be told what I may expect.'

A changed Below had spoken: his dignity was compelling: his voice rang out clean and strong. His mistress started and stared – and for once a prelate stared back.

So for a long moment, while Gaston and Acorn watched. Then Vanity Fair bowed, and her chaplain bowed in return. Deep had called unto deep – and had been answered.

Vanity Fair was speaking.

'Chandos came here to find out as much as he could. I suspected him from the first, but I held my hand. With the unhappy result that he did find out – quite a lot. How much, I am not quite certain: but from what he said this morning, he seemed very well informed. After three days he left here, and six nights later he carried my daughter off. That would have been enough for most men, but Chandos saw fit to come back – no doubt, to find out still more. But I was ready then, and I got him down. In a word, I'd pulled everything round. And then, while my back was turned, his colleague stepped out of the shadows and helped him up.'

'His colleague,' said Acorn, staring.

'His colleague,' said Vanity Fair. 'I didn't know he had one, till noon today – *when John Wright never turned up*.'

Acorn was half out of his seat.

'Wright?' he cried. 'Wright?'

Vanity Fair nodded.

'Explains such a lot, doesn't it? Jean's failure...the forged letter sent to Lafone...Chandos' escape. But those are details. *Wright's was the brain that conceived and directed matters from first to last*. What beat me all ends up was how such a fool as Chandos could do what he did.'

'Well, I'm damned,' said Acorn.

He filled his glass with brandy, and tossed it off.

'If you please,' said Below, and stretched out a trembling hand. The bottle passed.

Gaston said and did nothing. The man seemed sunk in despair.

There was a little silence.

Then Below cleared his throat.

'Madam,' he said, 'you have said that you cannot be sure; but how much do you think that they know?'

'More than enough. Lafone was arrested for murder – this morning at seven o'clock.'

That this was no news to Acorn was very plain, for the man sat perfectly still with his eyes on the board: but the others made no secret of their distress. Below was breathing most hard and beating his breast, while Gaston rocked in his stall, with his head in his hands.

'God shut her mouth,' he kept wailing. 'God shut her mouth.'

Vanity Fair regarded him.

'What God,' she said, 'are you delighting to honour?'

Gaston made no reply.

'If it's the God of your fathers, then Father Below would be the appropriate channel for such an appeal. I say "would be". Perhaps I should say "would have been". I am honestly happy to inform you that your request has already been treated as it deserves…

'Lafone was being taken to Gobbo – some weary miles. On the way, by the merest chance, she and her zealous escort overtook Marc. Now Marc was there because Marc had failed in his duty. Lafone knew this – and the sight of him sent her mad. There and then she let him have it – *in front of the police.*' She shrugged her shoulders. 'I don't know what she said, but of course they arrested Marc.'

'My God,' said Below.

'And Marc,' said Vanity Fair, 'has opened his mouth.' The priest let out a whoop of dismay: tremulous fingers to lip, he gazed at his dispassionate mistress with starting eyes.

'How much does he know?' he quavered.

'Quite enough to set the police thinking,' said Vanity Fair.

Gaston burst into tears.

'It is not fair,' he blubbered, and banged his head on the board. 'What wrong 'ave I done? Because I 'ave try to 'elp you,

because I 'ave kept your secrets which I 'ave not want to be
told...'

In a ghastly welter of sobbing the rest of the sentence was
lost.

The others regarded the creature with what, I suppose, was
surprise.

Then, as though ashamed of their manhood, the men
averted their gaze. But Vanity Fair looked on.

Her voice cut through the lament with the crack of a whip.

'Is this repentance?' she said.

Buoyed by God knows what hope, Gaston lifted a shocking
visage and swore at some length that it was.

'Then,' said Vanity Fair, 'there is joy in heaven. I imagine that
the joy is restrained, but joy there is. Let that be your
consolation. You're some way from heaven, of course, and soon
you'll be further still: but – '

'No, no,' screamed Gaston.

Vanity Fair sighed. Then –

'Pass him the brandy,' she said. 'I'm not through yet.'

Before this sinister statement, Gaston appeared to collapse.
At least, for two or three minutes he made no sound but sat in
his stall like a dummy, with his arms hanging down by his sides
and his chin on his chest.

Vanity Fair picked up the thread of her tale.

'Well, the police telephoned from Gobbo about eleven
o'clock, and I sent Acorn over to see how the wind was setting
and do what he could. Somehow he managed to bluff them – to
hold them off. I don't know how he did it: I don't think he
knows himself. But they won't be here till tomorrow, and he
said I was away from Jezreel...

'Now Acorn did his best, but, of course, it's a great mistake
to lie to the police. I mean, tell an obvious lie. Because, when
they find it out, your credit is gone. Acorn should never have
said that I was away from Jezreel: for now, the moment they see
me, the police will know that he lied. And that would be fatal. I

have therefore, no choice but to bear his statement out... And so, by the time the police come, I shall be "away from Jezreel".'

Even Gaston looked up at that, and for twenty seconds or more the three men stared at the woman, with open mouths.

Then –

'And what about us?' said Acorn.

'Exactly,' said Vanity Fair. 'What about you? That was what worried me. I gave it much anxious thought. And in the end I decided that in your own interests, and mine, it was better that you should – go.'

Now whether it was her inflexion, I do not know, but I think that the word rang strangely in all our ears. I know that it did in mine. There was something – not quite natural about it...something faintly suggestive of a pregnancy, unobtrusive, yet well advanced...

Mansel's words came into my mind – *It's too late. It can't be helped.*

I think the hair rose upon my head.

The three men sat still as death, with their eyes upon Vanity Fair. And she sat as still as they, with her head against the back of her stall and her eyes on the blaze of one of the chandeliers.

Below seemed to break the spell.

Shining red in the face, he shifted, to slew himself round in his stall. But though he opened his mouth, it was Acorn that asked the question which hung on his lips.

'Go? Where shall we go?'

'That's not for me to say,' said Vanity Fair.

Gaston's breath was rattling. White as a sheet, he started up out of his stall, but his legs gave way beneath him and down he went on his knees between his stall and the table, to which he clung.

The others observed him in silence – Acorn, with his hands to his knee.

Below returned to his mistress.

238

'Your words are equivocal, madam. I can hardly believe...
And yet, *his legs have failed him – and mine are dead.'*

There was a dreadful silence.

Then –

'That's the effect of the poison,' said Vanity Fair.

Though I cannot be sure, I believe that her saying killed
Gaston. Be that as it may, the fellow mewed like a cat – a very
shocking noise on the lips of a man – and then slipped down
from the table and out of sight.

The chaplain lifted his voice.

'Madam,' he said, 'in thirty-three years I have much to thank
you for. May God Almighty have mercy upon your soul.'

With that, he seemed to withdraw, for he laid his hands
together and lowered his eyes, and I do not think he knew what
came after, because his attention was gone.

Acorn glanced at his watch. Then he folded his arms and
looked at Vanity Fair.

'The brandy, of course,' he said.

His mistress nodded.

'I might have guessed,' he said. 'To tell you the truth, it did
just enter my head. And then...I couldn't believe that you'd do
me in.'

Vanity Fair sighed.

'Sorry, Acorn,' she said, 'but I know you too well. When it
came to the pitch, you'd have turned King's Evidence, Acorn,
and let me down.'

Acorn threw back his head and laughed loud and long.

Then he leaned forward.

'You're devilish shrewd,' he said. 'That's just what I've done.'

The woman sat as though frozen, staring ahead down the
table to Gaston's empty stall. And Acorn stayed still, as he was,
leaning upon the table and smiling into her face. And while they
were sitting in silence, I heard a knock fall upon the door.

Vanity Fair shivered.

'I see,' she said very slowly. And then, 'Is this them?'

Acorn sat back in his stall.

'I imagine so,' he said. 'They said they'd be round tonight.'

Vanity Fair nodded.

Again someone knocked upon the door – this time with less discretion.

Vanity Fair sat forward, finger to lip. Then she left her stall and, passing behind Below, picked up the bottle of brandy which stood on his left.

As she returned to her place, the knocking broke out again. It was loud and insistent now, and I heard the murmur of voices beyond the doors. As she regained her seat, a handle was turned – in vain. The doors had been locked.

Vanity Fair filled her glass – there was just enough brandy left. I can see her now, with the bottle reversed in her hand and her head on one side, regarding the winking crystal brimming with gold.

Then she turned to Acorn – and raised her glass. 'The trouble is,' she said lightly, 'we know one another too well.'

As the brandy went up to her lips, Mansel touched my arm and turned to the stair.

'By God, she's game,' I murmured, with my eyes on Vanity Fair.

'Come,' said Mansel. 'We shouldn't have stayed so long.'

When I turned to follow him down, Acorn had drawn out his case and seemed to be asking his mistress for her permission to smoke: and she was sitting back, smiling, with the empty glass before her and a napkin up to her lips.

Mansel led us the way we had come.

The lobby and stairs were empty – to my surprise: but the instant we gained the first floor, we knew the truth.

Vanity Fair's apartments were on fire.

'Good God,' said Mansel. And then, 'We can't let them burn.'

We pelted back to the lobby, but as we thrust into the hall, I heard the crash of woodwork and saw the sergeant-footman burst into the dining-room. Two other servants were with him: and since three were more than enough, we turned again and ran for the stable-yard.

No one saw us, for no one was left to see. At the first alarm of fire the rest of the staff had fled.

We passed by way of the meadows, skirting the seething village until we came to the path which would lead us down to the Rolls. It was as we were using this, that a car stormed up the zigzag, taking the bends so fast that its tires cried out.

'The police,' said Mansel. 'They've come by way of the pass and they've seen the fire. And that's as well. If they hadn't been in a hurry, they might have stopped to have a look at the Rolls.'

Had they done so, they would have found Virginia asleep, with the chambermaid's arm about her and her feet wrapped up in her apron against the cold.

Without a word I took my seat by her side...

Ten minutes later, perhaps, we stopped by the lonely stable and made our way up to the loft from which Carson had watched Jezreel.

The flames had spread now, nearly half the castle was well alight, but the fire was still fiercest about the roof of the tower which stood up like some monstrous stake set up for the burning of some Titan, whose body might have been there.

Had any attempt been made to prevent the flames from spreading I am perfectly sure that this would have met with success, for there was plenty of water and there were plenty of hands: but I afterwards learned that, because it was nobody's business, nothing whatever was done to fight the fire, but a good many books were carried out of the library and laid on the sopping grass of the meadows south of the house. And there they were left to rot, as they very soon did.

That there perished so many treasures, which might so well have been saved, will always seem dreadful to me: but they had been heaped together by Vanity Fair, and I think that perhaps for that reason they were accursed.

For a quarter of an hour we watched the spectacle, but though it was very striking and the blaze in its frame of black mountains filled the eye, I think that all three of our minds were still full of that other scene which we had lately witnessed – as now, unobserved and in silence, and, as now, from the mouth of a loft.

Then we went down to the car, and drove to the thicket where I had left Jenny and Bell...

And there Mansel set me down.

'I'm not coming in,' he said, smiling. 'For one thing we're late enough: for another, I'm not prepared to be cross-examined tonight: but what is far more important is that the two Virginias should be kept apart until we know where we are. I'm going straight to Bordeaux – to put my Virginia into a nursing-home. And you'll take yours to Anise, where I shall join you tomorrow, about midday. And now go in and find her. If everything's quite all right, tell Bell to switch on your lights. I won't go till I see them come on.'

I did as he said.

Five minutes later, with Jenny sitting beside me and Bell behind, I swung my car out of the thicket and on to the open road.

Some eighteen hours had gone by, and Mansel and I were taking our ease in the meadow where, six weeks before, he had told me that I was to visit a castle, which went by the name of Jezreel, and there be the guest of a woman, whose nickname was Vanity Fair.

Nothing was changed.

The stream was as lazy, the shadows of the poplars were taking their handsome order, the woodland was smiling as ever and the comfortable murmurs of the country neighboured the sleepy silence that ruled our council-room.

Bunyan's words came into my mind. *So I awoke, and behold, it was a Dream.*

And so, indeed, I might have believed our Progress, if my head had not been still tender and my hands still sore from the payment I made to Marc.

Mansel lay silent so long that I had thought he had fallen asleep, for though he had slept at Bordeaux, he must still have been very tired; but at length he lifted his head, propped himself on an elbow and felt for a pipe.

'You know,' he said, 'I've not a great deal to tell you that you haven't heard already – from the lips of Vanity Fair. Still, for what it's worth, you shall have what news there is left.

'You were to rescue Jenny: and I was to find Virginia and pull her out. In fact, you did my job, as well as your own: but that was because I was hoist with my own petard.

'Well, I was always sure that mine was a waiting job. And so it was. Virginia was in the tower, under lock and key. I couldn't reduce the door and I didn't know who had the key. I was pretty sure it was Acorn: but since I couldn't be sure I didn't dare hold him up. The only thing to do was to wait and watch. You see the point. Once I knew where the key was, I could do as I pleased – I'd a gun in my pocket and nobody knew I was there. But I had to be sure where it was, before I moved.

'I expected they'd take her some breakfast: but nobody did. And no one had been to see her when Vanity Fair returned. I heard her return – I was waiting for the sound of her car. And I entered that cursed chair as she was coming upstairs.

'You see, it was daylight now – when I could be seen: so I simply had to take cover – cover from view. The system, of course, was useless, for I had to see and hear: and the tower was out of the question – you might as well try and lie low on a bagatelle-board. But the chair was simply ideal. Bang on the spot – in the very holy of holies. I'd have laid a coach to a cornflake that before I'd been there five minutes I should know what I wanted to know.

'In fact, I knew it in one, for Acorn came into the room with Vanity Fair.

' "Got the keys all right?" says she.

'Acorn tapped his pocket.

' "Where did you put them last night?"

' "In the pocket of my pyjamas. Why do you ask?"

' "Curiosity pure and simple," says Vanity Fair. "Just run up and see they're all right, while I wash my hands."

'Well, there was my chance. I'd only to follow Acorn, lay him out and take Virginia away. As they left the room, I made to get out of that chair...'

As though the memory tired him, he put a hand to his eyes.

'I've only myself to blame, but you saw the dummy handles inside – to pull the doors to. I'd never dreamed they were false. Never mind. Let's skip that bit. I stayed where I was.

'I imagine that you can imagine Acorn's return... Vanity Fair let him wallow. And when he was out of breath –

' "You needn't worry," she said. "Chandos is out of reach. I've really only just left him. He said he hadn't killed Marc – I don't know why. But he's got Virginia all right – my daughter, Virginia Brooch."

'Acorn maintained that you were the devil himself. And his mistress shrugged her shoulders and asked him what he advised.

' "Not that I value your opinion, but I want to see what it's worth."

'I can't say my day was dull, for they stripped and were stripped before me again and again. Virginia was brought, to sign papers – a pitiful sight. The money question appeared extremely involved. She's been selling Jenny's reversion, hand over fist. The marriage had been arranged, as I thought it had: and, after much hesitation, Vanity Fair decided to let it take place. Gaston, as might be expected, provided the comic relief. It really was very comic, because *I saw the trap set* – by Vanity Fair and Acorn. I heard every word that was said and I saw them at work.

'They had a document there, setting out who Virginia was and whence she came, that she had pretended to be Virginia Brooch, that by this false pretence she had obtained the money on which she and her husband would live. And they had another paper, setting out who Gaston was and how he had served de Rachel and then stepped into his shoes. Well, Gaston was summoned and given these things to read. And when he'd read them through, he was told to write on their backs that he'd read them through. Well, of course, he refused. You can give a man a halter, but you can't make him hang himself. But Vanity Fair can – could. When he refused to sign, she simply raised her eyebrows and locked them up in her safe.

' "Look at your fingers," she said.

'The tips were white.

' "Those papers were powdered," says she. "You can swear you never read them, but I guess your finger-prints will give you the lie."

'You should have seen Gaston's face.

'He'd hardly gone, when Acorn came bursting in with the news that Lafone was taken and Marc was under arrest…

'Well, the day wore on. It was a day of intrigue, a day of alarms and excursions, a day of doubts and fears – and I was in the thick of it all. I knew where everyone was, and I had my finger on the pulse of Vanity Fair. The ball was not at my feet: it was under my arm. I could have made rings round the lot, again and again – if I could have only stepped out of that good-looking chair.'

He paused there, to pull at the blowing grass and stare at the sky.

'I won't dwell on what I went through, but it was…the most trying experience I've ever had. I've never enjoyed inaction: and once or twice, if I had been free to move, I might have…straightened things out. When I say "free to move", I mean it. I'd have fired through one of the air-holes, if I could have drawn a bead: but I was denied even that. Never mind…

245

'I saw Virginia doped – Esther and Acorn held her while Vanity Fair pumped something into her veins: I saw the brandy poisoned: and I heard the orders which Vanity Fair gave Esther, before she went down to dine.

'Now before I tell you those orders, I want to clear up one point. Vanity Fair, as you know, had meant to clear out. Well, that was all very well, so far as it went. But police will be police: and if they wish to – er – interview someone, they don't let the matter drop, because the person in question is not at home. And if they have reason to think that the person in question has fled, their wish to see him becomes a raging desire. Very well. Vanity Fair could clear out: *but the police must not think she'd cleared out*, because, if they did, she would be found and detained within twenty-four hours. Well, police are suspicious coves, and she very rightly decided that the only way in which to allay their suspicions that she had fled, would be to convince them that she was still at Jezreel. To that end she laid her plans...

'A car was to be in waiting from nine o'clock on. Her private suite was to be soused with petrol, and a train of sheets laid down to the postern-door. When this had been done, Esther was to visit Virginia, tire her head with one of those black silk hoods and set on her arm a bracelet belonging to Vanity Fair. She was then to bring her, by the system, into the private suite, give her a whiff of chloroform and, when she was down and out, pour a gallon of petrol over her clothes.'

'My God,' said I.

'Exactly. And when the fire had burned out and the body was found, everybody would know it was that of Vanity Fair.

'Well, happily you stepped in, so it didn't come off. What did come off, I don't know – and nobody ever will. Finding Virginia gone, Esther may have lost her nerve and decided to quit: I imagine that she started the fire, but whether she did so on purpose, I've no idea. When rooms are soused as those were, you've only to plug in a lamp to send them up.'

246

There was a little silence.

Then –

'Why did she take the poison? If she'd left the room by the terrace, she might have escaped.'

Mansel shook his head.

'Acorn would have called to the police and told them to make for the garage and wait for her there. It wasn't the police, as we know, but she didn't know that. But, even if she had known, I think it more than likely that her chauffeur had run with the rest. And even if he hadn't and she'd started off in the car, her departure would hardly have been private. I imagine most of the staff were jammed in the entrance gates.'

As I heard a movement beside me, Goliath nosed my shoulder and put his tongue up to my ear. And before I had time to turn round, his mistress was sitting between us with one hand on Mansel's shoulder and one on mine.

'You must go away,' said Mansel, 'because this is our house.'

Jenny laughed.

'I was a little girl then.'

'You'll always be my little girl.'

'Always,' said Jenny. She stooped to brush his hair with her lips. 'Jill sent me to find you for her. But now I've found you, I don't want to let you go.'

Mansel kissed her fingers.

'You were always much nicer to me than you were to William.'

'I'm not now,' said Jenny.

Her fingers slid from my shoulder and felt for my lips.

'Why were you then?' said Mansel.

Jenny lifted her eyes to gaze at the golden woods.

'I don't know,' she said slowly. 'Jill says I was shy. I always loved him best: but I wasn't easy with him, as I was with you. It meant so much more when I touched him. I did – I do love you: but I wanted him to love me.'

There was a little silence.

'D'you believe me now?' said Mansel.

'Yes,' said I.

'What didn't he believe?' said Jenny.

With a smile, Mansel got to his feet.

'That's for him to tell you,' he said.

'Tell me, darling,' said Jenny.

'Damn it,' said I, 'I thought you loved Jonathan best.'

'Oh, William, how could you?' She slid an arm round my neck. Then she looked up to Mansel. 'Isn't he funny?' she said. 'And yet he's been out in the world for the whole of his life.'

'It's not my fault,' said Mansel. 'I've done what I could.'

'No, no,' cried Jenny, fiercely, and held me tight. 'No, no, I don't want him changed.'

'Sweetheart,' smiled Mansel, 'don't worry. Heaven and earth may pass away, but, for better or for worse, Richard William Chandos will never change.' He stood up, squared his shoulders and snuffed the air. 'My God,' he said, 'I feel like a boy out of school. Come, Goliath,' and the two of them raced for the gate.

Her chin on her shoulder, my lady watched them go.

As Goliath came loping back, I touched her cheek.

'There goes a great gentleman, Jenny: a far finer fellow than me.'

'I know,' said Jenny. 'I know. But I love you best.'

I kissed her lips, and stood up. Then I put out my hands for hers and drew her up to her feet and into my arms...

After a long moment I held her off, to regard her – a rosy child.

I had not thought that she could look more lovely than she had looked those days in the belvedere: but Jill and Bordeaux, between them, had found her in clothes which better became her estate. Her beautiful legs were still bare, and so were her arms, but her shoes were of neat, white buckskin, her dress was a smart confection of blue and white, and a slice of embroidered silk was betraying a fine chemise. That these things enhanced her beauty, I cannot deny. The gold of her curls, the blue of her eyes, the bloom of her exquisite skin seemed rarer and more outstanding than ever before. But that is as far as I can go. You cannot sweeten sweetness itself; and the shape of her mouth, the light of her countenance, and the eager breath of her lips were ruled by 'a grace beyond the reach of art'.

'Do you like my dress, William?'

'I love it,' said I.

'D'you remember how I was dressed when you saw me first?'

'Perfectly,' said I.

'What was I wearing?'

'Nothing, my beauty,' said I. 'And very lovely you looked.'

Jenny's great eyes grew round. Then she caught my wrist with a cry.

'I know, I know. That was the day before. You were there at dawn – in the meadows…the morning that Jean came back.'

I could hardly believe my ears.

'That's perfectly true,' I said. 'But how do you know? I'll swear you never saw me.'

'No, but I had a feeling – a feeling I didn't know. And the moment I saw you next day I had it again. D'you think I smelt you, William?'

'I hope not,' said I. 'I was more than two hundred yards off.'

'Then it must have been love,' said Jenny.

I picked her up in my arms.

'The world's full of men,' said I. 'Perhaps one day you'll have that feeling again.'

A maiden smiled.

'If ever I do,' she said quietly, 'I'll know that it can't have been love.'

'Jenny,' I said, 'who taught you to say these pretty things?'

A child shook her lovely head.

'No one,' she said. 'But I'm glad you find them pretty, because that means that you love me. And that's what I want.'

'I'm mad about you,' I said.

'Splendid,' said Jenny, and put up her mouth to be kissed.

And that is very nearly the end of my tale.

Virginia passed from her trance to a nervous breakdown, and lay in the home at Bordeaux for nearly a month. For that time we stayed at Anise, fleeting the days 'as they did in the golden world'. When she was fit to travel, she went with Jill and Mansel to stay at their Hampshire home: and that, I am sure, was more to her taste than was my home in Wiltshire, for the very simple reason that she had fallen for Mansel and was ready to sell her soul to become his wife. This, as may be supposed, to my great relief… And when they went to Hampshire, Jenny and I went home.

Lafone was not brought to justice, but hanged herself in her cell, thus saving me inconvenience which I was most glad to escape. Marc was less considerate: but Mansel was clever enough to steer me clear of Jezreel, and, after a delay of six months, the ruffian was only charged with stealing my car. For this offence he was ordered to pay a fine of ten francs, the judges remarking that he had suffered enough. Indeed, I was sternly rebuked for having offered him violence of any kind. But when, encouraged by this, his counsel made bold to suggest that an action would lie against me for aggravated assault, the judges rose up as one man and, vowing most horrid vengeance for such 'contempt of their court', increased the fine by four hundred and ninety francs and awarded me costs which, of course, I never received.

Jenny took her true name, and Virginia came to be known as Virginia Wright. We let it be understood that she had been staying with Jenny as the guest of Vanity Fair and that they were the only survivors of the shocking affair at Jezreel. Of Virginia's marriage to Gaston nothing was ever said, and, thanks to the drug with which her senses were dulled, she herself never knew that for half-a-day she was that recreant's wife.

The whole truth was only disclosed to those at whose instance Mansel set out for Jezreel; but a part was told to the lawyers who dealt with Jenny's estate. Of the fortune which should have been hers not one-sixth remained, and when Jezreel had been sold and all debts and duties were paid, she was left with a sum which brought in two thousand a year. Half of this she gave to Virginia who needed it more than she. This property stood Virginia in very good stead. After falling in love three times in as many months, she met and married a Scotsman who in her eyes diminished all other men, and since his estates in Rhodesia were demanding most of his time, she has to a great extent passed out of our lives.

I had made up my mind that I would not marry Jenny until she had taken her place in the world I knew and so had become acquainted with other men. But this she declined to do, except as my wife. I do not mean that she refused to go out or to have to do with the men and women she met: but if Mansel or I were not present, she seemed preoccupied, and if we were, she never had eyes or ears for anyone else. In a way this was natural enough, for the ten years she spent in the pleasance had left their mark and there was between us three an understanding which nobody else could share. So after six weeks it seemed best to throw in my hand and to take up the shining honour which I had been done.

Jezreel was sold to the Roman Catholic Church: and from the remains of the castle there has risen a building which has the look of a school. In fact it is a seminary: and boys are now taught to be priests where Below bowed down at the altar of Vanity Fair. I hope they find the ground holy: for me it will always be the field of blood.

I have never seen it again, and I never shall, for the memories which it would kindle are vivid enough.

I can see the terrace laid with carpet, and the elegant figure in black with the eyes of steel: I can see Julie's pitiful corpse asprawl on the sunlit flags: I can see the Spaniard crouching, his face alight with that mountain-side: I can see my gorgeous bedroom, and the dying scream of the chauffeur whose death I caused: I can see Jenny sitting above me, and hear the slam of my heart as I fought with that mountain-side: I can see my gorgeous bedroom, and Virginia, pale and trembling to find herself trapped: I can see myself bayed in my cell, and the woman framed in its doorway, and the lazy light in her eyes: I can see the line of the drip-course, and can feel the sweat running on my fingers as I strove to face an adventure which wore the semblance of death: I can hear Lafone's hideous laughter and the crunch of her pick as it sent a soul to its Maker before its time: and then I can see that most amazing picture, that had the look of a film – where the three whom she had poisoned whimpered or prayed or laughed at the table of Vanity Fair.

There are nights when these things haunt me, so that I cannot sleep: and then I call to Jenny: and because she is kind as fair, she comes at my call: and always, because she is Jenny, they fly away.

THE END

DORNFORD YATES

AS BERRY AND I WERE SAYING

Reprinted four times in three months, this semi-autobiographical novel is a comic rendition of the author's hazardous experiences in France at the end of World War II. Darker and less frivolous than some of Yates' earlier books, he described it as 'really my own memoir put into the mouths of Berry and Boy', and at the time of publication it already had a nostalgic, period feel. A hit with the public and a 'scrapbook of the Edwardian age as it was seen by the upper-middle classes'.

BERRY AND CO.

A collection of short stories featuring 'Berry' Pleydell and his chaotic entourage established Dornford Yates' reputation as one of the best comic writers of his generation. The German caricatures in the book carried such a sting that when France was invaded in 1939 Yates, who was living near the Pyrenees, was put on the wanted list and had to flee.

DORNFORD YATES

BLIND CORNER

This is Yates' first thriller: a tautly plotted page-turner featuring the tense, crime-busting adventures of suave Richard Chandos. Chandos is thrown out of Oxford for 'beating up some Communists', and on return from vacation in Biarritz he witnesses a murder.

Teaming up at his London club with friend Jonathan Mansel, a stratagem is devised to catch the killer. The novel has equally compelling sequels: *Blood Royal, An Eye For a Tooth, Fire Below* and *Perishable Goods*.

BLOOD ROYAL

At his chivalrous, rakish best in a story of mistaken identity, kidnapping, and old-world romance, Richard Chandos takes us on a romp through Europe in the company of a host of unforgettable characters. This fine thriller can be read alone or as part of a series with *Blind Corner, An Eye For a Tooth, Fire Below* and *Perishable Goods*.

DORNFORD YATES

AN EYE FOR A TOOTH

On the way home from Germany after having captured Axel the Red's treasure, dapper Jonathan Mansel happens upon a corpse in the road, that of an Englishman. There ensues a gripping tale of adventure and vengeance of a rather gentlemanly kind. On publication this novel was such a hit that it was reprinted six times in its first year, and assured Yates' huge popularity. A classic Richard Chandos thriller, which can be read alone or as part of a series including *Blind Corner, Blood Royal, Fire Below* and *Perishable Goods*.

FIRE BELOW

Richard Chandos makes a welcome return in this classic adventure story. Suave and decadent, he leads his friends into forbidden territory to rescue a kidnapped (and very attractive) young widow. Yates gives us a highly dramatic, almost operatic, plot and unforgettably vivid characters.

A tale in the traditional mould, and a companion novel to *Blind Corner, Blood Royal, Perishable Goods* and *An Eye For a Tooth*.

OTHER TITLES BY DORNFORD YATES AVAILABLE DIRECT
FROM HOUSE OF STRATUS

Quantity	£	$(US)	$(CAN)	€
Adèle and Co.	6.99	11.50	15.99	11.50
And Berry Came Too	6.99	11.50	15.99	11.50
As Berry and I Were Saying	6.99	11.50	15.99	11.50
B-Berry and I Look Back	6.99	11.50	15.99	11.50
Berry and Co.	6.99	11.50	15.99	11.50
The Berry Scene	6.99	11.50	15.99	11.50
Blind Corner	6.99	11.50	15.99	11.50
Blood Royal	6.99	11.50	15.99	11.50
The Brother of Daphne	6.99	11.50	15.99	11.50
Cost Price	6.99	11.50	15.99	11.50
The Courts of Idleness	6.99	11.50	15.99	11.50
An Eye For a Tooth	6.99	11.50	15.99	11.50
Fire Below	6.99	11.50	15.99	11.50
Gale Warning	6.99	11.50	15.99	11.50
The House That Berry Built	6.99	11.50	15.99	11.50
Jonah and Co.	6.99	11.50	15.99	11.50
Ne'er Do Well	6.99	11.50	15.99	11.50
Perishable Goods	6.99	11.50	15.99	11.50
Red in the Morning	6.99	11.50	15.99	11.50
She Painted Her Face	6.99	11.50	15.99	11.50

ALL HOUSE OF STRATUS BOOKS ARE AVAILABLE FROM GOOD BOOKSHOPS
OR DIRECT FROM THE PUBLISHER:

Internet: www.houseofstratus.com including author interviews, reviews, features.

Email: sales@houseofstratus.com please quote author, title and credit card details.

Hotline: UK ONLY: 0800 169 1780, please quote author, title and credit card details.
INTERNATIONAL: +44 (0) 20 7494 6400, please quote author, title and credit card details.

Send to: House of Stratus Sales Department
24c Old Burlington Street
London
W1X 1RL
UK

Please allow for postage costs charged per order plus an amount per book as set out in the tables below:

	£(Sterling)	$(US)	$(CAN)	€(Euros)
Cost per order				
UK	2.00	3.00	4.50	3.30
Europe	3.00	4.50	6.75	5.00
North America	3.00	4.50	6.75	5.00
Rest of World	3.00	4.50	6.75	5.00
Additional cost per book				
UK	0.50	0.75	1.15	0.85
Europe	1.00	1.50	2.30	1.70
North America	2.00	3.00	4.60	3.40
Rest of World	2.50	3.75	5.75	4.25

PLEASE SEND CHEQUE, POSTAL ORDER (STERLING ONLY), EUROCHEQUE, OR INTERNATIONAL MONEY ORDER (PLEASE CIRCLE METHOD OF PAYMENT YOU WISH TO USE)
MAKE PAYABLE TO: STRATUS HOLDINGS plc

Cost of book(s): —————————— Example: 3 x books at £6.99 each: £20.97

Cost of order: —————————— Example: £2.00 (Delivery to UK address)

Additional cost per book: —————— Example: 3 x £0.50: £1.50

Order total including postage: ———— Example: £24.47

Please tick currency you wish to use and add total amount of order:

☐ £ (Sterling)   ☐ $ (US)   ☐ $ (CAN)   ☐ € (EUROS)

VISA, MASTERCARD, SWITCH, AMEX, SOLO, JCB:

☐ ☐ ☐ ☐ ☐ ☐ ☐ ☐ ☐ ☐ ☐ ☐ ☐ ☐ ☐ ☐ ☐ ☐ ☐ ☐

Issue number (Switch only):

☐ ☐ ☐

Start Date: **Expiry Date:**

☐☐ / ☐☐   ☐☐ / ☐☐

Signature: _____

NAME: _____

ADDRESS: _____

_____

POSTCODE: _____

Please allow 28 days for delivery.

Prices subject to change without notice.
Please tick box if you do not wish to receive any additional information. ☐

House of Stratus publishes many other titles in this genre; please check our website (**www.houseofstratus.com**) for more details.